T0209315

The Rest of My Story

HOPE HARTFORD

WESTBOW
PRESS®
A DIVISION OF THOMAS NELSON
& ZONDERVAN

WestBow Press books may be ordered through booksellers or by contacting:

WestBow Press
A Division of Thomas Nelson & Zondervan
1663 Liberty Drive
Bloomington, IN 47403
www.westbowpress.com
844-714-3454

ISBN: 979-8-3850-0332-7 (sc)
ISBN: 979-8-3850-0333-4 (hc)
ISBN: 979-8-3850-0331-0 (e)

Library of Congress Control Number: 2023913736

Print information available on the last page.

WestBow Press rev. date: 8/2/2023

"Freight train, freight train, run so fast.
Freight train, freight train, run so fast.
Please don't tell what train I'm on,
They won't know what route I've gone."

ELIZABETH COTTEN

Contents

Prologue

I am definitely going this time, Lydia thought to herself. Then she wrestled with the idea for the third time, *No! I can't leave my friends behind.* She knew that her suitcase wouldn't pack itself, but she couldn't start sorting through her clothes and belongings yet. She was scared, and she needed to sort through her thoughts first because she was planning to leave her home forever.

Running away was an option that had flashed through Lydia's mind only a few times before when life was going wrong. The kind of wrong that makes you feel as if nobody understands you, not even your best friend or your mother. Then sometimes she imagined leaving the annoying frustrations of being a teenager. How awesome it would be if she suddenly became a young adult who could live in her own apartment and get a puppy. So far, the running away idea was always just that: a flash of lightning, not a full-fledged thought that had purpose or practicality.

Well, once she had packed a backpack and left home for a bit. A very short bit. She had remembered to pack her toothpaste and toothbrush; who wants to get a cavity while they are on the run? Besides that, she had brought two pairs of socks, her favorite blue shirt with the ruffle, and her iPod. She had only been ten years old, so what could she know about running away? The October weather had been frosty that day; when the freezing rain started blowing into her eyes about five blocks from her green two-story home, Lydia had turned back. The argument with her parents over her roller-skating party hadn't been so awful after all, she decided as she shivered her way along the sidewalk. Her mom and dad were usually willing to compromise about birthday parties anyway. Her brothers were enjoying hot chocolate in the kitchen when she returned, and Mom had a steaming mug waiting for her too. She had only been gone ten minutes; no one knew that she had intended to be gone much longer.

Sitting on the edge of her wooden sleigh-style bed Lydia recalled how when she was even younger than that, only seven, she had an emergency "bag" ready and waiting to go. Just in case. She had attached a note declaring, "In case of emergency." She had kept it under her bed: a few packages of breadsticks and cheese and her children's Bible wrapped in a pink blanket. Stitched in the corner of the pink blanket was her name, LYDIA, in purple. The blanket she had been swaddled in as a baby. How sweet, she thought, that she had planned to take that faded pink blanket with all its happy memories when she headed off to make a new life for herself—at age seven. Thankfully, she hadn't needed that emergency bag after all. What could go *that* wrong when she was only seven?

She paused in the middle of this innocent thought, and her heart was gripped with uncertainty. Was it possible that something very terrible *had* occurred when she was seven? The conversation she had with her mother an hour before made her aware that something very awful had happened. Yet Lydia hadn't known. Well, she had known, but she hadn't understood. Not at all! And she wasn't sure she wanted to start understanding now. It seemed much too terrible to consider. She purposefully pushed these disturbing thoughts aside. Even if she tried to sort through her mother's revelation for the next week, she still wouldn't make sense of it. Anxiety flooded her heart like a monsoon. How were they going to get through this mess?

Lydia leaned farther back onto her bed and tried in vain to relax. She rested against the flannel pillows as she looked out her window to the community playground that she shared with her neighbors and friends. As she gazed, two images came in and out of focus— one close and one distant in her vision. If she allowed her eyes to focus beyond the glass windowpane, the low-branched live oak trees, the red picnic table, and the basketball court filled her vision. If she kept her eyes on the surface of the glass, there she was, 16-year-old Lydia Crew.

The morning sun was rising to the east of her northern-facing window, so her reflection was faint. She couldn't see the reddish highlights in her long hair or the blue-green of her wide eyes, but she could make out the delicate oval of her face. Even simply glancing at the muted image, Lydia could understand how everyone said she and her mother looked alike. On this November day, Lydia's almond-shaped eyes were even larger than usual. She looked more carefully; that was certainly fear she saw mirrored in her eyes. Wait a minute! The girl in the window—that was the very same girl thinking about running away! The one trying not to wonder about that horrendous event that happened when she was seven. It was confusing and disturbing to look at herself now that she had that new information about her life. Who was Lydia Crew anyway? Christ-follower, homeschooler, ballet dancer, flutist...victim? How could she possibly reframe her picture of herself to include *that*? She closed her eyes and took a deep breath.

Opening them again, Lydia let her eyes refocus on the view of her backyard in the distance. Seeing the playground helped her to momentarily quiet her heart. It brought so many carefree images to mind. Filling most of the yard was the basketball court where she raced her beagle, Stella, on her ten-speed bike. It was also where they had family kickball games and where her brothers, David and Jonathan, zoomed in daring circles on their scooters. To the left of the court was their favorite lunchtime spot—the red picnic table. On sunny days, noontime would find Lydia, her mother, and her brothers enjoying the fresh air as they munched on a homemade lunch such as apples and quesadillas. Lindsey, her mom, and her brothers often joined the Crew family as well.

She remembered how she had met Lindsey, her next-door neighbor. The girls were three years apart in age, yet they were inseparable friends. During four military moves in seven years, Lydia learned to make friends quickly. With the heat of a Florida summer came many trips to the officers' club pool; that's where she and Lindsey had met during the first week of July. Up and down the waterslide they had raced with their brothers in tow. Little had they known that their mothers were also becoming fast friends perched on their poolside chairs. One week later, Lindsey and her family moved in next door. How cool was that!

One of her favorite memories was of the game "Journey to Atlantis" that she and Lindsey had concocted out of their vivid imaginations. In their childhood diversion, the friends had pretended to have adventures at sea. Named after the heroine in a popular film, Lydia had been Elizabeth Swann. Lindsey had been Elizabeth's daughter. The nautical travelers had left the comforts of England to start a new and courageous life in America. Elizabeth and her daughter clung to the hope of their new life as they battled marauding pirates (their brothers) and faced the many other adversities of seafaring life. She could almost hear David shout as he leaped from his tire-swing pirate ship, "Rah! Your ship has been ransacked!" Often the girls swooned from lack of nourishment. Or worse. Once Elizabeth's daughter had tightened her corset dangerously snug, had fainted, and had fallen into the water where she had almost drowned. Thankfully, at that very moment, the erstwhile pirates had become the naval heroes who rescued the maiden in distress.

The summer they had arrived in Jacksonville she had been twelve and a half, and she hadn't been sure that it would ever feel like home. Now, three and a half years later, it was perfect. She loved everything about her east coast life and felt thankful for the years packed with delightful recollections. Then somehow, that very morning, her world had suddenly shifted. A five-minute conversation with her mother had changed everything! What would become of their pleasant memories? What would become of everything that Lydia lived for? It seemed as though her life had been made up of two disparate realities: the one she loved and understood, and the other that was suddenly turning the first completely upside down.

Looking around her upstairs bedroom in the morning light, Lydia saw the treasured mementos of her life in recent days. On the shelf next to her window, her ballet trophy from her last recital pirouetted in golden grace. To the right of the window, her music stand stood waiting patiently for another two-hour practice session. Playing in the Jacksonville Youth Symphony required a type of dedication that Lydia thrived on. Next, her roving eyes turned to her tall cherry-stained dresser with its sparkly glass knobs. Three photos stood side by side: the first of the Crew children, another of Lydia and Lindsey, and the third of Lydia with a group of her friends from church. A special keepsake bear sat atop the dresser as well. The bear was dressed as a pirate and held a mug of chocolate kisses—a gift from her boyfriend, Drew, on her sixteenth birthday only two weeks before.

Lydia's reminiscing could not help her to relax after all. She began to panic. She was going to leave this all behind? There was no way she would make it through this day on her own. She picked up the leather NIV Study Bible from her nightstand and clutched it to her chest. Only with God's help would she make it through this unwelcome journey. Holding her favorite book tightly, she breathed a prayer of desperation, "Please, help me, God." *Will God help me today as He has so many times before?* she wondered. Perhaps she would know by the end of the day; for now, she knew she needed to get back to packing. She would pack her Bible too. Certainly, its faithful wisdom could bring her the strength she would need in the difficult days to come.

She stood to put the book in her suitcase, and as she moved off the comfort of her bed, a wave of fear washed over her. Because this time thinking about running away was different—seriously unlike anything she had experienced before. She looked down at the pile of clothes clumped on the beige carpet. *This time she really was leaving.* She was sixteen now, and this wasn't a "Journey to Atlantis" game with her best friend. Now she was packing her suitcase for real and not merely a few crackers or a ruffled blue shirt. All the clothing and shoes that she could fit were going to be jammed into one large red suitcase. Summer's swimsuits and winter's Ugg boots and everything in between vied for space. Was it possible that this time running away was a reality and that it was the right thing to do? How could she leave her beloved home, her dear friends, her awesome church, her ballet classes, the youth symphony, and her first boyfriend? She knew she really didn't want to. In fact, she decided in a rush, she wouldn't after all. Lydia tried to reason with the barrage of thoughts crashing through her mind like a runaway freight train.

But it didn't matter what she thought; she had seen the look on her mother's face. She had no choice because this time her mother was the one telling her to pack. Her mom was the one telling her to run away as quickly as she could. There was no turning back now.

"From the lips of children and infants,
you have ordained praise."

PSALM 8:2

Chapter 1

ONE UNUSUAL THING

"Lydia! Lydiaaaa!" Lydia's mother called as she searched through the bedrooms, the closets, the living room, the bathroom—even the laundry room—looking for her missing daughter. The rooms were empty except for the calico cats sunning themselves in the cozy patch of light coming through the front window. The white kitchen was filled with the aroma of spaghetti and meatballs, and a large pile of clothes lay strewn about on the floor in Lydia's bedroom. Other than the heap of clothes, everything seemed to be in order. Where could she be?

It didn't take long to search through their home: Lydia wasn't there. One of the things Ettie usually loved about their apartment was how small it was; she could vacuum the entire place without moving the plug from the outlet in the hallway. It made cleaning on Saturdays quick enough to leave lots of time for playing at the park with Lydia. Right now, one of the things she didn't appreciate was how small their home was. Not a lot of hiding places here.

Ettie recalled the disagreement that she had with her daughter that morning. As they had gotten ready to leave for school, Lydia had begun to fret about what to wear. Lydia attended San Diego Country Day, the private school where her mother taught, and leaving the house punctually was a challenge. Ettie was prepared for a little drama from her daughter because it was a relatively normal occurrence, especially if it was about her hair. Lydia was particular about keeping her reddish-brown hair smooth and styled just right. However, this time it was her school uniform that had caused her distress.

"I have nothing to wear!" Lydia had cried mournfully from behind her closed door. Ettie had tried to be patient although it had been five minutes past the time they should have left to beat the traffic. Instead, when she knocked on the door and went into Lydia's room to help her, she had been seriously impatient. She had lost her cool completely. Lydia was still in her pajamas! Ettie remembered ruefully how their conversation had escalated.

"Mom, I do *not* have the right uniform to wear to school! And I don't want to go."

"Here, honey, try this white top with the blue pleated skirt. They will look pretty with your red shoes."

"No, I can't. Nobody wears that white top; the collar is too big. I want the same uniforms that my friends have!" Lydia had dropped the button-down blouse and blue skirt onto the beige carpet.

"Lydia Zeller. You have every different style of uniform that your school offers." And that is where the situation had gotten out of hand. Ettie had been frustrated enough with Lydia's selfishness that she had taken the whole bunch of yellow, blue, green, and white uniforms and their hangers out of the closet in one swoop and dropped them on the floor at Lydia's feet. "Here! Now, pick one! And let's go!"

Mother and daughter had made amends on the way to school, but now that Lydia was missing Ettie wondered if maybe she was still upset. She had been quiet on the way home. Her regular fifteen-minute enthusiastic monologue about her day had been reduced to a few sentences. At the time, Ettie had simply been thankful for their peaceful ride home after her hectic day. Maybe Lydia was hiding to pout? Were there any hiding places that she hadn't thought of? Could she have left the house? Ettie began to worry in earnest. She picked up the portable phone and stood in the middle of the living room, mind racing and heart pounding, wondering whom she should call for help.

Suddenly, Ettie heard a *thump* from the porch. The porch door was right next to the almond-colored couch in the living room, and it had a tall glass window. The curtain on the window covered the view of the outdoors. Another *thump!* The porch!

"Oh! I forgot to look on the porch!" With six steps, Ettie was opening the door and looking expectantly outside.

"Ah, there you are, sweet girl," Ettie whispered with a sigh of relief. Five-year-old Lydia was standing next to her plastic kitchen humming happily and smiling sweetly. The afternoon sun reflected off the pink sparkles on her short-sleeved shirt. *Why didn't I think to look out here?* Ettie chided herself. Yesterday, they relocated the play kitchen from the living room to the porch to enjoy the lovely weather. Ettie's heart filled with gratitude. Lydia was safe and sound right on their back porch. "Thank you, God," she prayed aloud.

Lydia looked up, her bright blue-green eyes shining.

"Hi Mama," she greeted as she finished putting several metal toy pots and pans and a variety of pretend foods into the shoebox she was holding and put the top on tightly. Next, she dropped the shoebox onto the cement porch floor next to her feet. *Thump!* It landed neatly next to two other boxes. Lydia looked up again, and mother and daughter both smiled as their eyes met.

"Hi, honey. I didn't know where you were. Believe it or not, I had forgotten that we had brought this kitchen out here, and I was looking all over for you. You didn't hear me calling?" Lydia shook her head. "Well, you are busy," Ettie chuckled now that her anxiety had passed. "What are you working on out here?"

"I am packing food for the poor people. See, this box is for Africa, and this one for India, and the big one is for the people right here in San Diego." She pointed to each shoebox in turn. "I put money in there, too, Mama. The people need clothes and medicine and vitamins and things, right? My friends from my dance class are helping me pack the boxes. See Emma and Anna are here now.

We are going to mail all of our nice things to World Vision." Ettie nodded in agreement, although she couldn't actually *see* Emma and Anna since they were Lydia's imaginary friends. "Do you think we can invent a special kind of vitamin to help the poor people who don't have healthy food like apples and carrots and broccoli? Maybe a spray vitamin that can give them all they need for a whole month. Anna thinks we can. And it was her idea to put money in these envelopes too. I hope that you don't mind—we used five of your envelopes." Lydia held up a yellow offering envelope from their church and paused.

Lydia didn't seem to be pouting at all. All her cheerful talkativeness had returned, and she was focused on a delightful and inventive game.

"What a wonderful idea, sweetheart. You and your pretend friends always have great plans," Ettie replied as she noticed the Monopoly money and collection envelopes lying on the countertop of the play kitchen. Across the front of the envelopes was Lydia's careful handwriting. Even at five years old, Lydia took great care in forming her letters precisely. Her invented spelling was adorable: one envelope was addressed to "Indeea" and another to "Sandy Eggo."

"Let's go in and have dinner now. Our spaghetti and meatballs are ready. After dinner, we have Bible study at the Novaks' house, remember?"

"Yes, I remember. I love going to their house; their puppy is the cutest! She is soft and fluffy like a cotton ball. Do you think she will play with me again? Do you think she likes me? I like her so much!" Without pausing to hear her mother's answer, Lydia picked up two of the shoeboxes and stepped inside. "The coffee table is going to be the post office, Mama. Can you please bring in the other box?"

Lydia and Ettie put the boxes on the low wooden table, and Ettie set down the portable phone as well. Thankfulness filled her heart again as she remembered her panic from a few minutes before. How grateful she was that she and Lydia were safe in their cozy apartment together. As a mother, keeping her daughter safe and healthy was one of the most important tasks she had; and Ettie took her responsibility seriously. Thus far, Lydia had never gotten lost, seriously injured, or even sick enough to need to see a doctor. They lived a simple life on her teacher's salary, yet Ettie knew that she was blessed to have her daughter. They had each other, they had God, and they had a lot of love.

As Ettie brought the plates filled with spaghetti and meatballs to the table for dinner, she looked around at the assortment of mismatched furniture in the living room and dining room. The almond-colored couch and the heavy oak table and chairs were all hand-me-downs from Ettie's relatives. They didn't need any fancy furniture with only 800 square feet of living space. Ettie knew that their home was modest compared to the homes of the friends that Lydia had made at her private elementary school. It had made them both laugh when one friend had come for a playdate and had wondered sincerely, "Where is the rest of your house?"

When Lydia's friend, Charlotte, had come to visit, she had been so enamored with their two cats, Rose and Violet, that she hadn't even noticed the size of their apartment. Charlotte had returned to her own home and implored her mother for at least *one* cat. Soon after, Charlotte and Lydia heard "Our House" on the radio: "Our house is a very, very fine house, with two cats in the yard. Life used to be so hard. Now everything is easy, 'cause of you." When the girls got together, they belted out the Crosby, Stills, Nash, and Young chorus. They called it their theme song.

While Lydia went to the sink to wash her hands for dinner, Ettie brought out Caesar salad from the refrigerator; and she thought about the truth of the girls' playful song. They did have a fine house, and overall, life with Lydia was easy. Rarely did they have arguments like the one that morning. When they did, they always worked through their differences in a way that brought them closer in the end. Ettie wondered if there was more that should be discussed about the uniform disagreement. They had both apologized during their car ride to school; however, she wanted to be sure the right lessons were learned. They sat down at the oak table to eat; and after they held hands for the blessing, Ettie brought up the situation again.

"Lydia, I'm sorry for the way that I handled my anger this morning. I never should have dumped all your clothes out of your closet. I need to be a role model for you. I am going to try to show you how to work through your emotions in a healthy way, okay? We need to talk things through nicely even when we are upset."

"I forgive you, Mama. And I'm sorry that I wasn't ready for school on time again. I sure like sleeping, and when I finally get out of bed, I don't want to get ready because my hair is bumpy and my uniforms are kind of yucky. Can't I wear regular clothes to school? Can't I wear my Barbie shirt instead?"

Ettie tried not to laugh. She loved the innocence and honesty of her pre-kindergartener. She knew how Lydia felt though—she would have loved to wear her jeans and flip-flops to work instead of her dressy work clothes. "Well, honey, while you are attending Country Day, you will need to keep wearing the same uniforms as everyone else; and you need to try to be thankful that we have such a wonderful school to go to and that we have clothes to wear. You know many children don't have those blessings. You can always change into your comfortable clothes when we get home. Remember that the important part isn't that you look pretty on the outside. The important part is that you have beauty and love on the inside. Let's make a plan that will help us in the mornings. How about if you pick out your outfit for school the night before?"

Lydia agreed, and they also discussed how listening to praise music as they got ready could help them start the day out positively. "Can we listen to Tammy Trent tomorrow morning? I love her song *My Irreplaceable*! That would be super cool!" Lydia was so enthusiastic about the idea that Ettie wished she had suggested it much earlier in the school year.

"May I please have a popsicle now?" Lydia requested when she had finished her spaghetti and salad.

"Sure." Ettie brought the dirty plates to the sink, rinsed them, and reached into the freezer for a raspberry fruit popsicle. Next, she sat down at the table with a piece of paper in her hand. "We got an important letter in the mail today."

"Oh cool, what?" Lydia asked between bites of her dessert. Her mouth was already turning a bright reddish-purple.

"It's from Mission Aviation Fellowship. Do you remember how we have been praying about whether God is calling us to move to another country to help children learn about Him?" Lydia nodded. "It sounds like God's answer is 'not right now.' This letter says that they only need families that have both a mommy and a daddy to help teach the children. I'm a little sad because it would have been an amazing adventure to serve God in that way. But you know what? We can keep having our adventure right here in San Diego for now." Ettie didn't mention that the letter had suggested that single parents needed more support than the organization could provide for them overseas. She wanted to keep things simple for Lydia's sake.

"Okay, Mama. Do you think we will ever have a daddy in our house? Then maybe we could go help the children, right?"

"If that is God's plan for us, yes. Someday we might have a nice daddy in our house. We can pray about it tonight at bedtime. It's almost time to leave for Bible study now. Let's go ahead and pick up that pile of clothes in your room before we head out."

Hand in hand, they walked down the hallway to hang the uniforms back up in Lydia's closet. Once the room was straightened, Ettie went into the bathroom to brush her teeth. She checked her hair in the mirror; wisps of auburn hair were resting around her oval face, but the French braid in the back was still neat. She decided to stay dressed in the navy-blue linen dress she had worn to teach that day. A brown and black beaded necklace that had been a gift from her homeroom mom graced her neck. She slipped on her blue suede Mary-Janes and grabbed her purse from the closet.

Ettie knew that Lydia was looking forward to the time at their friends' house because of their adorable new Border Collie. The puppy was well-behaved for seven months and loved the undivided attention Lydia gave her. Ettie was anticipating the evening for another reason: after a full day of teaching her four-year-old students, she enjoyed the opportunity for adult fellowship and conversation. Plus, the study they were currently doing on Romans was interesting and thought-provoking.

Carrying her purse to the kitchen, Ettie picked up her car keys from the silver heart-shaped hook by the front door. Lydia was all ready to go: her sparkly Barbie sneakers were on her feet, and she had her kitten coloring book and a box of 64 Crayola crayons on the coffee table next to her. She sat playing with seashells on the table. Spread out in several directions, shells of all colors, shapes, and sizes made a radial pattern. Lydia was taking more shells from the collection in the blue ceramic bowl on the table and adding them one at a time.

"What a cool pattern, Lydia! You are a great artist." Ettie loved seeing Lydia play with their shell collection. The two of them had spent many carefree evenings strolling along the lapping waves at La Jolla Shores. Often, they chased crabs and picked up seashells along the way. Sometimes they put the shells in a row on their legs as they sat in the sand. They giggled at what they called their "shell pants." A few special shells would be chosen to add to their collection.

Mother and daughter rode the ten minutes to their friends' house in their 1993 blue Volkswagen Jetta. Since it was evening, and the May Gray had passed, a warm wind blew through the open windows as they sang along with a couple of tunes on the radio. Natalia and Alex Novak lived in the neighborhood directly past San Diego Country Day School; the back porch of their condo overlooked the eighth green of their neighborhood's golf course. As Ettie and Lydia parked on the side of the street in front of the Novaks' house, they waved to their church friends who were arriving at the same time.

It was May 1st, 1999. That evening, Bible study was almost the same as usual. Lydia played fetch with the Border Collie in the side yard until the puppy was exhausted. After that they went onto the porch: Lydia was busy with her coloring book at the white wicker table and the tired puppy curled up by her feet. Ettie could see them through the large back window as she and her friends discussed chapter nine of Romans: Was God's plan predestination or free will? Or could it be both? Their conversation was lively as always. Only one thing was unusual that night.

A young man Ettie had never seen before had joined their group for the first time. He was broad-shouldered with neatly trimmed black hair, and he was dressed in a Naval officer's khaki uniform. A five o'clock shadow covered his chin and the bottom half of his cheeks. The name tag above his pocket read "Chip Crew." During the animated discussion about Romans chapter nine, Chip sat quietly listening. Near the end of the study, the conversation became more personal as people brought up their own experiences, and at that point, Chip told a story about his nine-year-old daughter. He shared that he had a daughter, Helen, who lived with her mother in Moreno Valley, which was an hour and a half north of San Diego. Helen attended a public school in Moreno Valley and was allowed to pray aloud in the homeroom at her school. Ettie was surprised to hear that; she imagined how exciting it would be if she could pray with her students at San Diego Country Day.

As Bible study ended that evening, Ettie decided to try to help the newcomer feel welcome. Making new friends came naturally to her, and the young man had seemed rather shy. Groups of twos and threes formed quickly after the closing prayer, but Chip still sat alone on the couch. She stepped over to where he sat and introduced herself.

"Hi, I'm Ettie. It's great to have you join our group tonight."

"Hi, thanks. I'm Chip. Nice to meet you. Did you say 'Eddie'?" Chip inquired as they shook hands.

"Well, it's short for Esther; so, it's Ettie with a 't.' Only my grandfather calls me Esther." Ettie added with a smile. "How did you hear about our group?"

"I've recently moved to San Diego with the Navy. I was driving down Southside Boulevard when I saw a sign for Christ the King Church. Sort of spontaneously, I parked in the parking lot and started to look around at the grounds and the buildings even though it seemed like no one was there."

"Really?"

"Yeah. Then a guy comes across the parking lot and calls out, 'Hey you! I'm Pastor Evan, and I want to see you here on Sunday morning.'"

"No way! Pastor Evan said that? That's awesome. What did you say?"

Chip smiled showing his straight white teeth, and Ettie noticed that it was a fine-looking smile. "I told him I would be there. On Sunday, he told me about this Bible study group that meets on Friday evenings, so here I am."

The two talked for a few more minutes; as they parted ways, Ettie was inspired to compliment Chip. He did look dashing in his uniform. She didn't intend to sound too forward or as if she was flirting with him. She shared words that she might say to a friend who looked particularly nice, "You look handsome tonight."

"Oh, umm," Chip mumbled. He had no other reply. In his embarrassment, he looked down at the brown leather uniform shoes he was wearing. Ettie certainly hadn't meant to make him feel uncomfortable. She quietly wished him a good night, gathered her purse and Bible, and went to the porch to get Lydia.

Under the twilight starry night, Ettie drove home to their apartment in Green Tree Square. Lydia chatted happily in the backseat about her visit with the puppy. Of course, they had no way of suspecting that back at the Novaks' house, Chip was hanging around until everyone had said their goodbyes. He was waiting for a moment alone with Natalia and Alex to ask a question: could he have Ettie's phone number? The Novaks hesitated; they didn't know Chip well yet. Still, he was a naval officer—a lieutenant, and that should be an indication of his character.

"All right, I guess; as long as you have good intentions," Alex joked. "Ettie is an awesome gal!"

Thirty minutes later, the silver bedside lamp was on in Lydia's bedroom, and Lydia lay tucked in bed under her flannel sheets and patchwork quilt. The bed was a low twin-size futon. Ettie sat on the edge of the futon, saying prayers with her sleepy daughter. They thanked God for all their blessings, then they requested His help with the hard things.

"And one more thing, God, if it is your plan, please help Lydia to have a nice daddy in our house."

Ettie prayed sincerely, however in her heart she did not feel much hope of this happening. She had not married Lydia's father and had been a single mom for five years. In those five years, she hadn't had any boyfriends. Not that she minded; she had experienced her fill of the complications of dating before Lydia had been born. Now she had the support of her parents, Evelyn and Sam Zeller, who lived only fifteen minutes away. They loved being available to help with Lydia anytime the need arose.

When prayer time ended, Ettie turned off the lamp and began to sing. At first, Lydia sang with her mother, their two voices blending sweetly together. As Lydia began to drift off to sleep, Ettie sang a Bible verse that their friend, Grace, had put to a tune, "I have set the Lord before me; because He's at my right hand, I will not be shaken. Psalm 16, verse 8."

Watching Lydia resting peacefully that night, Ettie felt her heart fill with an overwhelming sense of love and protectiveness for her delightful and innocent daughter. *God is at our right hand,* she mused; *He loves us and protects us too. What could shake us? Could anything shake our faith in Him?* The only thing that she could envision shaking their beautiful life together would be if something terrible were to happen to Lydia. Ettie was thankful that she couldn't even begin to imagine what that *something* might be.

"*Remember your Creator in the days of your youth, before the days of trouble come.*"

ECCLESIASTES 12:1A

Chapter 2
LEARNING TO RIDE A BIKE

May passed quickly as Ettie and Lydia finished up their school year. The school days were filled with friends, laughter, and learning. Lydia was learning the skills it would take to be a successful kindergartener the following year. Ettie was honing her abilities to teach and inspire in her second year as a pre-kindergarten teacher. It was a blessing for them to be at San Diego Country Day together.

Every day they saw each other on the playground after lunch. Lydia's class usually got to the playground first. She and her friends took turns on the swings, the monkey bars, and the slide. When they saw the other pre-k classes begin to arrive at the park, they began a waiting game for Lydia's mom. They would circle around a crepe myrtle tree, hold hands and sing, "We're waiting for Miss Mommy, we're waiting for Miss Mommy." When Ettie's class headed down the gentle slope towards the playground, Lydia and her girlfriends would dash towards her, and there were hugs all around. Lydia's friends were quite generous in their appreciation of their friend's mother, whom—when they weren't playing the "Miss Mommy" game—they called Ms. Zeller.

The pre-kindergarten and kindergarten teachers at Country Day chose a theme each year to unify their eight classes. This year they selected "The Zoo." Ettie's class was the bear class and Lydia's was the elephant class. At the culmination of the school year, the classes performed a singing extravaganza highlighting each class's mascot. Three children from the eight classes were chosen to represent their peers with speaking parts in the performance. These students were chosen based on their reading and memorization skills as they had many lines to recite.

One Friday in May, Lydia skipped into her mother's classroom at the end of the school day. Ettie's students had already been dismissed, and she was at her desk quietly preparing the assignments for Monday. Lydia came in with such excitement shining in her eyes, and so busily waving a packet of papers in her hand, that her mother guessed that she had been given a speaking part in the "Zoo Play" scheduled for June 10th. As soon as Lydia began to share the news, Ettie knew that her guess had been correct.

"Mama, look! This is the best day ever. Ms. Paxon picked me to be a zookeeper in the play!" Lydia handed the script to her mother and did a few bouncy jumps like a rabbit. "Matthew in my class is going to be a zookeeper too and so is Rosalyn from Ms. Wessler's class. Ms. Paxon said we'll get to wear a straw safari hat. Isn't that fun? I won't get to wear the floppy elephant ears all the other kids in my class will wear. They will look super cute. Did you know the homeroom moms came in to start making them today? I guess that's okay because Rosalyn says we will look pretty in our safari hats. Do you think I can memorize all these lines, Mama?" Lydia moved nearer to her mother's desk and pointed to the script. Ms. Paxon had already highlighted in yellow the lines that Lydia was to perform in the play.

"Yes, sweetheart," Ettie replied, "I have complete confidence that you will be able to memorize these. You're a smart girl; I know you will do a fabulous job! Should we start working on it now?"

The rest of Friday afternoon and evening, Lydia read and reread her lines. Lydia's lilting soprano continued to practice line after line-as Ettie finished preparing her room for class on Monday, as they drove home in their blue Jetta, and as she unpacked the three bags of groceries they had picked up on the way home. She even read the lines of her zookeeper companions and sang the songs that were in between each scene of dialogue. Into Saturday morning and early afternoon, as Ettie cleaned their apartment and folded laundry, Lydia's focus was nearly unwavering. She only took a break to eat, watch *Wishbone*, and have an impromptu dance class with her imaginary friends. At three in the afternoon, when Ettie suggested that they get some fresh air, Lydia agreed.

"Lydia," Ettie called from the porch as she rolled Lydia's pink sparkly Barbie bike out the back gate, "It's cool out here. The thermometer says it's 62 degrees. Will you please grab a sweatshirt for both of us?"

Ettie parked the bike on the sidewalk in the shade of the California buckeye trees that lined the walk. Then she went back through the porch gate and grabbed her roller blades from the tiny porch closet. Going back through the apartment, Ettie took her keys from their hook and her black sweatshirt from Lydia's outstretched hand. Zipping up their hoodies, they stepped out the front door into the brisk air. Lydia snapped on her helmet, took three steps in the direction of her bike, and gasped.

"Oh, Mama! I didn't remember that my training wheels were off. Grandpa took them off last weekend, didn't he? Oh my, now I can learn to ride without training wheels! Can we go all the way down to the duck pond? Can we bring bread to feed the ducks? I'm going to learn to ride my bike today!" Lydia declared this last sentence triumphantly several times as she danced in a circle around her bike.

After Ettie finished buckling her rollerblades, she glided towards her exuberant daughter. "Alright, cutie, let's give this bike ride a try. Sure, we can go all the way to the duck pond, but let's save the bread for another day. I'm going to need to hold the back of your bike and your handlebar while you learn to balance."

Lydia climbed confidently onto her bike as Ettie held onto the back of the seat with one hand and the left handlebar with the other. Slowly and carefully, Lydia pedaled down the sidewalk about 30 yards till they came to the driveway of their apartment complex. There they stopped and looked both ways before going again. The driveway wound through the entire neighborhood. For the first thirty minutes, Ettie held onto the bike with a firm grip as they traveled along their route. Eventually, she relaxed her hold and allowed Lydia to practice balancing on her own.

The first several times Ettie let go of the bike, Lydia wobbled quite a bit, and twice she fell. She shed a few angry tears and voiced her frustration freely. Ettie knew her daughter was used to learning new things quickly and easily, yet she certainly didn't seem ready to give up. Ettie was thankful that she had her rollerblades to help her stay alongside Lydia's bike. She knew she would never have been able to keep running for as long as Lydia wanted to practice riding. It was dinner time before they rode back to apartment 371—hungry and exhausted. As challenging as the bike riding lesson had been for Lydia, she had high hopes for soon becoming a successful cyclist.

Sunday after church, they practiced the script for a couple of hours until Lydia had each one of her lines completely committed to memory. Her intonation and enunciation were a delight to hear—she was a natural actress. What a proud mom Ettie was as she listened to her daughter. Feeling satisfied with their efforts, they once again headed outside to practice riding without training wheels.

However, Lydia's disappointment with herself at not being able to balance alone right away clouded the otherwise sunny afternoon. Time after time, her bike was close to toppling over. After her first fall, she stomped her foot and cried out that she would never learn to ride. Then Ettie realized if she rollerbladed close enough to the bike, she could catch it before it completely tipped over. She encouraged her daughter to try once more and the two continued to cruise around Green Tree Square.

When they arrived at the duck pond, they decided to take a rest. Lydia put the kickstand down on her bicycle and sat with her mom on a wooden park bench. In discouragement, she vented, "I don't know if I will *ever* learn to ride by myself, Mama. I mean, it's way harder than I thought it would be. It's easy with the training wheels on; I guess Grandpa could put them back on. Why are some things so hard to learn?"

"You will learn, Lyddie. I know you will. Soon you will be able to balance yourself very well. And until that point, I will be right there next to you. You are very good at learning new things. Look at how quickly you memorized all your lines for the zoo play."

"That's what I don't understand. Why was it easy to learn the lines, but it's *so* hard to learn to ride my bike?" Lydia emphasized the word "so" to make it sound about four syllables long.

"Well, that's how life is. Some parts are hard, and other parts are easy. If everything were easy, we would never learn to persevere."

"What does that mean?"

"It means when something is hard for you, you keep trying even if trouble gets in your way and even if you feel frustrated. You persevere because the thing you are trying to do is important to you."

"You mean like learning to ride a bike is important to me?"

"Yes, just like that. And you know what else? You know how I am with you, right by your side, while you are trying to ride your bike? God is right with us when we are going through trouble in our lives. He helps us to persevere because he gives us his strength and his joy to keep on trying. And he doesn't even need to wear rollerblades to keep up." Ettie chuckled at her own joke. Lydia was listening with her eyes on her mother's, and seeing her mother laugh, her blue-green eyes regained their sparkle.

"Thanks, Mama. I'm going to keep trying, and someday I think I will learn to ride my bike. It might take a super long time—maybe a whole year! Oh, there is Colton!" Lydia had spotted her friend who lived in the apartment next door arriving at the duck pond with his parents. "Can I go feed the ducks with him?"

"Sure, sweetheart." As Lydia skipped toward the pond, Ettie's phone vibrated in the pocket of her sweatshirt. She took the phone out and answered, "Hello?"

"Hi Ettie; it's Natalia. How's your weekend going?"

"It's going well, Natalia, thanks. We are outside enjoying this beautiful day. Lydia is learning how to ride her bike. How about you?"

"Aw, that's exciting! Well, Alex and I both worked such long hours this week—we are kind of taking it easy today. We have been brainstorming plans for our Bible study group. We have a few ideas for outreach that we want to discuss with everyone next week. We're also hoping to get everyone together this Thursday night."

"Okay, sounds good. What's happening Thursday?"

"It's Alex's birthday and we are going to celebrate at the new rock-climbing gym on Clarence Highway. We're planning to meet at seven. Can you join us?"

"I'd love to. Thanks for the invite. I'll plan to be there as long as my parents are available to watch Lydia for a couple of hours."

When Ettie and Natalia finished their conversation, Ettie called her parents to see if one or both were free on Thursday evening to spend time with Lydia. They had all seen each other at church that morning, and Lydia had been proud to recite some of her zookeeper lines for them in the courtyard after the service. When Ettie called asking if they could come over on Thursday, Evelyn answered the phone and said that she could. She was happy that she could have another opportunity to hear Lydia as she practiced.

Thursday's nightfall arrived, and Ettie welcomed Evelyn into their home. She smiled as Evelyn and Lydia quickly settled into comfortable spots on the couch and became engrossed in their mini-rehearsal. As she kissed her daughter goodbye, her heart was thankful that she could enjoy peace of mind knowing that Lydia was safe and happy with her grandmother for the evening.

Her thankfulness was quickly clouded by discomfort as she walked to her car. She felt conspicuous going out in public in her khaki shorts—the ones she normally wore for rollerblading. It seemed like they were too short to wear to a Bible study get-together. Her friend, Natalia, had suggested that she wear "workout attire" for rock climbing. The khakis were Ettie's only option.

The first person Ettie laid eyes on when she walked into the gym was the young man she had met at Bible study the week before—Chip Crew. She remembered his name from the name tag on his uniform, and she recalled the embarrassment she had caused him with her compliment. As the door to the gym closed, Chip looked over and waved. Now it was Ettie's turn to be discomfited; she thought about her khaki shorts and blushed. Now she wished she were wearing something else! Self-consciously, she waved back. Her legs were not her favorite feature, but at that moment she was grateful that at least they were in shape from all the rollerblading she had been doing.

Ettie joined a group of her friends who stood gathered at the base of one of the beginner-level climbing walls. The gym instructor had just started giving pointers on how to use the gear and how to climb safely. While listening to the instructor, Ettie looked around and noticed that her friends were wearing shorts that were similar in length to hers. Maybe they weren't as short as they felt after all.

When the rock-climbing teacher had finished his instructions, he handed out the equipment that they would need to wear. Ettie attempted to put the harness on around her hips and waist as he had demonstrated; it wasn't as easy as it had looked when he had done it. Fumbling with the straps and buckles, she stood at the base of the rock wall. She was looking down at the harness when she noticed someone standing half a foot away from her wearing a large pair of men's New Balance sneakers. Who was standing that close? She thought the instructor must have seen her confusion and come over to help her. What a jolt she felt when she lifted her eyes and saw that it was Chip Crew smiling and offering to assist.

"Hi, Ettie. Can I help you with that?" he asked kindly.

When Ettie returned his greeting and acquiesced, Chip stepped even closer and began adjusting the straps on the harness. His hands moved deftly as he made sure that the straps around her thighs, hips, and waist were snugly fitting. Her khakis were short enough that his hand brushed the skin of her thigh. His confident touch and his closeness took Ettie by surprise. This is not what she had imagined when she had agreed to go rock climbing. While she stood still as Chip snapped the last buckle, she realized she rather liked this surprise.

Chip stepped back grinning, and Ettie was suddenly aware of how charming his smile was. "Oh my, you are certainly practiced with putting on a climbing harness," she remarked, returning his smile. "I guess you've done this before?"

"Well, basically, yes. Rock climbing has been one of my hobbies for many years. When I was younger, I was part of a club that did a lot of climbing at Yosemite."

"Really? That's cool. I love Yosemite too! Our family does a lot of camping and hiking there but never any rock climbing. The hike around Mirror Lake is my favorite. Have you climbed Half Dome?"

"Yes, and what an intense climb that was. I haven't done any other climbs that compare to that one. You sure have to watch out on the ascent up the cables."

The climbing instructor motioned to Ettie to begin scaling the rock wall. Ettie got her next surprise when Chip stepped forward and began climbing next to her. Side by side, they reached from one handhold to the next. Midway up the wall, Ettie joked that Chip must be waiting for her since she was able to keep up with him—he with a lot of experience and she with none. Chip responded with a grin; when they reached the top, he confided in mock seriousness, "I never leave my climbing partner behind." Ettie found herself giggling like a happy schoolgirl at his silly sense of humor.

After they and their friends had all completed their evening of rock climbing, they gathered at the gym's tables in the lobby. Natalia had brought a cake to celebrate Alex's birthday, and to jest about Alex's affinity for a juicy burger, the cake was decorated to look like a cheeseburger. Ettie sat down next to her friend, Danielle, and began a conversation about Danielle's new job prospects in Seattle. As she listened, Ettie glanced across the table to where Chip was enjoying his piece of chocolate "cheeseburger" cake. He looked up at the same time, and Ettie noticed that his eyes were hazel-the same mix of green and brown that she had in her own eyes. Now she knew that they had three things in common: hazel eyes, a love for Yosemite, and a daughter in elementary school. Ettie wondered if over time they might find they had even more in common.

Ettie and Chip had that chance two weeks later when Bible study was relocated to Ettie's apartment. Apparently in receiving the message about the changed venue, Chip had not heard that the time was also pushed back a half hour; therefore, he arrived considerably early. Ettie was still cleaning up the dinner dishes and preparing to rearrange the furniture to make room for their friends to squeeze into her tiny living room when she heard the knock on the door. Chip must have seen the look of bewilderment on Ettie's face when she opened the door, because he immediately questioned, "Oh, hello, Ettie. Am I early?"

"Yes," Ettie agreed as she regained her composure. "That's fine. Come on in; how was your day?"

Chip, wearing his olive-green flight suit and black boots, explained that he had been flying a long mission that day, had assumed that he was late to Bible study, and had rushed across town to Ettie's apartment without heading home to change first. They both laughed at the misunderstanding because in their hearts neither one minded the mix-up. Chip offered to help get ready for their friends to arrive; Ettie explained to him how she was hoping to reposition the couch and chairs into a circle. As she finished cleaning the dishes, he quickly arranged the furniture. Working together, they finished efficiently and still had fifteen minutes before Bible study began.

Ettie started a conversation with Chip about his workday. He shared how their jet's flight pattern had taken them over Yosemite and how he had been able to see the two landmarks they had discussed the week before at the climbing gym. "The waterfalls are at their peak runoff this time of year, and I was looking down wishing that I was there hiking," Chip shared.

"Any time of year is awesome at Yosemite," Ettie agreed. "I have some fabulous photos from earlier this spring when there was lots of snow up at the White Wolf campsites. We saw a marmot for the first time too. Would you like to see a couple of the pictures?"

When Chip agreed, Ettie pulled out her photo album from underneath the coffee table. It was a wine-colored scrapbook that she had received as a gift from a friend. Ettie and Chip sat down next to one another on the couch, and Ettie flipped through the pages till she reached the most recent photographs. The Zeller family had all taken a trip to Yosemite together that spring; and after Chip admired the beauty of the scenic photos, he commented on how much Ettie looked like her sisters, Brittany and Molly, and also like Lydia.

Lydia, playing nearby in her bedroom, must have heard her name mentioned because a moment later she came traipsing out of her room carrying her favorite doll, Hope. Hope was wrapped carefully in Lydia's special pink baby blanket. Lydia walked over to the couch and stood shyly by her mother's side. Meeting new boys or men was perhaps the only time in her life that Lydia became quiet. Ettie introduced the two of them, and Chip tried to be friendly by commenting on the letters he could see on the corner of Lydia's pink blanket, "I like how you have your name sewn right on your blanket, Lydia."

Knowing Lydia's discomfort, Ettie answered, explaining how her mother's sewing machine had a special setting for making letters. She tried to think what else might help Lydia warm up to her new friend…the pictures of the zoo play! Country Day's zoo play had been the day before, and Ettie had been so excited about seeing the photos that she had stopped at the one-hour photo shop on her way home from work. She excused herself from the couch and grabbed the envelope from the kitchen counter. She was even more excited to share these pictures than she had been to show the Yosemite photos; she was proud of how well Lydia had done in her role as a zookeeper.

As they looked at the play pictures together, Lydia became slightly more talkative as she pointed out several of her friends in their animal costumes. The last photo in the stack was of Lydia riding her Barbie bike, taken three days before, right after Lydia had begun to ride independently. Looking at herself on her bike, Lydia began chatting in earnest: "There I am! I can ride my bike now! I sure didn't think that I was going to *ever* learn and then I got it! Isn't that funny? Mama, can we go bike riding after Bible study?"

"Hmm, it's going to be dark when Bible study is over. We can go again tomorrow. Lydia, did you know that Mr. Chip has a daughter too?" Ettie turned to Chip, "Do you have a picture of her with you?"

Chip did have one in his wallet. He pulled his black leather wallet out of the pocket on the lower leg of his flight suit. The photo showed a beautiful young girl, with wavy hair and a happy smile. "This is Helen," he announced proudly. "She is sweet and smart, and she definitely loves to ride her bike—just like you, Lydia." At that moment, the doorbell rang. As Ettie stood to answer the door, she realized the fourth thing she and Chip had in common: they were both thankful for their daughters.

Throughout the summer, Ettie and Chip began to be closer friends. Once, Chip offered to pick Ettie up for church. She was charmed by his thoughtful gestures of chivalry: he opened the car door for her and Lydia, and he offered to carry her Bible. Even though Chip's squadron traveled frequently during the latter part of summer and early fall, by October, Chip had finally decided to call Ettie on the phone number that he had gotten from the Novaks in May. If Ettie had known the darkness that was to follow, she never would have answered the phone.

"I know you,
I walked with you
Once upon a dream.
I know you,
The gleam in your eyes is so familiar a gleam,
Yet I know it's true
That visions are seldom all they seem."

PRINCESS AURORA

Chapter 3

REMEMBER YOU'RE GOD'S CHILD

A lovely October breeze blew in the open windows of Ettie's classroom as she sat at the table and worked with a couple of her students in the "Rabbit" class. A new school year had begun and the kindergarten theme for the year was "The Forest." Directly across from her sat Max, a lively boy with a mop of blond curls and an endearing lisp. Every time Ettie called him over to work at her table, he answered, "Yeth, Mith Thellah, I'll wowk wiff you."

Ettie smiled as she watched the three children at her table who were concentrating on their writing. Sometimes her students were so funny, and she loved working with her assistant, Ms. Sonya Renaldo. Her enthusiasm for cheering the children on was contagious. As the students worked on their art projects, Ettie often heard Ms. Renaldo exclaim, "You go, girl!" or "You're going to town on that drawing." That morning, Ms. Renaldo made Ettie laugh. Diligently painting a picture of a dog, Eric, one of their class artists, had asked innocently, "Ms. Renaldo, am I going to town today?"

Forgetting her phrase of encouragement, Ms. Renaldo replied sincerely, "I don't know, Eric. Is your dad taking you downtown after school today?" Ettie and Sonya had chuckled about it while their students were at PE. During the half-hour while their pre-k students were exercising with the coach, the two women had a chance to catch up on their personal lives. Sonya shared with Ettie about her doctor's visit the day before; her broken arm was mending well, and she would be able to get her cast off within the next two weeks.

"Do you think you'll be getting back on your rollerblades any time soon?" Ettie wondered as she searched through the classroom supply closet looking for a new box of colored pencils.

Sonya looked chagrined, "Well, not if my husband has anything to say about it. He's convinced that at my age roller skating isn't a wise choice for exercise. He thinks swimming might be a safer option; we haven't heard of anyone who broke her arm swimming laps!"

"True! Aw, sorry to hear that. I sure would miss rollerblading if something happened, and I couldn't go anymore. It gives me a wonderful sense of freedom. Hey, guess what? The guy that I met at Bible study, the one that I told you about—he called me last night."

Sonya took one look at Ettie's glowing smile and made a guess, "He invited you out, didn't he? Where is he taking you?" She added after Ettie nodded.

"We're going to an event for his squadron on Saturday night. He called it a 'Hail and Farewell.'"

"You have two days to decide what to wear, then? Maybe a little black dress?"

"Yeah, Chip said that the dress will be 'standard nice casual'—whatever that means."

"You could wear jeans and you'd still knock his socks off."

"Sonya, you're the sweetest. Thanks." She glanced at the large wall clock, "Oh hey, it's time to pick up the kids."

Walking down the open hallway towards the gym, Ettie considered Sonya's words of encouragement. Would she really make any sort of impression on Chip? She wasn't sure; she hadn't had a date in almost six years. There must be some reason that no one had asked her out. Although, it could have simply been that God was protecting her heart and Lydia's. She was certainly thankful that it hadn't been the opposite—a series of broken relationships. That would have been difficult for both of them. Maybe God had kept her single and happy until the right guy came along. Maybe it was Chip.

She stopped her musing and laughed inwardly at herself. She felt like a young girl fantasizing about her fairy tale life—Cinderella, maybe. *Why is it that a girl's approach to a first date is often shadowed with thoughts about marrying the guy?* she wondered. She had talked to many of her friends about it, and they agreed that it happened to them too. How silly! She wished she could change the pattern of her thinking! She resolved to work on it anyway.

Saturday evening came, and when Chip rang the doorbell, Ettie was ready wearing her favorite black dress pants and a simple white blouse. She also had her hair down. She almost always wore it in a bun or a braid, so it was the first time Chip had seen it down. His generous compliments sent her straight back to the fairy tale! "Your hair looks gorgeous, Esther. I love it down. Honestly, it's not about the hair. I think you're beautiful on the inside too."

Together they walked with Lydia out to Chip's blue convertible Mustang. Lydia was having her first sleepover at Grandma and Grandpa's house. Driving to Sam and Evelyn's house, Lydia seemed enthralled with her first ever top-down convertible ride: she watched the world whizzing by without her normal car ride chatter. This gave Ettie a chance to relive the compliment Chip had just given her: *he thought she was beautiful!* And he had called her "Esther;" only her grandfather called her Esther. Both of those things combined to make her feel very special. She almost floated right out of the car's open top like a helium balloon.

Of course, the top-down of the Mustang was causing her long hair to blow all over. The realization that her efforts to curl the ends of her hair would come to naught brought her right back down to earth. She was going to look quite a mess by the time they made it to the party. Oh well, she felt like a princess on the inside.

They reached Sam and Evelyn's wooden ranch-style home, and Chip carried Lydia's pink suitcase to the door. Chip greeted her parents with an amiable smile and a firm handshake. It was the first time they had met. Evelyn quickly made her granddaughter feel welcome by describing their fun plans to bake a cake that evening.

As they looked at the colorful sprinkles she had bought to decorate the top, Ettie could hear Chip telling her dad about a fellow pilot's fatal jet crash. Now that Ettie had known Chip for five months, she was aware that he would often embellish a story for effect—yet this particular tale seemed a bit incongruous for their first meeting. She was glad that her dad was a good communicator; he adroitly moved the conversation to a more suitable theme, football. They discussed how the Chargers were faring that season. They both had high hopes for the upcoming game against the Raiders.

Soon it was time to leave for the party. Ettie sat down on the brown leather sofa and hugged Lydia tight for a long moment; it felt strange to be leaving Lydia there for the night without her. Lydia was more than happy with the arrangement. She cherished spending time with her grandparents. During the first four years of her life, she and Ettie had lived with Sam and Evelyn, and their bond of love was strong. It was just in the last year that Lydia and her mother had ventured out to their apartment in Green Tree Square. Ettie knew it was a blessing that her parents were as supportive as ever.

Ettie leaned back and looked into Lydia's beautiful blue-green eyes, "Have a good night, Lydia, and be sweet for Grandma and Grandpa. Remember you're God's child. I will see you at church in the morning, okay?"

"Okay, Mama, you too; have a good night. Guess what? Grandma says tomorrow, in Sunday school, we are painting a still life of fruit. Because we are learning about the fruit of the spirit in Sunday school. You know: 'love, joy, peace, patience, kindness, goodness.'" Lydia merrily sang the verse from memory and Ettie nodded. Sam and Evelyn taught Lydia's kindergarten Sunday school class and they always had fun activities for the kids. "She says I can come with her to the grocery store on the way to church and pick out the fruit. I think pineapples are the best, don't you? I hope Lynn and Sarah will be there. They are my bestest friends at church, and they'll love painting a picture of fruit too. Do you think they'll be there, Grandma?"

"Yes, Lydia. I do; they are there almost every week. All right, Chip and Ettie. Have a nice time." Evelyn showed them to the door. Ettie turned to take one last look at her sweet daughter. She was happily working on a wooden Jack and Jill puzzle on the coffee table with her grandpa. Ettie knew that Lydia was going to have a great time with her grandparents; now she wondered how it was going to go with Chip at the squadron event. She had never spent time with a group of Naval officers before.

The ride to the other side of town was pleasant. Chip had noticed Ettie's hair blowing around on the way and put the top up before they started their ride. They had half an hour of quiet conversation about life and work. For the first time in their friendship, they each shared with each other about their past. Ettie told Chip how she had graduated from college when she was three months pregnant, and how her parents had been God's hands and heart to her during her five years as a single mom. Then Chip opened up and talked about his marriage during his early college years; the marriage had ended after three years, and now he found it very difficult to live apart from Helen. Sharing their stories seemed to be a natural part of their blossoming friendship, and Ettie felt closer to Chip than ever when they arrived at the officer's home where the party was being hosted.

The evening began with decorum: a lavish dinner was served buffet style from large tables on the patio near the pool. As the squadron photographer, Chip busied himself with getting candid shots of his fellow officers. Next, everyone gathered outside for brief speeches and poems to hail and farewell the transitioning officers. Ettie made conversation with a friend of Chip's whose beer was helping him to be especially gregarious. Although Chip wasn't by her side during the dinner hour due to his responsibility, when the speeches began, he sat down with his date near the front of the group in a prime picture-taking spot.

The poolside bench they sat on was crowded. Ettie was still surprised when Chip squeezed in so close to her that their bodies were pressed tightly together as if they were in a New York subway.

She considered easing to the right nonchalantly but reconsidered when she realized that the nearness to Chip was not unpleasant. The warmth of his shoulder and thigh was delightful next to hers in the cool evening air. She liked the scent of his aftershave as well and decided to stay right where she was.

When the speeches began, Ettie became uncomfortable with the off-color sailors' humor that filtered into much of the hail and farewell "poetry." After the third inappropriate reference, she and Chip glanced at each other; his concerned eyes and facial expression mirrored her discomfort. He cupped his hand by his mouth and whispered in Ettie's ear, "Sorry about the language. Some of these guys forget that there are ladies present." Knowing that Chip wasn't on board with that kind of talk helped Ettie to feel better. At least her date was behaving in a gentlemanly fashion. Ettie tuned out the officer who was speaking and began daydreaming about being somewhere more remarkable with Chip still close by her side. Maybe hiking the Bridalveil Fall Trail at Yosemite in June. They could stroll along the lush, green path listening to the beautiful, fluting song of the Mountain Bluebird. She imagined the spraying mist blowing onto their faces and dampening their hair.

Splash!

Ettie suddenly jumped; her reverie abruptly ended. That was real water wetting her face! She turned around and saw two grown men, fully dressed, splashing in the water behind her, and three more wrestling at the pool's edge. As she watched, two of the three tumbled into the water causing another large splatter of cold water that soaked the people standing nearby. The third man stood victorious on the deck laughing at his wet comrades as they spluttered to the surface.

Apparently, the speeches had ended while Ettie had been musing. She was grateful when Chip quickly ushered her inside away from the rowdy crowd; she did not want to go swimming in October! They collected their jackets from the entryway, and after saying thank you to their host and hostess, climbed into Chip's Mustang.

"Wow, Ettie, that was quite the initiation into Navy life. You know, those guys aren't always this boisterous." Chip chuckled. "You looked pretty shocked when they started throwing each other into the pool."

"Yeah, I guess I was. Growing up with a pool in our backyard, we were taught the number one rule was 'No horseplay on the pool deck.' My parents were very concerned that someone was going to end up getting seriously hurt. I guess these guys haven't heard that rule."

"I knew I should have brought you somewhere else on our first date," Chip joked.

"That would have been smart," Ettie teased in return. Then she added, "You might not want to take me to any more Navy events. Those guys are less mature than the four-year-olds that I teach every day. At least my students are still kind of cute when they act foolish."

The easy banter between the two friends continued during the drive across town. It wasn't until they reached Ettie's apartment and she took out her keys to unlock the door that Chip turned serious. "Thanks for coming with me tonight. I know it was more than you bargained for, but I liked having you by my side."

He leaned forward and tipped his face toward Ettie. His mouth barely brushed the corner of her lips. It was so gentle, it seemed to Ettie that a butterfly had kissed her. She smiled up into his hazel eyes and felt that something subtle had shifted in their acquaintance. She wondered if perhaps it was going to be more than a friendship. As she opened the door and whispered, "Good night, Chip," she began to hope that it would.

Ettie didn't have to wonder for long. The very next evening after Ettie had tucked Lydia into bed for the night, the phone rang. Chip was calling to invite her on a second date. It was another Navy event and since he was uncertain about how she felt about going with him, he phrased his invitation in the third person.

"Ettie, can I get your opinion?"

"Sure."

"Well, I have a friend who wants to take a woman to go with

him to his Dining Out, but he's rather nervous about asking her. He thinks maybe she doesn't want to go to any more Navy functions. What do you think? Should he invite her?"

"Oh, hmm, let me think." Ettie paused to collect her thoughts. She knew that she had been too outspoken and hasty in her appraisal of his coworkers the night before. Of course, she wanted to give them another chance, and certainly, she looked forward to spending more time with *this* dashing young officer. "Yes. Yes, I do. I think he should. I have a feeling she would love to go."

Thus, it was decided: in two weeks Ettie would accompany Chip downtown to the prestigious Ocean Club for an evening of formal squadron festivities. For most of the time between the invitation and the event, Chip was in Puerto Rico for work; so he and Ettie stayed in contact via email. He kept Ettie entertained with stories of his travels. His notes overflowed with kindness and compliments. Ettie returned his epistles with tales of her own from her adventures teaching four-year-olds. Two days before Chip's expected return, Ettie typed the following email at her school computer before she went home for the afternoon:

"Dear Chip, I hope that you are having an excellent day! I loved the email that I got from you this morning. You sure know how to make me smile. Your sweet words worked their way right into my heart and kept me smiling all day. Thank you again; each email you send seems to be better than the last one. How are you going to keep that up?! I am missing you too. It's nice that we are getting to know each other in a new and exciting kind of way through our writing. The trip you took to the gorge sounds cool! I love the picture you sent! I took a successful trip too; mine was to the mall. Ha ha. I found a gorgeous black dress for the dining out that is super perfect. No pictures: you'll have to wait and see. Here's one funny story from the school day before I head home: at the lunch table, Frankie was eating his salad with his fingers. I tried to encourage him to use good table manners, so I said, "Please use your Frank, forkie." Oops! We all got a good laugh from that one. May God fill your day with His joy. Love, Ettie"

Since her schoolwork was completed for the day, Ettie logged off the computer and gathered her things into her canvas book bag. Lydia had been playing an "I Spy" game on the classroom's second computer; she logged off too and picked up her purple backpack. On the way to their car, Lydia recounted the events of her day as she loved to do. She was still chatting happily fifteen minutes later as they pulled into their parking lot, "Ms. Chapman told us that we will get to go on a field trip to their farm at the end of the year! I can hardly wait because they have sheep and goats and horses and chickens and *everything*. Isn't Wesley lucky that he gets to live there all the time? He did say it is kind of stinky sometimes. Is your class going on the same field trip, Mama?" She paused and when she got no reply, she leaned forward and tried again, "Is your class going too?"

"Oh sorry, honey; yes, we're going. It will be a great field trip." Then she exclaimed the reason for her distraction, "Look, Lydia! Mr. Chip's car is here! How can that be? He is supposed to be in Puerto Rico till Thursday. I hope everything is okay."

They walked down the sidewalk quickly, and when they rounded the corner, Chip was waiting in front of their green front door with a bouquet of daisies in hand. He had come directly from the Navy base and was still wearing his flight suit, and he was laughing at the fun of surprising his two new favorite girls. His squadron had sent him back early for a special assignment. He hadn't wanted to notify Ettie ahead of time so that he could take her by surprise. And he did; she was laughing too, with delight. Her heart did a backflip when he gazed into her eyes longingly as he gallantly presented her with the flowers. "Oh, thank you," she whispered.

"I have something for you, too, Lydia, a special present that I got just for you in Puerto Rico. But it will have to be okay with your mom because it's a pet."

"A pet? Yes! I love pets! Mommy, please, can I?" Lydia gushed.

"Really? A pet? Chip, what kind of pet?"

"Trust me." His hazel eyes lit up with a sparkle.

"Okay; yes, then."

Chip pulled out a beautiful, carved stone turtle from the breast pocket of his uniform and placed it gently into Lydia's upturned palm. If she was disappointed at all that it wasn't alive, she didn't show it. Her vivid imagination took flight, and she began to think of a name for her new pet turtle. She skipped around the garden by their front porch with her turtle in hand. Ettie watched her daughter's endearing play with joy in her heart. When Ettie turned her head to thank Chip, she found him gazing intently at her. She blushed, yet she managed to say sincerely, "Thank you so much. Lydia likes it; I think you're her new buddy."

"I want to be *your* buddy." Chip's charming turn of phrase took Ettie by surprise all over again. He took her hand in his and an electric wave of pleasure went from Ettie's hand to her toes and back up to her face where the current turned up the corners of her mouth. "Will you let me?" he asked.

Of course, Ettie would; she was swept off her feet by this amorous young man. October ended with the new couple enjoying each other's company at the Dining Out on the top floor of the Ocean Club. November rolled into December. Chip gave his girlfriend a leather-bound NIV study Bible for Christmas inscribed with "To Esther—my best friend forever." For Lydia, he bought a Barbie fishing pole that came complete with fishing lessons in the pond at their apartment complex. Chip's daughter came down from Moreno Valley to help celebrate the holiday, and Lydia and Helen were fast friends. Together they enjoyed singing and dancing and playing dress-up. When Chip and Ettie took their girls out to eat for dinner one night, a woman mistook Lydia and Helen for sisters. They did have the same delicate oval-shaped face, the same wavy light brown hair, and the same bright blue-green eyes. Chip and Ettie were delighted with how well their daughters got along.

It seemed like a match made in heaven. Not only was Chip charismatic and romantic, but he was helpful and thoughtful too.

Ettie loved spending time with him and was excited when he took her out to dinner at her favorite Italian restaurant on Valentine's Day. She was even more thrilled when the maître d' presented her with a dozen red long-stem roses and a bottle of champagne at Chip's request as they sat at their table in a quiet corner. As the maître d' walked away, Chip pulled a gray velvet box from his pocket.

Opening the box to reveal a Tiffany cut diamond solitaire engagement ring, Chip got down on one knee next to Ettie. "Ettie, I love you, and I can't live without you. Will you share your life with me?" he requested. He stood and slipped the ring onto her finger. Now she was truly surprised; they had known each other for such a short time and had been dating for a mere five months. Yet how could she say no, since she had absolutely fallen for this guy? She couldn't say no, so she said the only thing left: "Yes."

Later that night, as Ettie lay in bed preparing to fall asleep, she replayed the events of the evening in her mind. The pictures paraded before her eyes like a happy family movie. She saw Chip smiling broadly as he drove them from the restaurant to her parents' home. There was her dad, Sam, in the driveway shaking hands with Chip to congratulate him on their engagement. Next, she saw her mom, Evelyn, in the green and white kitchen laughing about how they had known about the proposal for two weeks, and it had been hard to keep quiet about it. Finally came a vision of sweet Lydia, so tired that she had almost fallen asleep at her grandparents' house during all the congratulations. She had somehow managed to stay awake far past her bedtime. When they had gotten back to their apartment, Ettie had tucked her into her twin-size futon with a song and a prayer like she did every night. Then she whispered, "Remember you're God's child," and turned out the light.

Now, as Ettie started to drift off to sleep herself, that simple phrase stuck in her mind. It was a truth that she reminded Lydia of often. However, at the moment, it was she who seemed to need the reminder. Ettie knew that she was God's child too, and as His child, she had spent time praying to Him about her relationship with Chip. Yes, she had talked to God about the serious direction their dating was taking; *but* she realized with a sinking feeling, she hadn't waited to hear the still, small voice of His answer.

"They clothe themselves with violence.
From their callous hearts comes iniquity."

PSALM 73:6B&7A

Chapter 4

INIQUITY

Patcher, the petite black and white rabbit, hopped unhindered across the red tile of the screened-in porch. On quiet afternoons, he seemed to saunter about lazily on his large, padded feet; but this Saturday there was a flurry of activity coming in and out of the porch. Patcher's hopping had a much more decided *thumpity-thump* as he hid first under the asparagus fern and then darted under the low-backed white rocking chair when startled by the next footsteps approaching.

From her perch on a little red wooden footstool, Lydia giggled at Patcher's antics as he bounced from one hiding place to the next. *Wouldn't it be fun to be a rabbit hiding in the forest?* she wondered. The airy porch, with its profusion of foliage and flowering plants, was the perfect setting for her imagination. She moved off her seat on the stool and settled in the middle of the tile floor in the hopes that Patcher might hop by close enough that she could pet him on his next flight. As Lydia sat quietly waiting, she listened to the sound of clinking dishes and silverware coming from the open kitchen window.

It was the third Saturday that month that Lydia had attended a wedding shower for her mom, and in Lydia's opinion, it was the best shower by far. The first reason was that her best friend, Lynn, was there too. Lynn's mother, Ms. Ruby, was helping to host the party at

Ms. Grace Paxson's lovely home; and Lynn had been invited to keep Lydia company. The second reason was that it was fun to see Patcher again. When Lydia had been in Ms. Paxson's pre-kindergarten class the year before, she had seen Patcher in his rabbit cage every day since he was their class pet. Now, what a treat this was! She was getting to see him hop freely around on his porch.

Five minutes ticked by as Lydia waited patiently for Patcher. Then the porch door swung open with a creak and banged shut; Patcher bounced out of his spot under the rocking chair and off he went! He hopped in a path that was decidedly close to Lydia and as he passed, she put out her hand and briefly felt the soft, fine fur on his warm back. Lydia smiled as she looked up to see who had come out to join her on the porch. It was Lynn, and she was carrying a dainty china plate of cookies to share with Lydia.

"Hi, Lydia. That was cool! Did you get to pet Patcher?" Lynn asked before she took a bite of a sugar cookie covered in pink frosting and sugar sprinkles. Then she held out the plate to offer a dessert to her friend.

Lydia selected one of the pretty pink cookies too and nodded her head. When she had finished munching on the treat, she added, "Yes! I was sitting there like *forever!* When you closed the door, he came out of hiding and... ta-da!" She waved her hands with a flourish. "I got to pet him! Isn't Patcher so cute? Don't you love his little twitching nose and his fluffy, puffy tail? He is really soft. When I was in Ms. Paxson's class last year, we got to feed him carrots all the time. I wonder if we could feed him a carrot now?"

"Well, probably not right now," answered Lynn practically, "Your mom is about to start opening her presents, and she said that we can help her if we'd like."

"Oh, yes! I do! Did you see that big pile of presents? All right; let's go."

Heading through the kitchen first where Lynn placed the china plate near the sink, the two girls entered the front living room where all of Ettie's friends were gathered. Ettie sat in a floral wing back chair; dining chairs had been pulled in from the next room so that everyone could sit. It didn't feel crowded because of the broad window on the western side of the room. About twenty of Ettie's family members and friends had come to Grace's home to celebrate. As Lydia entered the circle of friends, she didn't feel shy as she sometimes did in a large group: these were women who had known her at church since she had been a baby.

Lydia didn't take a seat. She stood next to her mother on the right side of the wingback chair. She and Lynn waited till Ettie had finished chatting with Ms. Melanie and then handed her the first gift from the pile. Ettie unwrapped a flowered recipe box. Following Ms. Ruby's direction, she lifted the lid of the box and pulled out the card at the front of the stack. Written on the card, in Ruby's lovely, careful print, was a recipe which Ettie took a quick look at and began to read aloud for all to enjoy: "Recipe for Marriage. Ingredients: Two cups of true love. Two cups of faithfulness. One cup of thoughtfulness. One cup of kindness. Stir in laughter and forgiveness. Blend with humor and friendship. Sprinkle with hugs and kisses. Serve daily with warmth and kindness. Yields a lifetime of happiness."

When Ettie finished reading, a chorus of appreciative murmurs filled the room. Women chuckled aloud at the creative way Ruby had expressed her hopes for a blessed marriage. For the next hour, Lydia and Lynn presented Ettie with the presents that had been brought to the bridal shower. The theme of the shower was cooking; with her gift, each guest had also given a recipe card. At the end of the party, Ettie's recipe box from Ruby was full of directions such as how to bake homemade scones to serve with blueberry jam, how to prepare perfectly crisp pork chops, and how to concoct refreshing raspberry sherbet.

The recipes all sounded delicious to Lydia. The one that intrigued her the most was the recipe from Ms. Ruby. It seemed to have caught her mother's eye as well, for when they returned home to their apartment late that afternoon and began to unpack their bags of gifts, Ettie hung the recipe for marriage on the refrigerator. Ettie's heart was filled with thankfulness, and she was humming a little tune as she worked. As she pulled a shiny new muffin tin out of its packaging, she paused her song and asked Lydia, "Did you have a nice time at the party, sweetheart?"

Lydia's response was detailed and enthusiastic, and she repeated her favorite parts a couple of times before winding down and asking the questions on her mind about the recipe now displayed on the frig, "Mama, how do you cook a marriage? It doesn't really need to be cooked, does it?"

What adorable questions, Ettie thought as she tried to hold back the laughter that bubbled up inside her. She began explaining with a smile, "Well, you know, that card doesn't mean a literal 'recipe' for marriage. You're right; it doesn't need to be cooked. Just as in a recipe where there are certain steps to follow to make the food turn out right—in a marriage there are certain steps the husband and wife need to follow to make the marriage turn out right. The card gives some ideas about the things people need to do for each other when they love each other and want to be married forever. Things such as being kind to each other and always being forgiving and faithful."

Lydia listened to her mother as she carefully helped to unwrap the new white Williams Sonoma dinnerware they had been given at the bridal shower. She stacked three bowls without comment, so Ettie was thinking the conversation was finished, but soon Lydia looked up at her mother with her eyes squinted and her nose wrinkled up the tiniest bit as if she was trying very hard to figure something out. If she had seen herself in the mirror, she might have seen a resemblance to Patcher, the rabbit. She asked, "Like *we* are kind and forgiving to each other, right?" Ettie nodded and agreed, so Lydia posed her next question. "What about the faithful part, Mama? Aren't we supposed to be faithful to God?"

Ettie was surprised at how quickly Lydia's questions had transitioned from adorable to profound. She tried not to show that she was taken aback as she pondered the best way to respond. It was important to her as a mother that her daughter felt comfortable coming to her with life's questions, and she wanted to be sure her response helped Lydia to know that there were no "wrong" questions in their home. She put down the scissors she was using to trim the tags off their new fabric napkins; then she sat down at the table next to Lydia to be at her eye level.

"That's a good question, Lydia. When we are faithful to God, we make sure that we live in a way that shows that we love Him most of all. We put Him first in all that we do. In a marriage, the husband and wife are faithful to God first, and then they are faithful to each other. That means they will not have any other husband or wife; they will always stay with the one they have, and they will love only that one and no other. Does that make sense?"

Lydia agreed that it did, and now that these weighty issues had been clarified, she chatted merrily about the wedding shower once again. She began to compare it to the other two showers: one that had been given by the faculty at Country Day and the other given by the mothers of Ettie's students. Ettie couldn't quite focus on Lydia's ramblings; she had a nagging concern beginning to settle in her heart: *what if Lydia's naivete were to get her into trouble?* She had such a natural innocence that was refreshing to see in most circumstances; yet what if something bad happened, and Lydia didn't understand that it was wrong? Ettie knew this was very unlikely, but she couldn't shake the strange feeling of worry brought about by Lydia's guileless questions about marriage and faithfulness. She tried to refocus by being thankful that she would not be a single parent much longer. In one more week, she and Chip would be married. She felt sure that she would be able to count on him to help her teach and protect Lydia; he was a Christian man, a naval officer, and already a father to sweet Helen.

"Mama," Lydia's voice brought Ettie back to the present, "Can I wear my flower girl dress to church tomorrow? Please? It's so beautiful, isn't it? I am going to be Cinderella at the ball! I think it's too hard to wait a whole 'nother week to wear it."

Ettie explained patiently that they were going to have to wait to don their new lovely, beaded gowns; and wait they did. When the following Saturday rolled around, mother and daughter were both as lovely as princesses as they rustled around in their taffeta floor-length dresses. At ten o'clock in the morning, all the guests were in their seats, and the ceremony began. Dropping rose petals along their path, Lydia and Helen walked down the aisle and took their seats in the front row.

The three bridesmaids joined the girls at the front of the church. Lastly, Ettie walked down the aisle. Lydia thought her mother looked extremely happy; her smile was as bright as the stained-glass windows of Christ the King Church. Lydia's attention was intently focused on her mother and all the beautiful dresses and flowers; therefore, she didn't hear much of the service until Pastor Evan began his sermon. She loved Pastor Evan a lot, so she started to tune in. What was that he was saying? He was talking about how carefully we dress for special occasions. He must be talking about her mother in her gorgeous gown and her sparkly tiara. No, that was weird; he was saying that Chip needed to dress carefully. Was it because he was wearing his Navy uniform?

Well, Lydia reasoned, *I guess we all needed to look special for today.* Then, Pastor Evan explained what he meant. It was a Bible verse that Lydia had never heard before: "Therefore, as God's chosen people, holy and dearly loved, clothe yourselves with compassion, kindness, humility, gentleness, and patience. And over all these virtues put on love." Oh, that made sense to Lydia! The important part wasn't that they looked fancy on the outside; the important part was that they needed to dress their hearts up with love and kindness. Her mom had talked to her about that before, Lydia remembered, the morning they had that big argument about which uniform to wear to school. That was what Pastor Evan was teaching about: when you got married you had to be sure that you were beautiful on the inside too.

Pastor Evan's sermon reminded Lydia of Ms. Ruby's "Recipe

for Marriage." Between those two, the sermon and the recipe, she had learned a lot, and now she felt all ready to be a part of the new family that was being formed—she, Mama, and Chip. After the wedding, she was planning to start calling him "Daddy." That change felt like a pretty big deal because she had never had a daddy before. She looked down at her beaded white dress as she sat quietly in the church pew next to Helen, and she wondered, *Will anything else change when I call him Daddy?*

When the ceremony was over, and the newlyweds came and went on their honeymoon, Lydia realized that nothing was different after all, because her new Daddy left three days later on a very long trip with the Navy. Mama called it a "deployment," and she cried about it sometimes. All through the rest of the summer months, life was pretty much the same except for their once-a-week phone call from Lydia's new dad. Next came the fall and the winter holiday season. Lydia and her mother settled right back into the routine of going to school together during the week; they rode bikes and went to church together on the weekends. Nothing had changed—not yet.

When Christmas arrived that year, the changes began in earnest. With the festive twinkling lights and the gaily wrapped gifts also came Chip's return from his seven-month deployment. Two momentous announcements were made within a month after his return: first, the Crew family would be moving north to Washington state; and second, Lydia was going to be a big sister! The first bit of news filled Lydia with trepidation: she had never lived anywhere besides San Diego before. She would miss her grandparents and her friends terribly. However, the second announcement was so thrilling that it helped to ease the worry of the first. A baby! Lydia loved babies! She could hardly wait to be a big sister! Her mother loved babies just as much; together they began brainstorming baby names. Maybe David or Elijah for a boy? Hope or Hannah for a girl?

By February, everything in their little Green Tree Square apartment had been packed. On their last night in San Diego, Lydia was afraid. Her parents tucked her into her futon bed and when they went out of her room, it didn't feel right at all. Brown U-Haul boxes were piled along the wall, and none of her dolls or stuffed animals sat smiling at her from their seats on her bookshelf. She hugged Little Dumbo, her floppy stuffed elephant, closer and pulled her patchwork quilt tightly up under her chin. It didn't help. "Mama!" she called from her bed. She waited; she could hear her mother talking in the kitchen. It sounded like maybe she was on the phone. "Ma-maa!" she summoned more loudly.

In a moment, she saw Chip's figure outlined in the doorway. "What do you need, Lydia?" he asked gently. When she explained her fears about moving and the strangeness of her bedroom that night, he stepped into the room and lay down on the futon next to her. "Your mom is on the phone with your Aunt Molly; I can stay here with you till you feel better," he explained comfortingly.

At first, Lydia felt bothered by her new dad's presence beside her: she wanted the reassurance of her mom. Her mom would sit on the edge of the bed, hold Lydia's hand, and say a prayer with her. Probably even sing a song. This was different. Chip had gotten in the bed with her, and squeezing his large frame onto the twin-sized bed was a tight fit. Lydia had to choose to either hang halfway off the edge of the bed or snuggle close to Chip. She chose to snuggle. Chip was warm against her and was whispering to her about how Washington was going to be a great place to live. She didn't want to hurt his feelings. After all, he was her dad now, and she knew she should start to get used to his way of doing things. Even if they were different from Mom's way.

Her dad began to rub her back as he whispered. As he felt her begin to relax, he put his hand under the quilt, nudged her pajama shirt up, and tickled her back with the tips of his fingers. Lydia began to feel tired and loved; Chip's closeness and attention made her feel special. Lydia fell asleep dreaming of her new room in Washington where, once again, her dolls and animals would sit smiling on her bookshelf.

The drive from San Diego to Oak Harbor, Washington took

about three days. Lydia loved staying in hotels and eating in restaurants along the way. As they drove, she had a stack of her Uncle Ashton's hand-me-down chapter books next to her on the back seat; she had started reading the Boxcar Children series and felt very grown up as she discovered the adventures of Henry, Jessie, Violet, and Benny. It was fun reading about how they fended for themselves in their railroad car "home," and it also helped Lydia to feel more confident about the changes happening in her own life. She read several Boxcar stories until her dad began to tease her about always having her nose in a book. *Is there something wrong with reading?* Lydia wondered in confusion.

The closer they got to Oak Harbor, the more Lydia kept her eyes on the scenery rushing past the window. Mostly so that Chip would stop teasing, and also because she had never seen such a green landscape! San Diego had been beautiful with its brown hills and palm trees; the northwest was lush and verdant in a way that seemed more alive. Lydia's imagination began to stir as she watched for signs of wildlife in the passing fields, hills, and woods. *Oh, how Patcher the rabbit would love to live out here! He would have a lot of yummy things to nibble!* Lydia mused happily. Thinking of Patcher made her a bit homesick, so instead she asked her mom to turn on some music. They drove into their new town of Oak Harbor singing along cheerfully to their favorite Steve Green CD, *Hide 'Em in Your Heart*.

During Lydia's first weeks in Oak Harbor, her emotions continued to bounce back and forth between homesick and enthusiastic. She liked her new home on Chinook Drive with its bright open windows, but it wasn't close to her grandparents' home anymore. She loved her new school, Oak Harbor Day School, with its name like her old school, however, her old friends were nowhere to be found. She especially liked that her new room had a bathroom attached, yet she missed the familiar nighttime shadows in her old room. Her homesickness was worst in the evenings when her parents had said their goodnights, and she was alone in the darkness. The only light was from a stained-glass flower night light in the bathroom. Even though she snuggled her elephant close and even though she knew all her cuddly friends were smiling at her from their perch on the bookshelf, she felt small and alone. She felt even smaller because now she was sleeping in a bigger, taller bed that her dad had purchased for her after they had settled in. Night after night, she called out, "Mama!" hoping for that extra reassurance that her mother always gave.

Ettie had begun to suffer from a sickness too—morning sickness. Instead of feeling nauseous only in the morning, she experienced more severe bouts in the evening. At bedtime, she was often closed in the bathroom leaning over the toilet, relieving herself of her dinner; and it was Chip who responded to Lydia's cries for comfort. Chip left whatever work he was doing on the computer and lay down next to Lydia; he rubbed her back and whispered sweetly. Lydia got used to having her dad lie down in the bed next to her. She began to look forward to the moment when he moved his hand under the covers to tickle her back with his fingertips. After a few nights of snuggling together in her new big-girl bed, Chip's fingers began to move along Lydia's smooth skin in different places.

Having Chip pay attention to her in the bed made the homesickness disappear. She didn't feel small and alone anymore either; in fact, she felt quite mature. Even more than when she read chapter books. It made her feel loved, but the problem was that it also made her heart thump a little faster in a quivery sort of way when he was moving his hands around. This kind of heart fluttering was different than anything Lydia had experienced before, and she wasn't sure if she enjoyed it or not. Maybe her heart was telling her something was wrong? But Chip was her new dad, and he would know if what they were doing was wrong. And since he wasn't saying there was a problem, Lydia reasoned that his caresses must be okay.

The Crew family had moved to Chinook Drive in Oak Harbor late in February; Lydia's lack of resistance to the cold weather and her exposure to the new germs caused her to catch the flu in mid-March. When her mother felt her hot forehead one Thursday morning, she quickly pronounced her too ill to attend school that day. Lydia didn't mind; she drifted in and out of sleep, took her liquid orange fever medicine, and gazed out the window at the rain. She listened to the rain falling on the roof. For a while, her mom sat by the edge of her new white bed and read to her from the latest Boxcar book. As Ettie read, Lydia sat propped up on her pillows, sipping Gatorade, and thinking how exciting it would be to have adventures like the children in the story. Mid-afternoon, Chip came home from the Navy base, and Ettie took that opportunity to lie down and take a nap. Although she didn't normally sleep during the day, the pregnancy hormones had Ettie feeling completely exhausted.

Lydia wasn't alone for long. About ten minutes later, Chip came into her bedroom. He had already changed out of his olive-green flight suit into his forest green bathrobe. He came toward Lydia as she lay propped up on her pillows and asked her if she was feeling any better. When she replied that she was, he queried, "May I join you?" Without waiting for her reply, her dad lay down on the bed next to her. They lay quietly together, and Chip began to tenderly touch Lydia's face and hair. Gradually, the rain fell harder, and Lydia commented on the soothing sound of the rain pattering on the roof. Her voice sounded old to her own ears— not like a seven-year-old. When Chip kissed her on the mouth, she felt that she was kissing him romantically just as she had seen her mother kiss Chip. Lydia had never had a father before; and in her innocence, she did not know that boundaries should be in place to keep her virtue intact. Her heart began a wild dance as his fingers roamed all around her warm skin. His fingers caused a wave of expectant tingling to wash over her as if something exciting were about to happen.

Unfortunately, Lydia did not know to push Chip's hand away when he continued to disregard the boundary placed by God to protect children. She didn't know; and because the fondling felt very tingly, she didn't want him to stop. Lydia was confused by the way the touching felt good but somehow a little icky at the same time. Her emotions were all mixed up again similar to the way they had been about their move to Oak Harbor. Should she tell her dad how she felt? She wasn't sure; he was the boss and what he did *must* have been okay.

So she didn't tell him—which made it easier for it to happen again. A week later, Lydia lay sleeping in her big white bed. Her arms were hugging Little Dumbo as she peacefully dreamt about running through a field full of black and white rabbits. The sleeves of her favorite long-sleeved Tigger nightgown were peeking out from under the quilt. Her hair lay fanned out on her pillow. The night passed quietly without event until, at two in the morning, a *bump* in the hallway woke her. Her eyes fluttered open, and as they adjusted to the darkness, she made out the shape of Chip's broad frame once again silhouetted in her doorway. He entered the room and lay down under the covers with her. It was almost completely dark in the room except for the faint bit of night light glow from under the bathroom door. In the darkness, Lydia couldn't see her dad's face; she could only hear his soothing voice whispering endearments and feel his gentle fingers tickling her and rubbing her in the same places as before.

Five minutes later, when she was fully awake and her emotions were spinning madly, Lydia realized that she needed to go to the bathroom. She got up and went into the bathroom; when she came back, Chip spoke again. This time his murmured words shocked her. "You know, Lydia, we're going to have to tell Mom."

"What?!" she cried out, "No! I don't want to tell her!"

Chip shushed Lydia by putting his finger to her mouth. "Not right now." He reassured her quietly, "Later. I have to tell her; she's my wife."

Lydia's stomach sank. She was so embarrassed! She knew right away that he meant "tell Mom about him touching her private area." She did NOT want her mom to know; Lydia felt as if *she* had been the one to start the snuggling and fondling. It was all her fault. And now that Chip was saying that they had to tell, Lydia knew without a doubt that her feelings of discomfort had been correct. If they told her mom, her mom was sure to be disappointed with her. Why had he done it then? Lydia was confused, and she was mad too.

Putting her hands on her hips, she pouted in the dark bedroom. She didn't want to climb back into the bed with him now that he had decided to tell. Maybe she could convince him not to? No, that wouldn't work. Even though he had been her dad for a few short months, she knew that there was no arguing with him once he had his mind made up. She pretended not to care, and whispered back with passive aggression, "Fine! You can tell her if you want to."

Lydia stood by the side of her bed waiting until Chip got up. After a few moments, he stood to leave. On his way out, he leaned over and kissed Lydia lightly on the mouth, the gentle kiss of a butterfly. When he had gone, Lydia climbed back into her bed. She was still upset. She pulled the covers up, rolled onto her side, and tried to fall back to sleep. With her eyes closed against the darkness of the shadows in her new room, she struggled to make sense of what was happening. It was all so confusing that she began to think maybe it was a good thing after all that her mother was going to find out. Yes, that would help, Lydia realized as she readjusted her thoughts. Her mother was always there to help her figure out the hard things. Maybe it would all be straightened out tomorrow.

"Woe to those who call evil good, and good evil."

Isaiah 5:20

Chapter 5

The Lie

Tired from a sleepless night, Chip came home early from work the next day to find the house empty. Lydia had recovered quickly from her 24-hour flu, and he hadn't expected to find her home since it was only one-thirty. He was surprised that Ettie was gone. He was sure she hadn't left to pick Lydia up from school, and she hadn't told him that she had any errands or appointments that afternoon. He wandered through the living room and dining room in a bit of a sleep-deprived daze until he entered the kitchen. On the counter, Ettie had left a note on the back of an envelope; in her graceful print she had shared her last-minute plans for the day: *Chip, I have been called in to substitute at Lydia's school today. You're my hero! Hope your day was wonderful! I love you! Yours forever, Esther*

Opening the refrigerator door to get out the homemade iced tea Ettie had brewed for him, Chip recalled that three days ago she had turned in her application to substitute at Oak Harbor Day School. He was glad that they had called her in; he knew how much she loved teaching. Plus, it kept her busy earning some money while she was waiting for their baby to be born. As he poured himself a tall glass of tea and snacked on a handful of peanuts, he considered his relationship with Ettie: it was awesome, it was fun, and it was passionate. He couldn't let his mind even begin to accept that his choices with Lydia during the past week could wreck his marriage.

There was no way that he was going to let fifteen minutes of losing his self-control get in the way of his life. During his insomniac night, he had come up with a plan.

Common criminals might get caught and sent to jail for what he had done to Lydia twice that past week, but he would not. Not an upstanding gentleman like him. Anyway, he had known when to stop, definitely no penetration. That way there was no proof at all. Even if Lydia were to tell anyone, it would be her word against his. Thankfully, she was an imaginative child; he knew that would work in his favor if anything were to be suspected at all. Everyone would think she was telling another one of her fanciful stories. Chip realized that he had overstepped his boundaries as Lydia's new father, yet that didn't mean his misbehavior needed to have lasting consequences. He would make it up to her sometime soon. For now, a foolproof plan was what he needed; and after considering his options for a few wakeful hours, he knew he had it. He was ready. Nothing was going to come between him and his lovely wife and his burgeoning career, not even his perverted behavior.

Chip yawned. He was finally feeling more relaxed since he had his perfect scheme ready, and he decided he could catch a quick nap before his loved ones returned home. When they came home, he would follow through with his plan and then put this mess behind him. He would forget that the whole thing had happened at all. Unzipping his flight suit as he went, Chip headed down the hall to his bedroom. He undressed and lay down under the white quilt his wife had hand-stitched for him during their first deployment as a married couple. As he unstrapped his black Timex to place it on the nightstand, he noticed that the military time on his watch read 13:13; *uncanny*, he thought.

Suddenly, Violet, the calico cat, meowed from under the bed. *That annoying cat bit me yesterday*, Chip recalled angrily. It was the second time that month that the normally docile Violet bit him on the hand, and this time she had drawn blood. Could she possibly sense that Chip had mistreated Lydia? The idea disturbed him but seemed too far-fetched to keep him awake. Sleep came quickly, and before he knew it, two hours had passed. He was awakened by the sound of the front door opening and closing.

When Chip opened his eyes a few minutes later, Ettie was standing on the side of the bed looking concerned. "Hey, honey. Is everything okay? Are you sick?" she asked sympathetically.

"I'm fine, baby. I didn't sleep well, and then I had a six AM flight. I got off work early, and a nap was just what I needed." In relief, Ettie sat down on the edge of the bed next to Chip, and he reached up and stroked her hair lovingly. "I didn't mean to worry you. Wait a minute—have I told you today how beautiful you are?" His voice was thick with sleep and emotion as he grinned that slow, charming smile that Ettie loved.

Ettie laughed lightheartedly and returned the compliment, "You look pretty handsome yourself, Mr. Crew." Suddenly, her smile turned to a grimace of discomfort, and she rubbed her hand on her belly in a circle. "Ugh, that cafeteria food at Lydia's school did *not* agree with my morning sickness. I loved substituting there today, and I hope they call me back. I've learned my lesson though. Next time, I need to remember to pack my lunch!"

"Really?" Chip murmured distractedly. He had suddenly woken up enough to remember the plan that he had come up with. It was time to make it happen. He rolled over on his side and propped himself up on his right elbow. "Listen, honey, I need to talk to you about something that came up with Lydia last night at bedtime. It would probably be best if you and I could talk to her about it together."

"Of course. Sure. What is it?" Ettie asked while continuing to rub her stomach.

"Well, she was remembering how at her old school in San Diego they had been teaching about something called 'good touch versus bad touch'." Chip paused as Ettie confirmed that she recalled Lydia's class covering that difficult topic with the help of the guidance counselor at their school. It had been shortly before their move to Oak Harbor.

Chip's lie continued to roll effortlessly out of his mouth. It sounded so plausible that he almost believed it himself. "She asked me a couple of questions about what a good touch is and what a bad touch is. And I made a mistake, Ettie; when she asked me where someone might touch her if it was a bad touch, I showed her by tapping her on the front of her pajamas in her crotch area. I think we were both surprised that I had handled it that way. She was feeling worried about it, and I told her we were going to need to talk to you about it. Do you think that we could do that this afternoon?"

Ettie was surprised too. That would not have been the way she would have helped Lydia with those questions. Come to think of it: why was Lydia asking Chip anyway? She usually came to her mom with all her queries. Ettie spoke neither of these things aloud; she certainly wanted to encourage Lydia's relationship with her new dad, and if her daughter was already going to him with questions that was a good sign that she was learning to feel comfortable with him. Even though he seemed to have handled the moment inappropriately, at least he had realized that and had wanted to talk about it right away. No, she decided, she wouldn't chide him about his minor lapse in judgment. They could work through it together. That's what husbands and wives did. She was thankful that he had shared it with her quickly; it helped her to know that she could trust him.

All these thoughts moved through her mind as she searched for the right way to respond. Fortunately, Chip didn't seem to notice that it was taking a while for her to answer; he was busy scratching a bumpy rash on his thigh. He glanced up when Ettie began sharing that she agreed that they should talk to Lydia together; however, her first few words were interrupted by a rapid succession of knocks on their bedroom door.

"What do you need?" Chip called in response to Lydia's knocking. He spoke brusquely as if he were annoyed that their conversation had been interrupted.

"Can I talk to Mama? Please?" Lydia called back through the closed door.

"Come in, Lydia," Ettie replied; and once Lydia had opened the door, she asked, "What do you need, honey?"

Despite her aversion to her school uniforms, Lydia had not changed into her play clothes. She looked scholarly in a cute sort of way in her khaki pants and white polo shirt. Changing wasn't first on her list of things to do that day, because all she could think about was inviting her friend from next door over so that they could continue the game they had started the day before. She explained in a rush, "Mama, Daddy! Marissa's mom's car just got home! I didn't think Marissa was going to be home today, and now she is. We are playing this cool game where our stuffed animals are camping, and we're using books as tents. It's so much fun! Can I please go see if she can play? Can Marissa come over?"

Ettie was fine with it; she looked at Chip to ascertain his feelings about it. As she was waiting for him, the nausea that had plagued her since midday suddenly overwhelmed her. She jumped up and raced across the bedroom to the master bathroom. Although she shut the door behind her, Chip and Lydia could still hear the sounds of her discomfort as she lost the lunch she had eaten at Oak Harbor Country Day.

Because he wasn't completely focused on Ettie's plight and was instead caught in the trap of his predicament, Chip was also hit by a sudden overpowering feeling. However, this was a depraved kind of sickness: it was lust for a child. It swirled around him like the scent of a freshly baked pie tempting him to have one more taste. He couldn't resist the innocent beauty of the young girl standing beside his bed. In fact, at that moment, he didn't even want to resist, his desire had seized him so completely. His heart thumped faster as he lifted the covers and patted the bed with his hand to signal to Lydia that she should join him. Would she? Even though he had already suggested to her that they were going to tell Ettie?

Yes, she would. At that point, he knew for certain that she enjoyed the way that it felt to be caressed. If only he could take her farther, he schemed, they would both be satisfied. As he touched his young daughter, the demons inside him coaxed him to try it right then, before he lost his chance, before Ettie came out of the bathroom. The spontaneity of the moment and the fear that he felt at possibly being caught added an extra edginess to his excitement. His biggest hesitation was that he certainly didn't want to leave any trace of his actions behind. He could hear Ettie on the other side of the door continuing to heave and cough. Those unpleasant noises were the only other thing that held him back. That was his sweet bride in there, after all. Hold back he did, and he felt proud of his self-control. He was always one step ahead of trouble.

He knew that his pregnant wife took about ten minutes to vomit, wash her face and hands, regain her composure, and thoroughly brush her teeth. When he heard Ettie flush the toilet and afterward heard the sink water running, the licentious fire died out of Chip's eyes. The moment of his wicked craving had passed. Now he was left feeling a bit guilty. He smiled half-heartedly at Lydia as she climbed out of bed and walked out of the bedroom. He wouldn't let himself feel too guilty because he would make it up to her soon. He would make it up to both of them very soon.

Lydia walked straight from the bed to her bathroom. She looked in the mirror and saw the mess her hair had become from lying in the bed with her dad. Her thoughts were in the same confused jumble as her hair. What had just happened anyway? Hadn't he told her they were going to have to tell Mom? Maybe he had changed his mind? She wondered when she would have a chance to ask him about it as she went to work on her hair. Her compulsion to fix her hair took almost all her attention: no bumps, no flyaways, simply smooth, pretty, and perfect. She was still standing at the mirror five minutes later when Ettie knocked on the door.

"Come in," Lydia called out.

Ettie opened the door and looked at her sweet daughter carefully smoothing her auburn hair. She had arranged it with a ponytail on either side of the middle part. The ponytails were holding back the bangs that were halfway finished growing out. Ettie's love for her daughter swelled in her heart; she was so proud of Lydia. That day at Oak Harbor Day School, Lydia's new teacher had stopped Ettie in the hallway to tell her how wonderfully Lydia was adjusting to her new classmates and the schoolwork. When Ettie spoke to Lydia that afternoon as she watched her brush her hair, it was out of a heart of love and thankfulness. Had Ettie known what was really happening in her home, she would have spoken out of a heart of panic and dismay.

"Honey, I'm sorry I didn't get a chance to answer you about Marissa. She may come over to play. First, your dad and I need to talk to you about something. Can you please come into your room when you've finished with your hair?" Ettie asked.

"Okay," Lydia replied, "In a minute, Mama."

Lydia knew right away what her parents wanted to talk about. She wondered if they were going to be upset with her. She didn't think so; Mom had agreed that Marissa could come over, so she couldn't be in too much trouble. Nervousness began to flit around in her stomach anyway. She quickly decided to be done with her hair. She put her hairbrush down on the counter and passed through the door into her bedroom. Her parents came in a moment later, and they all sat down together.

Ettie began, "Lydia, Daddy told me that you were worried because he touched you a little bit on your private area?" As she asked this question, she had no idea that the meaning behind what she was saying was being understood in a completely different way by seven-year-old Lydia. Poor Lydia was confused and frustrated; this wasn't the way that she had imagined her mother handling the situation. She had expected that maybe Mom would tell her that she had been wrong to let him touch her. Lydia was too embarrassed to voice her confusion and too confused to know why she was ashamed. She trusted her mother completely; if Mom said the touching was only "a little bit," that's what it must have been. So instead of voicing the concerns racing through her mind, she simply whispered in the affirmative.

The normally enthusiastic and chatty Lydia was subdued and still. While she waited with her head bowed, silence filled the room. Ettie sensed how uncomfortable her daughter was; she certainly didn't fully understand why. Rather than dragging out the conversation and making it into a big deal that would embarrass Lydia further, Ettie summed up the matter in the most succinct way she could, "Well, Lydia, do you remember what you learned in your good touch versus bad touch class? No one should touch you where your bathing suit covers. That's not the way a daddy is supposed to touch his daughter, and it's not going to happen again."

Glancing up from under her long eyelashes, Lydia spoke softly, "Yes, Mama."

Wanting to encourage her daughter to move out of her discomfort, Ettie continued, "You know, Grandma and Grandpa are coming to visit soon so I don't want you to worry about what happened. Uncle Ashton and Aunt Brittany are coming too. And Aunt Molly is bringing your cousin, Charlotte. They are all going to come to see our new house on the golf course, and we're all going to have lots of fun together, okay? I'll bet Grandpa will even take you out riding in a golf cart."

Lydia paused to think about all this. She was comforted to hear that her grandparents had a plan to travel to Oak Harbor, yet she didn't want the snuggling and caresses from her new dad to be over. Maybe they would say yes if she asked again really nicely? Chip's attention had been making her feel special; and although it also made her feel a bit uneasy, the natural feelings of physical pleasure outweighed her discomfort. She wondered how she could word her question without being embarrassed in front of her mom. She couldn't think of a way. Instead, she agreed, "Okay. You're right, Mama, it will be fun when Grandma and Grandpa and all our family are here."

After she answered, her question still felt like it had to be asked or it would pop out of her mouth like a jack-in-the-box. She leaned over towards Chip, cupped her dainty hand around his ear, and whispered "Daddy, will you please ask Mama if you can still touch me on the front?" As soon as the question was out of her mouth, Lydia was ashamed of her desire to be touched. She quickly plopped onto her bed, stuffed her face into a fluffy feather pillow, and stopped up her ears with her fingers.

At that moment, Chip realized that Lydia had almost no understanding of what her mother had explained. Ettie had clearly stated, "It's not okay, and it's not going to happen again;" however, Lydia didn't get it! Instead, she had innocently asked if he could still rub her in her private area. Hiding his surprise behind a poker face, Chip glanced casually at his wife. If he could make it through this moment without letting on what was happening, he would certainly deserve an Oscar for best actor. Ettie was looking at Lydia with concern; her daughter was curled up in a ball with her face completely hidden in her pillow.

"Did I say something wrong?" Ettie queried.

"You did great, honey. You were perfect," Chip comforted smoothly. He spoke in a low voice so that Lydia wouldn't hear that he was not asking her mother *that* question. "She said she's embarrassed. I think you're right; we need to get her to focus on something else now. She's going to be okay." Chip smiled reassuringly and the love in his eyes melted Ettie's worries away. Ettie touched Lydia's shoulder gently; and as Lydia turned her head and looked up, Ettie held her arms out in an open invitation for a hug. Lydia unplugged her ears and sat up. Then she too held out her arms toward her mother, and they met in the middle in a tender embrace.

Lydia stole a glance over her mother's shoulder to see what Chip's reply would be. Chip saw her questioning look and managed to shake his head "no" the slightest bit in a way that wouldn't draw Ettie's attention. As he shook his head, he also opened his eyes wide in a warning sort of way to deter any further incriminating questions. Seeing that his foolproof plan was nearly complete, he sighed deeply in relief and offered a gentlemanly hand to help Ettie and Lydia to their feet. Before she reached for his hand, Ettie kissed Lydia and peered into her eyes. "I love you, sweet girl. Are you okay now?"

"She's good now," Chip asserted lightheartedly, "because she and I are going to go share a bowl of chocolate chip ice cream. How about that, Lydia?"

Ice cream and popsicles were Lydia's favorites, so she agreed that she was all right. Chip smiled to himself, once again applauding his cleverness; he knew the way to redirect Lydia for sure. Even though he felt that he had been putting on a bit too much weight lately, he could indulge in a small bowl too. Or maybe even a medium one to celebrate his victory over that close call.

As they sat down at the kitchen table with their treats, Chip let his mind shift back to their recent conversation. He was exhilarated that Ettie had suspected nothing! It made him feel that he must not be a bad person after all since he had a wife who trusted him completely: with child rearing, with their finances, with their spiritual walk as a couple. Even when he spent late nights and early mornings on the computer, she never checked up on him which was good for him, or she would certainly discover his affinity for pornography. Unfortunately, he did realize that he did have a problem with porn ever since he was ten years old, and his Boy Scout leader had introduced him to his stash of racy magazines. Not that he would call it an addiction necessarily, because he knew that he could stop whenever he wanted to. Certainly, he would sometime soon—before Ettie found out. He didn't want to break her trust; he loved her that much.

As he was enjoying his ice cream with Lydia, he had the perfect idea of how to indulge his girls with a special day to make up for this confusion with the good touch versus bad touch mishap. After church on Sunday, he would take them to Michael's, the pricey seafood restaurant that he had recently discovered at an officer's luncheon. It was right on Crescent Harbor and had crab cakes that melted in your mouth. He could almost taste their tanginess over the bittersweet chocolate chips. He wouldn't tell them about their surprise yet. Better to impress them with it when they were walking out of church looking lovely in their graceful dresses.

Two days later, Chip followed through with this next plan of his and it was as successful as the first. His girls enjoyed the lunch on the harbor and showed their appreciation with thanks, hugs, and kisses. For the rest of the week, life moved along peacefully, until the next Friday when Chip's in-laws came to visit. Chip had always felt intuitively that perhaps his mother-in-law did not trust him as completely as his wife did. He nevertheless made the mistake of snuggling with Lydia under the covers of his bed in the middle of the morning during Evelyn and Sam's visit. How could Evelyn know that he had no intentions of being inappropriate with her granddaughter? He simply felt the need to hold Lydia close and tickle the smooth skin of her arms and legs. He knew he had enough self-control so as not to repeat his past behavior. No use putting himself in that precarious position again.

Evelyn made quite a fuss about how he needed to be appropriate with her granddaughter and not lay under the blankets with her. Chip was grateful that Ettie stood up for him. She explained to her mother that he was simply an affectionate father. The result of that mix-up was that Chip realized he needed to be more prudent with where and when he showed his love for Lydia. Not everyone believed in him as much as his wife did.

When the school year ended at the beginning of summer, Chip took steps to adopt Lydia as his daughter. The attorney he had met with earlier that year had informed him that he needed to wait until he and Ettie had been married one year. Soon after their first anniversary, they completed the necessary paperwork and had taken it to the courthouse in downtown Oak Harbor. What pride he felt when the judge asked Lydia if she wanted Chip to be her legal father, and she chirped in her cheerful, forthright way, "Yes, I would!" The newly formed Crew family, now both physically and legally, needed to commemorate this occasion; once again, they headed to Michael's for a delicious seafood lunch.

The momentous day warranted thankfulness; however, Chip left the restaurant feeling dissatisfied with himself and with his life. He had noticed a fellow officer at Michael's and had tried to catch his eye to nod hello. The man had looked right at Chip without acknowledging his presence. This slight, compounded with the way that he often felt shunned and unappreciated by his peers at work, exacerbated the frustration that had been building since he had gotten his last set of orders to Oak Harbor. What was going wrong with his career lately? He was unhappy and moped all the way home.

Arriving home on Chinook Drive, all Chip wanted to do was recline in his Lay-Z-Boy and close his eyes to block out the negative emotions that were pestering him. He tried to get comfortable, but the snugness of the waist of his dress pants was beginning to give him indigestion. Maybe if he got rid of those extra pounds that had been piling up, he could begin to receive the respect he deserved from his comrades. Moving off the recliner, Chip went to change into athletic shorts with an elastic waistband. He picked up the Protein Power diet book from his nightstand. All month, he had been reading the book with the intention of starting the diet. It was a difficult transition to make since he would be doing it alone. His pregnant wife didn't need to shed any pounds; even at six months along, she was still looking petite. That didn't seem particularly fair to Chip either.

Ettie was supportive of his goal of healthy eating, and Chip did acknowledge that to himself as he settled back into his chair with the diet book in hand. She had even been willing to change many of their favorite recipes to accommodate the protein diet. The problem was that he didn't want to change recipes; he wanted the change to be within himself, some inner motivation to be better, stronger, and more fit. He began to flip the pages of the book randomly looking for inspiration to begin the life change he desired. Nothing caught his eye in the self-help book. Suddenly, Lydia bounded in the front door. She traipsed into the entryway and unknowingly banged the door shut behind her.

At first, Chip was annoyed at being interrupted in his quiet moment; and even when Lydia came over and sat on the couch close to him, he remained grouchy. It wasn't until she finished her monologue about why Marissa couldn't come over to play that day, and she began to describe the song that she had written for him that he began to perk up. Lydia explained that she knew that he had wanted to start his diet, so she had made up some words and a tune to go with it to be an encouragement for him.

"It's called the "Protein Power Cheer," Daddy." She chattered happily. "Do you want to hear it? It has a dance to go with it too!"

After he agreed that he wanted to hear it, Lydia began. "Protein power, protein power! Every day and every hour! Drink your shake! Eat your meat! Protein power can't be beat! Protein power, protein power! Every day and every hour!" As she chanted, her arms and legs moved in a peppy cheerleader-type routine of waving and jumping. When she finished, Chip chortled and clapped his hands with appreciation. Now here was the push he needed to get started: if only he could see her perform that cheer again sometime when it was the two of them alone at home. He would ask her to try it in her birthday suit. The rise he felt with this new idea was a mix of tingling anticipation and forbidden pleasure. *When can I make that happen?* he wondered even though he knew deep in his heart that the desire was sinful and despicable.

Coming up with a plan was simple. He seemed to be full of ideas these days. That evening after dinner, Chip mentioned to Ettie that he wanted to run to the grocery store to get protein shakes so that he could begin his diet in earnest the next morning. As he had hoped, Ettie offered to go pick them up for him. He loved that his wife was so accommodating. She would be gone at least thirty-five minutes, he figured, since the store was almost fifteen minutes from their home. Plenty of time for him to be inspired by Lydia's protein power cheer.

Chip stood in the driveway and kissed Ettie goodbye sweetly. After he watched her depart down Chinook Drive, he turned and went back into the house calling Lydia's name.

"Yes, Daddy?" she answered as she came out of her room.

"Let's go ahead and get you ready for bed while Mommy is at the grocery store. Are you ready for your bath? I can use my watch to time you tonight and see how long you can hold your breath underwater." Lydia was ready for a bath; her energy level increased as she got enthusiastic about trying to beat her record for holding her breath. She brushed her teeth first with her Cinderella toothbrush, then she began undressing while Chip turned on the bath water and plugged the drain. Her cheerful voice rose and fell above the sound of the rushing water as she chatted about whether she could beat it. Chip didn't hear what she was saying; he was studying the firm virgin lines of her seven-year-old figure and feeling a mounting excitement about what he was going to ask her to do next.

The bathtub was halfway filled with warm water when Chip turned off the tap and interrupted Lydia's chatter. "Do you remember your Protein Power Cheer, Lydia? The one that you did for me this afternoon?"

Lydia giggled, "Of course, I do, Daddy."

"Would you do it again for me? It was so special, and I loved the dance that you did with it. Could you do it again right now?" Chip requested cunningly.

Lydia's face lit up with pride. Her happiness that her dad had enjoyed her cheer dance enough to want to see it again shone through her blue-green eyes. There wasn't much space in the small bathroom, but she happily started singing her song and going through the motions she had choreographed with an extra bounce in her step. Chip watched her with delight. Here was the pornography he had perused for all those years—now it was moving and alive! The desire he felt rippling through him like wildfire needed an outlet. He ached to touch her, to hold her close, and to kiss her soft skin.

When her cheer dance ended, Chip did not resist the voice of caution in his spirit. He opened his arms wide in an invitation for a hug. Lydia moved into his arms without resistance. Her heart was beating quickly from her exertion, and Chip held her close enough to feel its quick rhythm through his white undershirt. He held her tight and still for a long moment. Hugging Lydia this way was the high point of his week because for the moment he felt unconditionally loved. No one was expecting him to perform, fulfill a duty, or complete a task perfectly. All week long, he felt that his comrades and his wife expected that of him. He basked in this moment which felt the way he had always yearned to be loved.

Even more, the hug was a new thrill. He resisted the sexual urges surging through him so that Lydia would have a reason to trust him. He would remain a gentleman. He viewed himself as a Christian man after all. It was just a hug, he decided, and a hug was a completely fatherly gesture. No one would ever know the rush it gave him. If his wife or a friend questioned him, he could explain to anyone who had a problem with it that a naked hug was simply a boundary issue. He lied to himself so convincingly that he felt there wasn't anything intrinsically wrong with this type of hug. It was nothing compared to what his mother had done to him.

He simply stroked the warm skin of Lydia's back and told her how much he loved her cheer. He pressed his mouth against hers tasting the freshness of her minty breath. As she stepped into the steaming water, Chip made up his mind. A naked hug would have to happen again—repeatedly. The name "birthday suit hug" popped into his mind. Yes, that's what he would call it. He and Lydia could have an inside joke called the "birthday suit hug;" he would wait until the next time he hugged her to tell her the name for it. That could be his surprise for her. He loved giving his girls surprises.

*"When friends betray us, when
darkness seems to win..."*

LAURA STORY

Chapter 6

A Beautiful Family

Nine-year-old Lydia sat on the blue velour couch with the sweetest, coziest bundle that she had ever seen in her arms. She rocked gently back and forth and hummed a lullaby about roses and slumbering till day. She wasn't sure what all the words meant, but she had heard her mother sing it to her two younger brothers many times. What a joy it was to be a big sister, she reflected; it was just as fun as she had imagined. As she watched her infant brother, his eyes opened the slightest bit, and he smiled a spontaneous toothless grin. It made Lydia's heart feel as light as a drifting cloud, and she smiled happily in return. She was glad to be holding him while her mom got her other brother, David, ready to head to the bookstore.

As baby Jonathan began to stir and coo, David toddled into the living room wearing a navy striped polo shirt with khaki pants. His dark hair was damp and combed neatly to the side. The toy lawnmower he was pushing along made an insistent *pop! pop! pop!* noise that abruptly woke Jonathan. Jonathan's blue eyes opened in earnest, and he began to cry. Following close behind David and his mower, Ettie came with her finger to her pursed lips, "Shh."

"It's okay, Mama; Jonathan had started to wake up anyway. And guess what? He smiled at me! I think he was smiling in his sleep. Is he too young to smile for real?" Lydia paused briefly and continued talking before Ettie had a chance to respond. "I'm so glad he smiled!

I think it was real even if he was sleeping; he must have liked my song. Right, Mama? I remember when David smiled his first smile. I can't believe I have two brothers now! I'm going to get ready too. Should I wear my velour dress with the satin ribbon?"

As she gushed about her baby brother, Lydia gingerly placed him into her mother's arms. Ettie sat down with Jonathan where Lydia had been seated with him moments before. She answered, "Your velour dress will be perfect. I can't wait to hear you read your story at the bookstore, Lydia; we're very proud of you. And yes, certainly, I think Jonathan's smile was real. He is blessed to have a sister who loves him so much." As Lydia skipped toward her room, Ettie propped her feet up on the footrest and relaxed as Jonathan began to nurse. David stopped mowing the living room carpet and climbed up on the couch next to Ettie. From the basket on the coffee table, he pulled out a construction vehicle book and began to turn the pages contentedly.

Ettie was grateful for a quiet moment. The past two months had certainly been eventful: Christmas, Jonathan's birth, family visiting, and teaching Lydia third grade at home had all kept Ettie busy. The homeschooling began after Lydia completed her first-grade school year at Oak Harbor Day. Ettie and Chip decided since Ettie had her teaching degree that it could be a good fit for their family. Lydia was enthusiastic about giving it a try since back in San Diego her best friend, Lynn, was learning at home as well.

Ettie and Lydia realized that they loved it. They appreciated the flexibility it gave them to study topics they both enjoyed. They grew lima beans, studied the phases of the moon, read through the book of Ruth, and created portrait collages. Lydia had a few moments where she melted down about getting her handwriting perfect, and Ettie would need to go outside to do yard work and take a break; yet overall, the homeschooling experience had been very positive. The end of this third-grade year had been more challenging since Jonathan had been born only seventeen months after his brother David. Thankfully, Lydia loved her brothers tremendously and was delighted to help with them in any way she could. As one of Ettie's homeschooling mentors instructed, "The baby is the lesson."

Glancing out the front window as she continued to reminisce, Ettie saw Chip's white pickup truck pull into the driveway. When David had been born, Chip had pragmatically traded in his convertible Mustang for a Ford 150 with three rear seats. Now he had driven it home from work in time to bring them all to the Book Haven bookstore across town for Lydia's award ceremony. She had written and illustrated a story about her baby brother, David, and had entered her story in a *Reading Rainbow* writing contest. As a first-place winner in their district, Lydia had been invited to read her story aloud at the local bookstore.

The front door opened, and David looked up from his book. When he saw his daddy enter, he slid off the couch and ran to the door. Book in hand, he jumped up into Chip's arms for a bear hug. When Chip put David down again, he got down on one knee at David's eye level so that David could show him all the "diggers" in his book. Even at nineteen months, David knew the names of all the different excavators, backhoes, scrapers, and rollers. As she watched the two of them, Ettie's heart was filled with thankfulness. Her handsome husband took such a genuine interest in their children. He had even left work early that day to be sure that he could hear Lydia read her story at the bookstore. His integrity and his love for his family seemed to radiate right out of his bright smile.

After David toddled away to finish his carpet lawn care, Chip put the mail on the kitchen counter and joined Ettie on the couch. He kissed her sweetly, and she asked him about his day. "It was decent, but it's better now," he teased with a grin. "And I have news. Unfortunately, it's going to have to wait." Shifting his eyes to his watch, he stood up again. "I'd better change out of these boots if we are going to get to the bookstore on time."

Soon after, the Crew family all piled into the white truck: Lydia snuggled in the middle of the back seat between her two brothers in their car seats. Arriving at Book Haven, Ettie was surprised to see how many people were there for the award ceremony. The bookstore was packed. What a blessing that Lydia was the one reading the story aloud! It seemed she never got nervous in front of a crowd. Even at five years old when she had a speaking part in their zoo play at San Diego Country Day, she had been sure of herself. Ettie knew that God had given her daughter the gift of confidence; now, Ettie had enough butterflies in her stomach for both of them.

The Crew family joined the other participants and their families seated in the rows of chairs that had been set up in the children's section. When it was her turn, Lydia stood and read in a strong, clear voice. The beginning of her story brought tears to her mother's eyes even though she had read it a dozen times before.

"My brother, David, is six months old." Lydia began. "I love him very much. The best day of my life was when I met David at the hospital the day after he was born." Lydia held up the first page of her book for everyone to see the carefully detailed picture she had drawn of herself holding her baby brother. She was wearing a pink dress, and David was swaddled in a blue blanket.

Then she continued to read, "Now that David is six months, he is sitting up and is getting ready to crawl. When he sits up, he reaches for toys. He likes to press the buttons on his musical toys." That page had a drawing of David sitting on a patchwork quilt in their yard. Toys were on the quilt; trees and sky filled the rest of the page.

"I like to help take care of David. I help give him a bath almost every night. He kicks hard when there is just a little bit of water in the tub. He gets mommy pretty wet!" Lydia giggled as she read this page as if she were reliving the moment of her brother's splashing. "Pushing David in the stroller is fun. He babbles and coos while I push him around the block. He loves to watch the pretty birds fly by."

"My favorite thing to do is to feed David in the highchair. David eats apples, sweet potatoes, rice cereal, oatmeal, and apricots. He likes them all!" At this point in her reading, the audience was momentarily distracted because David had slipped from his seat and had walked up the side aisle to stand beside his sister. Lydia looked up from her reading with surprise and exclaimed, "Oh! Here he is! Here's David!" Laughter erupted from the crowd. The timing of David's unrehearsed appearance was perfect! Lydia lovingly took his hand and continued to read, "David is so sweet. I love being his big sister. In six more months, when David is a year old and knows how to walk, I hope he will follow me everywhere!"

The final page had a picture of Lydia and David walking hand in hand on a trail in the woods. Except for the background, it was a complete match with the image of Lydia and David in real-time at the Book Haven bookstore. The participants and their families gave Lydia and David a rousing round of applause. When all the children had taken their turns reading their stories and receiving their awards, Ettie and Chip made their way to the front of the room to thank the two women who represented *Reading Rainbow* and who had facilitated the awards ceremony that afternoon.

The two women seemed delighted to meet the Crew family. The older woman, whose snowy hair coordinated with her white eyelet dress, congratulated Lydia once again on her story as the younger woman shook hands with Ettie, Chip, and young David. Together, they admired Jonathan who was sleeping peacefully in his denim Maya wrap sling. His round, rosy cheeks, and his chubby fingers were the topic of conversation for a few moments. Finally, as they turned to leave, the older woman exclaimed warmly, "What a beautiful family you have!" She looked squarely at Chip and admonished, "Now, you make sure you take good care of your lovely wife and these precious children."

Chip's reply was equally earnest, "Yes, ma'am. Quite honestly, I agree. With God's help, I plan to take care of this family better than any family has ever been taken care of before." He looked into her bright blue eyes with a sparkle in his own. "And I think I'd better bring them home now. My beautiful bride is waiting to hear my good news." He winked at the white-haired woman as he took Ettie's hand and steered her and the children through the crowd.

It was a thirty-minute drive home; however, Chip did not share his news with his family until they were almost pulling into the driveway. The white pickup rounded the corner of Chinook Drive. Their brick home nestled in the Western hemlock trees was in sight when he looked over at Ettie and then craned his neck back farther to see Lydia in the back seat. "Here's the news," he began as he turned to face Ettie once again. He put his right arm around her affectionately as the truck bumped up the curb and pulled to a stop. He cleared his throat and continued, "I have been given orders to PCS to San Diego. I will need to check in at my new squadron on the first day of…"

"What?! San Diego?! We get to go back? Woohoo!" Lydia interrupted. She unbuckled quickly and leaned over the seat so that her arms and head were draped over Chip's arm. "I can't believe we're heading back home! That's the best news ever, Daddy! I have to call Grandma and Grandpa right away. Oh my, I can hardly believe it. I get to see Lynn and Sarah! Everyone is going to be so excited, right?! Thank you, Daddy!"

In her excitement, she forgot to assist her parents in unbuckling her brothers' car seats as she normally did. Instead, she popped right out of the side door and started to dance toward the red front door. Her dance consisted of a hop and a skip, a pirouette, and a grand jeté; and her face shone with all the excitement of the day: first, her award ceremony at Book Haven, and now, this! Her artistic, enthusiastic nature exulted in moments such as these when her energy could find a positive outlet and become the song and dance of the joy in her heart. Ettie watched lightheartedly as Lydia continued to choreograph her spontaneous "happy to be moving" dance on the front lawn.

Then she glanced over at Chip and realized with a sinking feeling that he too was watching Lydia's performance; however, there was no twinkle in his eye now. He was scowling in a way that seemed completely unwarranted considering his good news. "Hey, honey, what's the matter?" she queried in a worried voice.

Uncharacteristically, Chip did not even turn his head her way as he spoke. "That," he spat out in an angry tone. He kept his glaring eyes on Lydia moving gracefully from the lawn to the sidewalk. "She interrupted me. She did not let me finish my sentence. She did not help with her brothers, and now she's wasting her time jumping around out there like a grasshopper. Really, what does she think? That we're here to carry her things in from the car for her?"

When he did finally turn to look at his wife through lids half closed in anger, it was as though he was challenging her to argue. Ettie was on the verge of defending her daughter; there were many things she wanted to say on Lydia's behalf. For instance, *don't you think we should be glad she is excited about moving?* Or *it's okay that she left her trophy in here; I'm proud of her story writing and that's the main thing.* And even, *hey, I love her dancing! Her new dance classes seem to be teaching her a lot.* When she considered how furious he looked with his brow furrowed, she decided to keep quiet. No sense in taking the risk of making it worse. After a tense moment of silence, Chip slammed the car door and stalked into the house.

Lydia followed him inside, and Ettie moved to the back seat to begin unbuckling David and Jonathan. She spoke to them reassuringly as she prepared to take them out of the truck and kept her tone light despite her concern with Chip's strange mood swing. She had seen him get frustrated before, but he had never been quite this angry. *What was different?* It was the cold, calculating way he had kept his eyes trained on Lydia. Ettie shivered unconsciously as she pictured how his face had looked moments before. She figured they would talk more about it when he had calmed down a bit.

After she set David down, and he toddled toward the front door, she picked up Jonathan who had begun to cry. "It's all right, sweet guy," Ettie said soothingly, "Don't you worry. Are you hungry?" She knew it had been about two hours since he had nursed, and she planned to sit down with him on the couch and rest until she needed to get up and make enchiladas for everyone else. Perhaps she and Chip could discuss his feelings while she was cooking.

Then she heard an unwelcome noise that dashed her hopes like the vase she had accidentally dropped yesterday on the tile floor in the kitchen. Glass had been everywhere. Now, hope flew in all directions and lay shattered at her feet. As they approached the front door, heated yelling drowned out the sound of Jonathan's crying. Ettie could hear that Chip was fuming mad from the volume of his voice. She couldn't make out the words over Jonathan's insistent request for dinner.

She hesitated to open the front door until she realized that another discordant sound was resonating through the red door—the door Chip had painted "Cardinal red" because they had discovered that a red front door symbolized welcome. No feelings of warm welcome reached out to embrace her now. Instead, fear's cold fingers were gripping her heart; what she heard was Lydia's weeping. That sound woke her protective mothering instinct, and without further pause, she quickly opened the door.

She pulled Jonathan closer and held David tightly by his hand and stepped into the entryway. The sight before her could not possibly be happening in her home! Chip had always been a loving father; he had never treated Lydia so rudely. Lydia was so frightened she was sitting on the couch with the entire upper half of her body folded over into her lap. Her head was tucked into her knees so that her slight frame took up less space than normal, yet her sobs filled the whole room. And there was Chip, standing over his daughter, menacingly pointing his finger at her. "No, Lydia!" he hollered with a distasteful emphasis on the last syllable. "You are not calling your grandparents right now, and that's final!"

Storming away without a backward glance, Chip exited the living room leaving a dismayed Ettie behind. A hollow feeling settled in her chest as she joined Lydia on the couch and began to rub her daughter's back comfortingly. *Why did he have to yell that way?* she wondered. *Couldn't they work out their problems with gentle words?* Ettie knew what had happened; Chip had blown up because Lydia had interrupted him. He hadn't been able to tell them about his new job or about when their move would be. Although Ettie did not feel that the interruption warranted a volatile reaction, she wanted to explain Chip's side to Lydia, with hopes that the situation would never repeat itself. The role of peacemaker between Chip and Lydia fell into her lap more and more often.

Immediately contrite when her mom explained Chip's need to be respected by not being interrupted, Lydia's sobs subsided, and she expressed a desire to apologize. "Let's wait a bit, honey," Ettie counseled, remembering past arguments with Chip. "I think he may be too upset right now to accept your apology. And you know what else? In a short while, he's going to be sorry that he spoke to you that way, and I bet he's going to ask for your forgiveness as well. Later tonight, you can call Grandma and Grandpa and tell them our good news."

Lydia nodded as she accepted her mother's advice. Ettie's understanding of what would happen later that evening couldn't have been any more wrong, but how could she know? Why would she ever have imagined that Chip's routine for making amends with Lydia was to sneak into her bathroom with a little tap on the door as she was undressing for her shower? That he would hold her close in her innocent nakedness and whisper endearments? That he would kiss her tender mouth? That he would thank her for the chance to share another wonderful "birthday suit hug" with her? And that with each birthday suit hug, he was cunningly preparing her for his next ungodly violation of her privacy and her body.

The beautiful family existed only as an illusion. The betrayer in their midst changed their beauty into ashes. Would anyone ever know what darkness lurked behind his charming smiles?

"And the tree was happy. But not really."

SHEL SILVERSTEIN

Chapter 7

Behind Closed Doors

Snip, snip, snip. The subtle noise of the scrapbooking scissors was barely audible over the animated sounds bouncing off the walls in the Crews' two-story home on Sea Robin Street. Their homeschooling session had ended for the day, and it was Friday: the one afternoon of the week when Ettie and her three children did not need to hurry to David's baseball game, Lydia's flute lesson, or her ballet class. That certainly didn't mean it was quiet in their home. It was quite the opposite. David and Lydia were practicing a piano duet to the accompaniment of Jonathan and his friends, Benjamin and Ryan, racing up and down the stairs calling boisterously to one another in their play. To add percussion to the mix, Benjamin's puppy, Walker, was barking to his own beat each time the children came bounding back down the steps.

Ettie didn't mind the bustle. It felt good to have her children playing nearby as she worked on the family photo album at the dining room table. It almost seemed as if some of the sounds had popped right out of the pages she was working on. The pictures she was currently arranging were from their recent move to Mandarin in Jacksonville, Florida. Bright sunny days and many smiles graced the photos of the Crews and their extended family that had traveled east to help them get settled in their new home. This was their fourth move with the Navy in six years. Ettie enjoyed the adventure of living in a different city or state; yet, it was always comforting to have family help with the transition.

This move had also coincided with the tail-end of Chip's latest six-month deployment. Not only had Evelyn and Sam come to help as usual, but Meg and Helen had also arrived to spend time with Chip since he had been away so long. As Ettie trimmed a photo of the three youthful grandparents posing in the front yard with their four smart and healthy grandchildren, she whispered a prayer of thankfulness. God had given them a special week together to celebrate their move and Chip's homecoming. After she had affixed all the photos to the page, she began writing brief explanations next to the pictures. Below a candid shot of herself and Chip smiling into each other's eyes, she began to write "Happy to be together again." Instead, she intercepted the "H" mid-stroke and wrote, "Home at last!"

Pausing in her scrapbooking, Ettie gazed out the window as she questioned her motive. Why had she not wanted to use the word "happy" in the caption? If she was honest with herself, she realized that something had changed. She looked back at the picture. Chip did look different; he always managed to lose weight and get in shape on deployment. That certainly wasn't the change she was thinking about. No, there was a deeper, darker shift that was occurring. *What could it be?*

Before her ideas had time to arrange themselves, Lydia called from the living room, "Mama! Jonathan! Can you come to hear our song? David has gotten his part! Come and hear!" Excitement filled Lydia's voice. She had started teaching David simple keyboarding about three months before when they had first moved to Jacksonville. As a mature thirteen-year-old, she was a dedicated teacher; and David was a diligent student. Already, they had moved into their second piano instruction workbook.

Smiling, Ettie got up, stretched her legs, and joined the children in the living room. From the open booklet, she could see that the duet they were playing was titled "The Circus." It appeared to be an appropriate anthem for the day considering the antics of Jonathan and his friends thumping and bumping on the stairway. The boys also took a break from their work of capturing the bad guys and sat down with Ettie on the couch to listen to David and Lydia's simple melody. Side by side, brother and sister sat up straight and tall on the wooden piano bench. Lydia counted out the beats in the intro, and they began.

"The Circus" was a rollicking success. Neither student nor teacher missed a note, and they stood to take a lighthearted bow. Clapping enthusiastically, Jonathan and his friends in the makeshift audience gave their approval and then invited the performers to join them in their game. David agreed. The boys' new friend, Benjamin, rallied them back on duty with the rousing call, "Aw wight men, get your webbons!" The brave heroes gathered up their Nerf guns and foam swords to head out to the backyard to battle with their toy weapons on the basketball court. Lydia had declined the invitation and instead went next door to invite Benjamin's sister, Lindsey, for a bike ride.

Ettie watched the five boys tumble out the sliding glass back door, and she reminded Lydia to wear her helmet while she rode her bike. The house suddenly felt still and silent as if a blaring boombox had been switched off. The dramatic change in the house reminded Ettie of the shift she had been wondering about ten minutes before, and she decided to continue working on the photo album while solitude reigned. Although her pen normally flowed freely, she couldn't think of any more witty captions or sentimental phrases to add under the pictures. Instead, she put her pen down and started flipping back through the pages of the album. Maybe looking back through the past year or two could give her insight into what seemed to be changing.

The first page she turned back to showed their family playing in the yard of their home in Pensacola: a moss green two story on NW Rosebud Loop. These colorful photos that had been taken a month before their move to Jacksonville showed David and Jonathan playing in their red and yellow sandbox wearing the bright orange swimsuits that Meg had sent as Easter gifts. It had been a hot and humid day, and Ettie had encouraged the boys to fill their buckets with water to cool off. The water had of course made it into the sandbox too. A series of photos displayed the creative progression of the "sandman" building that had ensued when Lydia had finished her schoolwork and had joined her brothers in their play. They had taken wet balls of sand and piled them three high like snowmen. Next, they used rocks and leaves from the yard to decorate their characters. Lydia had named her sandman "Mr. Doodle-head."

Flipping back another page in the scrapbook, Ettie found more family memories smiling at her. A camping trip to Cade's Cove National Park in Tennessee had been a true highlight of their move to the east coast. The scenery had been a glorious variety of shades of green and blue. The trip had been an amazing family time of hiking, relaxing, and laughing together. One night at the campfire beside their tent had been life-changing for David. Their family trip had coincided with his fourth birthday, and as they sat around the fire on the evening of his birthday, they had discussed the day of his birth. Ettie could see the campfire glowing in her mind's eye.

"Oh, I sure remember the day you were born," Lydia had shared enthusiastically. "Mommy could hardly wait to meet you! She had been counting down the days till your due date. Well, we all had been counting down. And you came one day late, and it wasn't very long to wait. Did you hear that? I made a rhyme!"

Ettie chuckled and interjected, "I guess it didn't seem long to you, Lydia! Whew, another day felt like a whole month to me. David, you were such a special baby that after you were born, I forgot all about that hard pregnancy. All I could think about was what a joy it was to hold you in my arms and look at your sweet, peaceful smile."

As they reminisced, David's face shone with pride in the flickering light of the fire. He loved hearing the stories about when he was born, and he knew it would be neat if he could relive those moments. With a wistful look, he had said, "I wish I could be born again."

Chip and Ettie had locked eyes and nodded to each other. It was the perfect time to explain to David that Jesus gives everyone who believes in Him the gift of being born again. David had heard the Bible story of Jesus talking to Nicodemus before. That night as Chip had explained it to him once more, the story had taken on new meaning. "Your body won't be an actual baby again," Chip had expounded, "Your spirit will be made new in God's kingdom."

Ettie added, "You will be His child forever if you believe that Jesus died to forgive your sins and that He rose again to conquer sin and death."

Without pause, David exclaimed, "I want to do that!" With joyful hearts, Chip and Ettie had led him in a simple prayer talking to God about how he believed in his son, Jesus.

Always the photographer, Lydia had gotten the camera out of the tent and snapped a photo of Chip sitting in his camping chair with his arm around David. The lighting wasn't great in the picture, but the smiles were, and now they had a memory of that notable birthday. Ettie was thankful that Lydia had gotten the gift of photography from her Grandma Evelyn.

That thought was still in Ettie's mind as she turned back the pages of the album once more, and the book opened to a panorama of photographs taken primarily by Evelyn. Ettie's mother had flown east to attend Lydia's ballet performance of "Snow White and the Seven Dwarfs." En pointe for the first time, Lydia had danced the roles of two woodland animals: a feathered blue bird and a graceful deer.

Suddenly a blur of color whizzed past the dining room window: Lydia and Lindsey on their bikes heading toward the basketball court. Even on her bike, Lydia's gracefulness was evident. No wonder her ballet dancing was lovely to watch. Ettie looked back and forth from the dancer in the performance pictures to the bike rider outside the window, and oddly a sad memory entered her mind. The day before Evelyn had arrived for "Snow White and the Seven Dwarfs," Ettie had taken Lydia to a day-long rehearsal at the high school where the performance was to be held. Chip had generously stayed home from work that day to be with David and Jonathan. However, his back began to hurt and by the time Ettie had returned in the evening, he could barely stand. The scene replayed itself without being beckoned; in fact, Ettie would have gladly forgotten what had happened next. Instead, the evening was captured in her mind so vividly that it seemed to happen again right before her eyes.

Ettie and Lydia walked into the living room to find toys, clothes, diapers, and half-emptied plates and cups strewn around on every surface—tables, countertops, couches, and even the floor. Chip stood hunched over the kitchen sink holding his back. He glanced over his shoulder with a grimace of pain on his face when he heard Ettie's stifled gasp. "Are you surprised to find the house a wreck?" He began defensively.

"Well, a little," she admitted, "But it looks like you're not feeling well. What happened?" As she questioned Chip, she also picked up Jonathan who had toddled over and was holding up his arms to her. "Hi, sweet guy! How are you? How was your day?" Chip scowled at her and gave no explanation; therefore, she continued to focus on Jonathan which meant checking his diaper. "Oh, your diaper is wet, buddy. Let's go upstairs and get you a dry one." She turned to go.

Despite his pain, Chip moved quickly and intercepted her. He snatched the baby and reproached Ettie, "Don't worry about this mess. Or the diaper. Listen, you think I can't handle things around here while you're gone, don't you? I saw the look on your face when you came in. You think I'm incapable."

He only took a dozen steps away from her when his back gave out again, and he was forced to put Jonathan down at the foot of the stairs. Still clutching his back with one hand, he grabbed Jonathan by the other and nearly dragged the reluctant child up the stairs. By the time they had reached the top, Jonathan was crying in earnest, and Ettie hustled up the steps to intervene.

"Chip, you look like you're in a lot of pain. I understand; it's okay. Please let me change him," she suggested.

"*You don't understand! Nothing is ever easy for me like it is for you. It doesn't mean I'm useless. I don't need your help. Now get out of my way!*" *Chip's statement felt like a slap in the face. What in the world is he doing talking to me like that? she wondered. They had always been a great team in taking care of their children. She didn't like that he was yelling in front of the kids or that he was taking out his frustrations on her. It seemed awful. How could she have known that the situation was about to get much worse?*

As he reached down to get a diaper from inside the changing table, Chip was gripped with another wave of pain. He roared in frustration and fell to the ground. His discomfort snapped his self-control in half, and pent-up rage came pouring out. Unfortunately, the wooden step stool that Meg had built and engraved with David's name was the closest object in reach. It splintered into unrecognizable pieces of wood as Chip swung it back and forth smashing it first into the wall and then into the changing table.

Ettie didn't wait to see what would happen next. Holding Jonathan tightly in her arms, she ran back down the stairs and gathered up her purse and car keys that were still on the kitchen counter. "Let's go," she managed to squeak out in a frightened voice to Lydia and David. The four of them quickly piled in the truck and drove away to safety. They didn't go far. This had occurred in Pensacola where they had no family, and Ettie did not want to involve any friends in their misunderstanding. She merely drove out of the neighborhood and parked in an empty parking lot knowing that Chip could not follow them since they only had one car at the time.

Sitting at the dining room table with the photo album in front of her, Ettie took a deep breath. It sure made her sad that Lydia's ballet pictures would bring back that nightmarish day. The horrible memory seemed like it belonged to another family. Reliving it so clearly had drained her; ready to move on, she turned the page back once more. This page displayed a collage from when the Crew family moved back to San Diego when Jonathan was six months old. With their frequent military moves, this one had been a tremendous blessing since they had been close to family and Ettie's long-time friends for almost two years. Their brick house on Tarpon Court had been only a mile and a half from Sam and Evelyn's home; and Teresa, one of Ettie's best friends, had been Lydia's first flute instructor.

However, as Ettie looked at the page, a strange thing happened once again. Instead of simply viewing the adorable faces of her children and remembering the joyful moments from their days on Tarpon Court, the two memories that arose were ones she would have liked to erase. In her mind's eye, she saw Chip throwing over their heavy wooden coffee table in anger; and she saw him pitch every tool from his workbench onto the garage floor in his rage. What an unusually bizarre experience she was having as she worked on the family album!

For the first time, she began to realize there were two realities present in her scrapbooks. The one reality was evident on the surface of the photographs: the smiles, togetherness, and fun. The second reality existed as the memories behind the glossy photos. And sometimes those remembrances matched the smiles, and sometimes they didn't. Those were the things that would never make it into a photo album. Maybe that defined the change she was experiencing.

She certainly didn't want everyone to know about Chip's outbursts. Their parents knew, and her sisters, but the fact that Chip lost his temper in a scary way about every six months wasn't something Ettie was proud of. Mostly because she felt that it must in some way reflect her relationship with him as his wife and best friend. He had gone to anger management counseling for a while after the awful incident when he had pulled Jonathan up the stairs. He only agreed to go because they had recently begun the process of adopting a baby girl from China, and their social worker had suggested counseling. The counselor guided Chip as he worked through issues in his relationship with his father. Neither Chip nor the counselor had pointed a finger at Ettie saying that the outbursts were related to their marriage. Still, she felt that she must be responsible in some way.

The counseling hadn't seemed to help; and it was no way to live—wondering when he was going to explode at them again. Maybe that's why she had simply written "home at last" as the caption on their reunion photo. Too much had happened behind closed doors. She was starting to feel that they were living a lie.

Not desiring to dwell on the past any longer, Ettie was relieved when she glanced at the clock and saw that it was time to make dinner. Her plan that night was to make her grandmother's baked chicken recipe. After putting her scrapbook materials into neat piles on the dining room table, she went into the kitchen and began peeling and chopping garlic. She had just reached into the pantry to get out the olive oil and the breadcrumbs when the doorbell rang.

"Hi Joy," Ettie greeted her new friend at the door, "Come on into the kitchen. I was starting to make dinner. How are you?"

"Mmm, it smells good in here," Joy complimented. "I love the smell of garlic. What are you making?"

Joy followed Ettie into the kitchen. From the open kitchen windows, they could see their children playing together on the community basketball court.

"We're having baked chicken tonight," Ettie replied. "How about you? You're always making such yummy dinners. By the way, can I get you something to drink?"

"Yes, a glass of water would be great. I'm trying to get hydrated for my race tomorrow. And we're having angel hair pasta with garlic and tomatoes for dinner. Hopefully, the carbs will give me the boost I need in my 5K." Joy explained as she swept her long bangs behind her ear. "I am planning to do at least as well as I did in the Run for Autism Awareness that I ran last month. I came in second in my age bracket in that."

"Whoa, that's awesome!" Ettie exclaimed.

Joy started laughing. "Ha-ha, not really. Since there were only two of us in that age bracket."

Ettie joined Joy in chuckling over her silly joke until suddenly Joy stopped. The emotion that was bubbling over became a choked sob. She hung her head and held onto the kitchen counter tightly as if it were the only thing keeping her from falling. Ettie quickly put down her chopping knife and moved closer to Joy.

"Oh no. What's wrong, sweetie?" She asked in concern as she put her hand on Joy's arm.

Joy looked up. A dozen unshed tears filled her eyes as she struggled to reply, "It's Don. We had another fight. He came home early from work today, and we started talking about our plans for the weekend. He never wants to spend time with me and the kids. When I told him that Justin, Lindsey, and Benjamin need him, he started yelling at me." She paused and looked down; when she looked up again, the tears were gone, and instead, she had a fire in her eyes. "Ettie, you know how feisty I am. When I started hollering back at Don this afternoon, he lost it. He broke the handle off the refrigerator door. Right in front of the kids." The fire died out of her green eyes, and she sat down at the kitchen table and put her fingertips to her temples.

Sitting down beside her, Ettie considered what she should say to support her friend. In the three months they had known each other, their friendship had blossomed quickly. It helped that they lived right next door to each other and that their kids got along well too. She had a feeling that they would soon be best friends if their relationship continued to grow. Even their husbands seemed to hit it off. That gave Ettie an idea. Sharing a few of her own experiences with Joy seemed right, although telling people about that darkness in their lives was uncomfortable for her. Hopefully, she and Joy could be a source of encouragement for each other.

"I'm so sorry, Joy," Ettie began. "That's awful. Marriage can be extremely challenging. I was actually sitting here thinking about a few of the times that Chip has gotten that angry."

"Really? He does that too?" Joy asked in disbelief. "He seems so... I don't know, nice? Like he truly cares about you and the kids."

"Well, he is usually nice," Ettie agreed with a half-smile. "He does have anger issues sometimes. Can I tell you a story that helps me get through those blow-ups?"

"Sure."

"A few years back, when Jonathan was one and a half, Chip was deployed for six months to Japan. After only three months of deployment, I got a phone call in the middle of the night from Chip. He had suffered a heart attack after working out at the gym and was being medevaced to Hawaii for surgery. He asked me to meet him at Tripler Hospital in Oahu the following day."

Now it was Joy's turn to be sympathetic, "Ettie, I had no idea. I'm sorry to hear that. It must have been shocking."

"It sure was. Chip was only thirty-two years old. We didn't understand how he could have a heart attack at thirty-two. When Chip and I got off the phone that night, I could hear Jonathan crying in his room. I walked across the house to get him, and when I picked him up out of his crib, he put his head on my shoulder and immediately relaxed. His crying stopped, and I heard God say to me, 'Ettie, this is what I want you to do too. Put your head on my shoulder and trust me.' Hearing God's voice say that to me is something that has stuck with me clearly over the years; and even when hard days come, I try to remember that he wants us to rest in him and trust him."

"That is powerful, and you're right." Joy answered, "The problem is that I get so caught up in the moment, and I can't handle the way he disrespects me. When he brings the kids into it, forget it, I swing into action. I know how much it would mean to our three children if Don would simply spend a Saturday afternoon with them. Especially Justin now that he's getting older; he needs a good male role model in his life. Don says he's too busy. I don't even know what he does out there, puttering around in the garage or sitting on the computer for hours at a time."

Ettie certainly understood the part about sitting at the computer, and she nodded her head in sympathy. Then she had another idea which she shared optimistically with Joy: "You know, we have plans to go on a hiking trail on Little Talbot Island tomorrow. Maybe Chip could invite Don to bring you and the kids to join us? Do you all like hiking?"

"Yeah, we do. Before Justin was born, we used to hike the Appalachian Trail together. I would love to go with you. I think you're right—Chip should be the one to ask Don. Coming from me after our fight, Don would be sure to say no."

Later that afternoon, when Chip invited Don to bring his family hiking, Don agreed. Saturday dawned sunny and warm, and the blue Florida skies smiled down on the Crew and Brighton families as they trekked along the pristine dunes and under the Live Oak trees. Walker, the coonhound puppy, and the six children found adventure at every turn—one moment running ahead to hide in the tall grass and the next moment lagging behind to climb a tree. Ettie and Joy shared thankful smiles when they saw Don pointing out ospreys and fiddler crabs to Justin, Lindsay, and Benjamin. Fresh air and exercise made everyone cheerful, and the two families had such a blast in each other's company that they made plans to get together for church the following day. The Brightons were still looking for a church in Jacksonville and were enthusiastic about checking out Ocean View Christian Fellowship with the Crews.

Back at Sea Robin Street, after a round of goodbyes and a chorus of "see you tomorrow," the Crews went inside. Ettie helped David and Jonathan bathe and put on pajamas while Chip and Lydia washed out the water bottles and put away the backpacks, binoculars, and shoes they had used on their hike. When Ettie and the boys went back downstairs for stories on the couch, it was Lydia's turn to head up for a shower. The boys chose a favorite story that night, *Whose Tracks Are These,* a forest animal book with deer, chipmunks, raccoons, and more darting across the well-loved pages.

Chip was in his study when Ettie began to read the book, and she looked up expectantly when he immediately stepped out. It seemed as if he would join them. David and Jonathan loved it when their father read this particular book to them. When all the clues had been given, and you found out whose feet had made the tracks, Chip always made the boys laugh at the mimicry of his funny voices parroting out, "I am a squirrel!" or "I am a chipmunk!" Yet, this time, Chip simply walked by with a grin and a wave.

Chip had considered joining story time that evening. He had changed his mind because he was more interested in a different bedtime routine that was happening upstairs. At the top of the stairs, he tried the bathroom door. Unlocked. Just as always and just as he liked it. He and Ettie had disagreed about the issue of the unlocked door early on in their marriage—Ettie saying that Lydia needed to have the feeling of privacy in her bathroom, and Chip arguing that for safety issues the door should remain unlocked. What if Lydia were to slip and fall in the shower and bump her head? How would they be able to quickly get in to help her? Safety won out. How thankful Chip was that Ettie implicitly respected his authority as head of their household. He would make it up to her soon and show her that he loved and appreciated her. A nice back rub would do the trick, he decided. For now, he was focused on showing Lydia that he loved and cared for her.

Lydia wasn't surprised in the least to hear the door handle turn and a tiny tap on her bathroom door. If it had been out of the ordinary, she might have been a bit startled, but it wasn't. She usually took a shower before it was time for bed since she liked to take her time washing up, and she enjoyed reading a chapter book afterward as well. A lot of times before she got in the shower, there was something else that took up a bit of her time, especially if her family had taken a hike or had gone on a camping trip.

That evening, she didn't respond when Chip tapped lightly on the door. She knew he would come inside anyway. Lydia saw the door crack open slightly, and she looked over at the mirror to see his grin in the reflection, peering through the little opening. He peeked in further and asked quietly if he could come in. She didn't want him to enter: she was getting older and didn't feel comfortable in front of him anymore. But she nodded hesitantly because she didn't know what else to do. She had never told him no before, so in a way, it seemed like the only option. He came inside, shut the door behind him, and moved close.

Lydia knew what was coming, and she felt a sickening feeling when Chip whispered, "Hey, do you want to do that tick check now?" Even though she didn't want to, she murmured "yes" and took off her underwear. She knew how this process would go, and that he would want to look at her and touch her all over to make sure that she didn't have any ticks buried in her skin.

Five minutes later, Chip smiled at her and announced, "Tick free again. Wonderful!" Finally, he gave her a lingering hug, rubbing her back again as well. He left the bathroom, and she took her shower. It lasted longer than usual. Their hike on Little Talbot Island must have left her feeling dirty, she reasoned; and she hoped that standing in the hot water would guarantee that all the dirt got washed away. Lydia waited several minutes in the steaming shower for the clean feeling to come. However, when she turned off the water, she realized that somehow she felt as soiled as when she had begun.

I lift up my eyes to the mountains—
Where does my help come from?
My help comes from the Lord,
the Maker of heaven and earth.

PSALM 121:1&2

Chapter 8

SURPRISES

Lydia peered at her reflection in the dressing room mirror. It wasn't at all how she had imagined she would look on the day of her first kiss. Her face was doused with an inordinate amount of makeup, whereas she normally wore none. Her long straight hair had been replaced by an abundance of ringlets. And the dress she was wearing, oh my— it was much too short and covered in ruffles. Not at all like the jeans and tank top she would be wearing on a regular day.

Even though she looked rather unlike herself, Lydia was thrilled that it wasn't an average day. It was such a special day that she could hardly sit still to finish applying her "really rosy" lipstick. She stood and moved to the other side of the room to see how she looked in the full-length mirror. Executing a sauté arabesque and a pas de chat, she swished the satiny pale pink skirt and smiled. The dress fit her quite well despite being short. Twirling in a chaîné turn, she realized that the whole ensemble was much more flattering than she had thought. It was going to be a wonderful day after all—December 15, 2007.

A group of giggling dancers came into the room and joined Lydia. Seven of the girls began coiffing their elaborate hair, costumes, and makeup. With them was Lydia's good friend, Marcella, who didn't even glance at her own image; she focused instead on Lydia's bright smile.

"Ooh, Lydia, you look perfect! You must be excited!" Marcella complimented sweetly. "Has your mom seen you yet?"

"Thank you, Marcella. You're looking beautiful too! I absolutely adore those white tulle tutus that Miss Daphne found for your 'Waltz of the Flowers.' I kind of wish that I could be dancing that part with you so I could wear one of those too." Lydia added this last part wistfully before addressing Marcella's question. "Yes, my mom came in and helped me with this bow on the back of my dress. I couldn't quite get it straight."

"Did she get any pictures?" Marcella asked.

"No, but that's all right; my grandparents will arrive tomorrow, and Grandma will take a couple dozen. She loves taking pictures as much as I do. I definitely got that gene from her. That reminds me, my mom told me to tell you that she is going to be taking a walk with your mom during the next part of the rehearsal. They'll be back in like an hour. Hey, Marcella, can we talk for a minute?"

"Umm, we are talking, Lydia," Marcella replied with a gentle grin.

"Right, ha-ha, I guess we are. Okay, well," Lydia lowered her voice which normally carried above other conversations even in a busy room, "I'm super excited about today, but there is one thing I'm kind of nervous about." She paused dramatically.

Marcella guessed that Lydia was referring to dancing the lead role and gave her friend some words of support. "Don't worry; your dancing is going to be amazing. Ms. Daphne knew what she was doing when she chose you for the part of Clara. She says that you float across the stage."

"Thank you! I do feel confident about all the dancing. The awkward part is the kiss. When I've imagined what it will be like to be kissed for the first time, it's always with a boy that I care about— not like this! Not by a classmate on stage!" The volume of Lydia's voice rose with her emotion, and she blushed when she saw a couple of her other friends glance her way. She quieted her voice again, "I keep feeling like it's going to be a fabulous day and an awesome show. Then the idea of that silly first kiss keeps getting in the way."

Like many of Lydia's closest friends, Marcella had a more reserved personality than Lydia. Lydia's outgoing nature generally attracted girls who liked to listen more than talk; and although this was true of Marcella as well, she also had a mature outlook and wisdom that helped her to calm Lydia's concerns. "It's all right, Lydia," she encouraged, "Ivan has kissed your hand a couple of other times in class when you were rehearsing that scene. I don't think those count as a first kiss, and this one won't either. You know, just because you're all dressed up doesn't mean that it's official. You'll have a real first kiss someday when you're older—more like sixteen than fourteen probably."

Taking Marcella's advice to heart was easy for Lydia, in part because Marcella spoke earnestly, and because Lydia knew that what she said was true. It helped to hear it from someone she trusted. She was able to completely enjoy the rest of the Nutcracker dress rehearsal after sharing her concerns with her friend.

At the same time that Lydia was feeling thankful for the camaraderie of Marcella, Ettie was walking on Jacksonville's downtown Riverwalk feeling grateful for her friendship with Marcella's mother, Deb Brown. The two women had connected the first time they met at the Civic Youth Ballet because of the similarity of their lives: they were both homeschooling moms with one older daughter and two younger sons. During the two, three, or four classes and rehearsals that their daughters attended each week, Ettie and Deb would often meet for a brisk walk along the St. John's River. They could usually be seen accompanied by their four boys—David, Jonathan, Derek, and Carter—zipping forward, backward, and all around on their Razor scooters. The boardwalk was a bit bumpy for the scooters; however, the foursome didn't seem to mind. They jostled along energetically as their mothers talked and exercised from one end of the Riverwalk to the other and back again.

Knowing each other for a year had brought Ettie and Deb close.

Their friendship had begun to reach the point where they each felt comfortable sharing the deep things that were on their minds, not only the superficial conversation that exists between acquaintances. Ettie felt blessed that between Joy and Deb, she had two dear friends whom she could count on for a compassionate listening ear and godly counsel.

On December fifteenth, their walk began at their typical starting point: Friendship Fountain. As the four boys zoomed ahead, Ettie began by asking Deb about the job opportunity that had fallen into her lap the previous week. "Have you decided whether you will take the job at the martial arts studio?"

"No decision yet. Todd and I are still praying about it. It seems like it would be a good fit for me; I love advertising and word processing. The company says they would give me creative license as well. Plus, if I'm not here at the ballet with Marcella, I'm at martial arts with Derek and Carter." Deb chuckled as she replied. "The most important thing is whether it is God's will. And that's what I'm waiting to hear." Deb paused as she took a quick drink from her water bottle and continued, "One other thing I've been wondering about is how well I can balance our homeschooling hours with the part-time job. How have you been doing with that since you started working as the early childhood director at your church last month?"

"Super well!" Ettie began enthusiastically. "It has been a great fit since most of the hours are during the weekend. The day we had a staff meeting, I made sure that the kids all had work they could do independently for the hour and a half that I would be gone. I am loving getting to know the staff and families of Ocean View Christian Fellowship better, and the babies are adorable! And guess what?"

"What?"

"Chip has been one of my best volunteers! He loves being with the babies almost as much as I do. Each time someone has canceled at the last minute, Chip has been willing to fill in. One thing that has been hard about being the director is all the emails. They're taking more time than I had anticipated. For now, it's fine; I save that work for when the kids are in bed. Once we bring Eva home from China, I'm going to want that time to be rocking her to sleep. Or even sleeping myself. Who knows how much sleep I'll be getting with a new baby in the house."

Without breaking her stride, Ettie unzipped her black velour sweatshirt and tied it around her waist. "Whew, it's warm out here for December," she remarked. "I still haven't gotten used to this Florida winter."

Having grown up in the southeast, Deb was used to the heat and therefore didn't comment on the weather. Instead, she brought the conversation back around to the Crews' plans to adopt. "How are things going with your adoption? Last time we spoke, you mentioned the possibility of considering a special needs child."

"Oh, yes; I have the sweetest story to tell you about that. Well, as you know, the process has taken much longer than the six months we expected. Now after almost three years of waiting to be matched with our daughter, we started praying about whether it was God's plan for us to bring home a little girl with a medical condition. You wouldn't believe all the children available on the website. And I fell in love with one of them. A beautiful baby girl with the roundest cheeks and the darkest eyes. Her name is Siqi. Lydia says the name reminds her of the verse, 'Seek ye first the kingdom of God.' When I asked the boys how they would feel about having a sister whose arms and legs didn't work so well, David's response brought me to tears."

"He does have a tender heart. What did he say, Ettie?"

"'I would like that, Mama, because then I could help her.'" Tears welled up in Ettie's eyes once again as she repeated David's affirmation of love for a sister he hadn't even met yet. She watched him zoom up ahead on his scooter and thought about how both he and Jonathan would be awesome big brothers once they brought Eva home.

"I'm thrilled for you, Ettie. What happens next?" Deb asked with sincere interest.

"We'll keep praying and talking. The hard part is that Chip and

I don't seem to be on the same page about it. I feel strongly that this is our daughter! God is affirming it for me in His word. Chip, on the other hand, is worried about the severity of her medical needs, and his father has been counseling him against adopting a child with any special needs at all." Ettie sighed. "Will you be praying with me for Eva? Whoever she is."

"Of course, sweetie, you know I always do." Deb agreed with a smile. Then she began sharing some exciting news with Ettie. She and her husband had been inspired by the Crews' adoption and had decided to expand their family as well. After researching international adoptions, they were leaning toward the idea of traveling to Ukraine to find their daughter.

During the rest of the hour-long walk, the conversation stayed focused on the Brown family's developing plans. Ettie and Deb were so engrossed in their heart-to-heart, that they didn't pay attention to the fact that they had returned to their starting point and that the four boys had begun to attempt a few daring tricks around the outside of the fountain.

Ettie looked over in time to see Jonathan falling headfirst into the water. His scooter had crashed into the edge, and it flipped in behind him landing with a splash. She ran over to see if he was okay, and as she reached him, he came up laughing. Fortunately, the fountain was very shallow, and the water only came up to his waist. He was soaked from his shirt to his sneakers and had minor scrapes on his knees and elbows. The other three boys joined Jonathan in his laughter and began to press their mothers to be allowed to hop in the fountain with him for a swim.

"Please, Mom! We're super hot," began Derek.

"And look—Jonathan is lonely in there!" added Carter.

However, the public fountain had "No Swimming" signs posted; so rather than becoming an impromptu December swim party, the event simply became a great story to tell and retell to family and friends. Four-year-old Jonathan couldn't wait to share all the details of his escapade with Grandma and Grandpa and Uncle Ashton the following day when they arrived to celebrate an early Christmas and to watch Lydia in the Nutcracker.

A week later when Chip returned from a month at sea, he chuckled long and hard as Jonathan told of his epic stunt and attempted to demonstrate it by tumbling off the couch.

"Honestly, I don't know if I can top that, buddy," Chip said as his laughter subsided. "But I do have a surprise for you. I am going to take our family on a camping trip to Gold Head Branch State Park in Keystone Heights. Have you heard of it, Ettie?" He asked without waiting for an answer. "I took an extra week of leave after the holiday so that we can go and do some fishing. It's been too long since I've been able to use my rod and reel; I've been dying to catch a largemouth bass while we're stationed here in Florida. What do you think, guys?"

Everyone in the Crew family was excited about the trip. David and Jonathan liked having sword fights with sticks in the woods, and they loved sleeping in the tent. Ettie was ready to be refreshed by the crisp air and the family time, and she was especially grateful for a vacation because it meant that Chip would probably be in a good mood for several consecutive days.

Camping with the family was something that Lydia always looked forward to greatly. She enjoyed being with the people that she loved in the most beautiful places she had ever seen. There was always a new mountain to climb, a cool stream to wade in, or a shady forest to explore. During the day, they might drive to a trailhead and hike from there or hike from the campground itself to a waterfall or scenic overlook. When they arrived back at their campsite, her family would share a simple meal cooked over the portable stove. Dinner was followed by a restful evening by the fire, roasting marshmallows, and talking about life or the day's events.

On the third night of their trip to Gold Head Branch, Lydia relaxed in her canvas chair in the dancing light of the fire. As she looked up at the sparkling stars, she realized that as much as she loved the exercise and camaraderie that they experienced each time they left the campsite to explore together, her two favorite parts of the day were the s'mores and the discussion by the fire after dinner.

By nine-thirty on that evening, her mom had already taken David and Jonathan into the tent to tuck them in for the night. S'more time had passed; Chip and Lydia still sat talking by the fire. For a while, Lydia could hear slight rustling noises from inside the tent as her mom and her brothers settled down for bed. When she heard no more talking for fifteen minutes, she assumed that the boys had fallen asleep. She wondered if her mom was going to join them back out by the campfire, and she wished that she would. She liked spending time with her mom.

Chip must have been wondering the same thing. After five more minutes, he stood and stepped toward the tent. "Ettie?" he called in a pseudo whisper; then again, a bit louder, "Ettie, are you coming back out?"

When silence was the only response, Chip added another medium-sized log to the fire and returned to his seat within the circle of light cast by the flames.

After a while of talking and sitting, Chip mentioned to Lydia that they hadn't done a tick check yet since they had been at the campground. Lydia wondered why all of a sudden he wanted to do a check at the campground rather than waiting until they got home. Always before, he had waited. That made more sense anyway since she knew that getting a tick was a possibility while they were still camping. Yet she didn't want to argue, and she figured it would be better to get it over with rather than think about it longer than she had to. He asked if they could go ahead and do one now, and she complied.

Chip suggested that they walk towards the bathroom a bit, so they set off toward a light that was a short distance away through the trees. They walked through the groups of dark tree trunks standing like sentinels in the night. When Chip stopped at the edge of the trees close to the bathroom, Lydia wondered why he had chosen this as a good place since someone could walk by at any point. She was used to doing these checks inside with the door closed—what if a camper came walking along the road on their way to the bathroom? She really hoped it was late enough that no one would walk by.

First, Lydia pulled her shirt up and let her dad look at her upper torso. He used a flashlight to look at her chest, stomach, back, and underarms. He looked a bit more quickly than usual. Maybe he was also nervous that someone would walk by. Next, she pulled her jeans down and bent over to let him check in her bathing suit area. Chip held the flashlight with one hand so the light shone on her bottom and used his other hand to touch her private area to make sure that there were no ticks. The whole tick check caused Lydia's skin to tingle and her stomach to flutter. This last part always made her palms sweat and her insides feel strange in ways she didn't understand.

When he finished, Lydia pulled her pants up quickly and looked around. There was no one coming. What a relief! That would have been terribly embarrassing! In a rush, she wondered if he would want to check her legs at all. Thankfully, he didn't. He only hugged her and told her that he loved her. Father and daughter walked back to the campsite together. Lydia tucked herself into her sleeping bag and waited for sleep to come.

After another three nights of camping, the Crew family headed home to Jacksonville. Halfway home, Chip left the main road. Ettie guessed that he was probably stopping for gas or a Diet Coke until he pulled the F-150 into the parking lot of the Middleburg Safe Animal Shelter. She looked over at him in surprise to see that he was looking right back at her with a grin. "Chip! Really?" It was all Ettie could manage to say in her disbelief.

For the past two months as Christmas had approached, she and Chip had been discussing the possibility of surprising the children with a puppy as a Christmas gift. The calico cats, Violet and Daisy, had both passed away in the last six months. Ettie had been completely ready to add a new furry member to their family knowing that the children's lives would be fuller with the lovable addition. Chip had been more hesitant. He said that he didn't want her to have to add another responsibility to her already full plate especially considering all his work travel. Their discussion had ended with Chip making the executive decision that they would wait another year. Now here they were. Although Ettie wondered why he had changed his mind, she decided she wouldn't ask him about it—in case she made him change it back again.

In the rear seat, the children started to chatter and giggle with anticipation. As they all piled out of the car, Lydia began thanking her dad with a hug. "Well, don't thank me yet, Lydia. We don't even know if they will have a puppy that we can all agree on at this shelter."

The red-haired woman at the receptionist's desk, however, seemed to be expecting them. When Chip introduced himself, she began talking about a certain litter, a Beagle/German Shepherd mix, that he apparently had called to inquire about. "Come right this way," she requested. She smiled warmly at the three children. "You must be pretty excited about today. These puppies are precious."

Following close behind the woman whose name tag read *Frieda*, Lydia and her brothers explained cheerfully that coming to the animal shelter was a complete surprise to them. Chip was holding Ettie's hand and caressing it gently. Ettie knew that he meant to convey his joy at being able to share this moment with her. She was excited yet also feeling betrayed, and she wished he would let go of her hand. Chip had lied to her. He had told her that they could not have a family pet, and yet he had been looking for one without her. The situation reminded her of the September past when she had asked for a picture from the Christian bookstore for her birthday.

Chip had called from the store asking for particulars about the gift.

"It's a black and white photograph," she had described. "With an oak tree in a field. A fence runs along the edge of the field. Along the bottom is Psalm 121, verses one and two. I love those verses."

Chip had paused for several moments as if he was looking

around at the display of wall hangings. "Well, sorry," he began disappointedly, "It's not here. Honestly, they must have already sold that one. Don't worry, baby, I have a different gift in mind that you'll like."

None of that seemed strange until she opened her birthday present the next day. It was the beautiful photograph she had asked for! When she had questioned him in delight about where he had found it, he had guffawed with a gleam in his eye and explained that the bookstore had it all along. He hadn't wanted her to know. Suddenly, the whole situation did seem strange to Ettie. Couldn't he have been like, "Oh, alright, thanks for telling me which picture you like;" instead of "I can't find it"? Since when had Chip started hiding things from her? She had believed that they told each other everything. *That's what best friends are for*, they often promised. Yet, he seemed to think that it was okay to hide things from her when he wanted to give her an unexpected pleasure.

She wanted to ask him about both situations now that it had happened again, yet this certainly wasn't the right time to discuss it. It could wait till they got home that night. Frieda had reached the outdoor kennels where dozens of dogs were barking their welcome. Canines in all sizes and colors were saying hello. The Crew family followed the animal shelter attendant to a cage filled with six brown, black, and white wiggling puppies whose tails waggled like dancing bees. "This is the litter you have seen pictures of on our website, Mr. Crew. If you'll let me know which one you like, I'll bring him or her into our 'meet and greet' room so you can get acquainted with one another."

It didn't take long to decide which pup to choose for the "meet and greet." All five of the Crews quickly agreed on a petite female with dainty white paws and a splash of white on her chest. After bringing her inside, they sat down with her and began to offer her toys. She made a few fumbling attempts to chase the tennis ball but only managed to run right over the top of it. She sniffed around in the corners of the room a bit, had a bathroom accident in the middle of the floor, and then chose to sit down in a cozy spot between David and Jonathan. They rubbed her floppy velvet ears and the fluffy ruff of fur under her neck.

"Oh, Mama, Daddy! She loves us already! Look! She snuggled up here right between us. We have to get her! Can we? We can, right?!"

The vote was unanimous and within the hour the newest member of the family was riding in the backseat of the truck with her sister and brothers. They each took turns trying to help her sit quietly for the ride as they discussed what to name her. She eventually wore herself out and fell asleep in a makeshift towel bed on Lydia's lap. As they were nearing home, they had the name pool narrowed down to two choices, Grace or Stella, both of which had been Chip's suggestions.

Ettie had looked through half a dozen baby name books when choosing their children's names and recalled that the name "Stella" means star. Stella got the vote. It seemed like the perfect name for the new shining star of the family. They arrived home soon after the name had been chosen. As everyone climbed out of the truck, they were greeted by the boys' friend, Justin. He had been sitting on his front steps and came over when he saw David and Jonathan returning from their camping trip.

"Hey, guys! What's up? How was your...whoa! Who is this?" he exclaimed as Stella trotted over and started sniffing his bare toes. "That tickles! Ha-ha!"

"This is Stella. She is our late Christmas present. She's going to sleep in my room." David shared proudly.

"Our room," Jonathan corrected. "And she'll sleep next to my bed because I'm on the bottom bunk," he added happily. "Justin, do you think Walker will like her? Mama, can we bring her over to Justin's house?"

"I think he will. He likes almost everything." Justin agreed. When Ettie gave her consent, he carefully picked up Stella and started walking back to his house.

Ettie glanced over at Chip and announced, "I guess I'll go over with them, honey. I'd love to say hi to Joy."

That left Chip and Lydia to begin unpacking the camping gear and luggage from the pick-up. They unloaded the tent and a few kitchen supplies for about five minutes, and then Chip sat down on the couch to take a break. Lydia followed him inside and sat down next to him as she chattered about what she had enjoyed about their vacation. Chip barely listened to the words since his mind was instead focused on how it was the perfect time to surprise Lydia with a kiss. He knew that Ettie and Joy were outside with the boys and the puppies. They would be preoccupied for quite a while catching up on a week apart. Chip was glad that Ettie had Joy right next door. It was convenient. If Ettie were to come back too soon, he would certainly hear the glass door slide open—even though it was on the other side of the house. He smiled and leaned over to place his open mouth on Lydia's. His kiss interrupted her monologue about the music they had been listening to on the ride home.

Lydia smiled too as Chip pulled back from a lingering embrace. She reasoned that if he was kissing her, it must mean that he liked the songs, and maybe he would be more likely to agree with her idea.

"So, is it okay, Daddy?"

Stroking her hair and her neck for a few moments before he answered, Chip asked distractedly, "Is what okay, Lydia?"

"You know, the songs we were listening to on the radio. They were ones that I think Marcella will like too. We've been sharing music a lot. She gave me *A Whole New World* from *Aladdin*, and before our camping trip, I shared Natasha Bedingfield's *Unwritten* with her. Marcella's mom thinks it's fine that we keep sharing music. Is it okay with you too? Those two Joy Williams songs we heard on the way home—they were so great! Don't you love the opening lines in *Hide*? 'To anyone who hides behind a smile, to anyone who holds their pain inside.' I mean we all do that sometimes, you know? Can I use my iTunes money to get *Hide* and the other one we heard by her, *Say Goodbye*? Would that be okay? I could share them with Marcella too."

"Well, now," Chip began teasingly, "You know, each one will cost you; the low, low price of 50 hugs apiece." As he spoke, he caressed the bare skin of Lydia's upper arm lightly with his fingertips. His fingers trailed their way up and down again along the inside edge of her arm.

"That's a hundred hugs! That's really a lot! Are you sure? When do you need all those by, Daddy?" Lydia cried in disbelief.

They had played this game before. Chip had bartered for the promise of more birthday suit hugs when Lydia had asked for simple things like a book from the library or a popsicle at bedtime. If they were keeping track, she owed him about 1,000 by now. Or maybe more, since as she got older, she was asking for more complicated things like rides to flute classes, ballet classes, or church; new shoes; and sleepovers with Marcella and Lindsey.

"No special date, Lydia. Don't worry about when you need to pay. I will come in and surprise you when the time is right. You never know, it could be tonight."

Chip slipped his hand under Lydia's shirt as he spoke and began to rub her back. The feel of her smooth skin and the idea of sneaking into her bathroom that night inspired him to begin to kiss her again. He closed his eyes and became lost in the moment until he heard the clatter of pots and pans in the kitchen.

His eyes flew open like a deer in the headlights. He backed away from Lydia just in time to see Ettie walk into the foyer. How had he missed the sound of the sliding glass door? He was usually so careful! He covered his tracks by laughing as if Lydia had shared something funny. His laughter rang false even to his ears. Would Ettie suspect something was amiss?

Ettie didn't notice the guilty look in Chip's eyes. Nor did she have any inkling of what had occurred to cause the look. She simply smiled and remarked, "Thanks for bringing in the kitchen stuff, guys. You wouldn't believe how happy Stella is out there with

Walker. They are playing like they've known each other forever. Joy is going to watch her for a bit while we finish unpacking. Is there still more to get from the truck?"

"Yes, sweetheart; I needed to rest a bit since my back is starting to seize up," Chip moped, hoping to garner sympathy. If Ettie was busy worrying about him, she wouldn't have time to be suspicious, he reasoned.

"Oh, bummer! Well, you keep resting, honey. Lydia and I can bring the rest in."

"I am not going to let you do all that by yourself." Chip stood, stretched his back deliberately, and added, "All right, Lyddie Bird. Let's go help your mother."

Lost in her thankful thoughts, Ettie was clueless about how close she had been to the shock of her life. She had not the slightest suspicion that she had almost walked in on her husband French kissing her fourteen-year-old daughter—or that his chuckling had merely disguised his deviant conversation, bribing Lydia to hug him when she was naked.

Instead, Ettie walked out the front door feeling blessed. She was thankful to see Chip and Lydia enjoying each other's company. Many days it seemed as if Chip didn't even like Lydia, especially when he complained about her behind her back. He would say, "Why does she talk so loudly?" or "Why is she better at baseball than me?" Ettie would play the role of peacemaker once again; at the same time, she wondered how he could dislike his own child. Here was proof, so it appeared, that he did have a fondness for Lydia. He had even used a sweet nickname for her: Lyddie Bird. It was one that he usually reserved for his daughter when he called her Helena Bird.

Ettie had intended to talk to Chip after they had unpacked. She wanted to get back on the same page with him—the one where best friends tell each other everything. But as she picked up two sleeping bags from the bed of the truck, she started to change her mind. *Why upset him and put him on the defensive when he's obviously in a good mood? Anyway, there's the adorable new puppy for Christmas and the lovely photograph he had given her for her birthday.*

Ettie watched her husband and her daughter each take a handle of the heavy blue cooler and carry it together into the house. They were still smiling at each other, and it warmed Ettie's heart like a ray of sun. As she followed them through the front door with a sleeping bag tucked under each arm, she continued to reason with herself. *If I try to talk to him about how I feel tonight, not only will I ruin his good mood, he might even have one of those scary yelling fits where he throws things. There's no way I want to risk that. It takes such a long time after those outbursts for life to feel normal again.*

Lydia and Chip put the cooler down on the kitchen counter and headed back out to get more gear. Ettie decided to stay in and put the perishables into the refrigerator. As she opened the top of the cooler to take out the milk and lunch meat, she paused and studied the black and white photograph on the wall. She loved the way the sunlight filtered through the leaves of the large oak tree. And she knew that she would be glad to have that verse to focus on after Chip's next blow-up. Their help truly did come from the Lord. If He could make heaven and earth, He could surely give them peace and strength for the tough days.

Maybe there won't be another blow-up? Wouldn't that be a nice surprise? Maybe with Chip and Lydia starting to get along, things would begin to change. Ettie was hopeful. She didn't see the dark storm gathering all around her family; all she could see was sunshine pouring down on the people she loved.

"Is there worse evil than that which goes in the mask of good?"

LLOYD ALEXANDER

Chapter 9

A DESPERATE PRAYER

Ettie didn't mean to start a fight that night; it happened because of one imprudent, impulsive decision. The full week of early mornings and late nights had left her feeling like a rag doll, and she had passed out at ten thirty with high hopes for sleeping in the next morning to regain her energy for the busy holiday ahead.

She rolled over groggily when Chip climbed into bed an hour later. Through one open eye, she saw him reach for the alarm clock and begin to press the buttons. "Hi, honey. What are you doing?" she asked sleepily.

Chip's eyes stayed on the glow of red numbers till they stopped at six-thirty a.m. "Oh, I'm just setting the alarm so I can get up for a run in the morning."

"A run? On Easter morning?"

"Right."

Images flashed through Ettie's mind from previous mornings—the alarm beeping incessantly until she woke up and turned it off; Chip rolling onto his back and putting the pillow over his face; herself at dawn wishing she could fall back to sleep while instead, she listened to Chip's snoring.

"Hmm. Well, I was kind of planning to sleep in tomorrow. They don't need me at church until ten, and we had talked about bringing the kids to the eleven-thirty service, remember?" Ettie coaxed in what she hoped was a persuasively sweet tone.

"You go ahead and get your rest, baby. I'm going to start a new training program first thing tomorrow."

Now Chip had Ettie's full attention, and she sat up quickly trying to figure out whether he was joking with her. The faint moonlight shining through the window wasn't enough to make out his facial expression. His voice had sounded serious enough, yet she felt sure he must be teasing.

"Well, all right, that's great," she began hesitantly. "Then why didn't you want to come with me when I invited you to exercise with me and Stella this evening?"

Chip didn't have a reason. He made a few attempts to find an excuse; however, nothing he said made sense to Ettie. The hurt she had felt when Chip had declined her invitation a few hours before began to turn into frustration. It was hard for her to voice her ideas to him if they were negative. Two weeks before, they had a question in their bible study that challenged them to express one thing they wished their spouse would change. Ettie hadn't mentioned any of the real issues. She was too afraid that she would anger him. Instead, she shared her desire that he would shut his closet door before he went to work in the morning. *How lame was that?* she wondered.

The red lights of the alarm clock seemed to mock her weakness. How many times had she wished that she could ask him not to set the buzzer since it never woke him up anyway? In the darkness, something inside her shifted, and she found the courage to speak.

"Honey, I'm happy that you want to start a training program. That is great; I know you've been thinking about doing that for a long time. Can we please not set the alarm early for tomorrow at least? This week has been awesome having Helen here for her spring break. It has been a whirlwind of Sea World and Daytona, Fort Clinch, and St. Augustine. Now, I'm exhausted. Can we sleep in for Easter? Maybe till eight-thirty?"

"No. Like I said, you sleep in. I'm going running."

The strength that Ettie had finally found reared up in response and galloped away towards another solution. Before she had fully processed what she was going to do, she was walking quietly in the shadows—feeling her way along the edge of the quilt, across the smooth wood of the sleigh bed, and back up Chip's side. Her hand moved to the nightstand. Leaning over slightly, she felt around, grasped the plug, and pulled. There. The red lights died. She hadn't known she had it in her.

Her passive-aggressive triumph was short-lived. Within two seconds, a sickening *thwack* jolted her out of her moment of bravery. The cords of the alarm clock and the metal lamp on the nightstand had been intertwined. Unplugging the clock had knocked the heavy light fixture over.

"How dare you? How dare you hit me with the lamp?" Chip roared.

Ettie did not know what he meant. She hadn't hit him! The night had shrouded the event. It couldn't hide the violent resonation of its aftermath. *Smash! Bam! Whack!* Were those awful noises coming from Chip's attempt to break the lamp on the headboard of their bed? She heard the sound of the lamp crashing to the floor. Chip howled in anger; then there was the awful *thud, thud* of his fist pummeling the wall. His last cry was in pain. In the dim light, Ettie could make out Chip's hulking shoulders disappearing through the doorway.

For several minutes Ettie sat in dismay on the side of the bed. What had she done? She feared what she would find when she turned on the light, yet her legs seemed to move of their own accord back to the other side of the room where she turned on the cloisonne lamp on her dresser. The damage was worse than she had imagined. The lovely smooth surface of the sleigh bed that Chip had painstakingly sanded and stained for their first anniversary was no longer lovely or smooth. Chip's attack with the heavy lamp had gouged out chunks of wood and had left a splintered mess on both the headboard and the footboard. The lamp itself, which had been a wedding gift, was bent; the lampshade was crushed. The decorative leaves that had graced the lampstand were knocked out of whack.

Finally, Ettie's eyes moved to the wall. Oh, no! A hole the size of Chip's clenched fist now gaped in the middle of their bedroom wall. The realization that her decision to stick up for herself had turned out to be a hapless mistake hit her with the force of a grizzly bear. As she sank to the floor, silent tears began to fall. Soon, faint whispering called her out of her funk.

Tiptoeing across the dark hallway, Ettie checked the boys' room first. Thankfully, they were fast asleep and had missed the meltdown. The whispers must have been coming from Lydia's bedroom. The door was open more than its usual small crack. She realized as she stepped into the room that of course, the girls were awake. It was eleven-thirty during their spring break week; they had probably been up talking and giggling. They weren't giggling anymore. The lights from the basketball court shone brightly into Lydia's window, and Ettie could see the wide-eyed fear on the faces of the girls. Ettie moved to where they sat shoulder to shoulder on the edge of the bed and embraced them both at the same time. The three held onto each other tightly for a full minute.

"Girls," she reassured in a hushed tone, "everything is going to be okay. Your dad and I argued. It's over now, and I'm sure we're going to make up. It was a mistake, and it was probably my fault. Somehow Daddy thought I hit him with the lamp." She paused and stifled a laugh. The situation certainly wasn't funny, but that sounded ridiculous! She had never even raised her voice at Chip—never mind try to hit him.

First, she explained to Lydia and Helen how she had wanted to sleep in and how the lamp and clock cords had been tangled up. She wanted them to hear the story so they would know that the fight had been over a misunderstanding. She knew that children often imagined that their parents' disagreements were over something that they, the children, had done. Next, Ettie prayed with the girls that they would feel God's comfort and protection through this difficulty. After their "Amen," the two girls reassured her that they weren't scared anymore and that they would be able to fall asleep.

It felt as if she was swallowing a lump of clay, but Ettie gulped down her pride and went to apologize to Chip. They reconciled lovingly as they always did. Before they made their way back up to bed, Chip got an ice pack for his hand; he griped that it was throbbing horribly. By six o'clock in the morning, the pain was so intense that he drove himself to the emergency room.

Easter breakfast was on the table when Chip returned with a white cast covering his right hand and lower arm. An x-ray at the ER had shown that only his pinkie was broken. As he gobbled down his breakfast, Chip expressed his annoyance that the doctor had insisted on putting such a large cast on such a tiny break—and now he was stuck drinking his orange juice and eating his homemade cinnamon rolls with his left hand. David and Jonathan ate happily, unaware of the drama of the night before. Because they hadn't asked any questions about Chip's cast, Ettie had thus far been spared an explanation of its cause. The boys had gotten a 1,200-piece Star Wars Lego ship the day before and were completely focused on going back to their building.

"Can I be excused, Mama?" David asked while still chewing his last mouthful.

"Me too?" Jonathan chimed in.

"Try again," Ettie corrected with a gentle smile.

David finished chewing. "May I please be excused, Mama?"

"Please, may I me too?" his cohort added in a comical attempt to use his best manners.

Ettie glanced at Chip to see if he was fine with the boys leaving the table or if he too was tickled by Jonathan's adorable diction. Chip was reaching for seconds with a scowl, so Ettie went ahead and answered. "Yes, you may. Are you almost done with your ship? I can't wait to see it," she added.

Carrying their plates to the sink, the brothers spoke in undertones to one another. Grinning, David gave these instructions, "Mama, please don't come in the dining room till we're done. We want you to wait and see the Millennium Falcon when it looks completely awesome!"

After the boys exited the kitchen, the only sounds left were the clinking of glasses and silverware. No one spoke until Chip cleared his throat loudly and pushed away from the table to head to the bathroom. Then Lydia and Helen began their usual chatter about their plans for the day: what are you wearing to church, who is coming to the Easter picnic in the backyard, and what time is the baptism starting? At first, there was no mention of last night's argument. As the three began to clear the table, Helen brought it up.

She set the salt and pepper in the cabinet above the stove and paused. Tilting her head to one side, she looked questioningly at Ettie with her clear blue eyes. It took a moment for her to formulate her question; finally, she asked, "Ettie, how is my Daddy going to get baptized tonight with that cast on his arm? When I had a cast for my broken ankle, I couldn't ever get it wet. I had to wear a plastic bag over it to take a shower."

"You know," Ettie began, "I had started wondering the same thing. Maybe a plastic bag would be the right solution if we taped it over the cast carefully. That's a good idea, Helen. Do you want to suggest it to Dad?"

Helen agreed that she would. The day zipped by, and Ettie and Helen didn't have another chance to discuss his response. After church, about thirty friends and neighbors gathered on the community playground behind their house for a festive afternoon picnic. Afterward, there was the flurry of Helen packing her suitcase and her Vera Bradley backpack. Immediately following the baptism at their pastor's home, Chip would be taking her to the airport for a red-eye back to Moreno Valley. Ettie had guessed that Chip would take Helen's advice; therefore, she was completely surprised that evening to see Chip step into Pastor Greg's hot tub with no plastic bag.

Later that night, while Chip was driving to the airport, Ettie called to say happy Easter to her parents. While talking to her mom, she attempted to process why the baptism had seemed unusual to her that night. Baptism was different at Ocean View than it had been at the Anglican churches where she and Chip had been sprinkled with water as infants. Ocean View taught that adults and children—who were at least eight years old—should decide to follow Christ's lead of baptism by immersion. On hearing this, Chip, Ettie, and Lydia had all been enthusiastic about being baptized. They spoke with Pastor Greg and set a date to be immersed on Easter, a perfect day to remember that their sins were forgiven and their hearts made new.

It wasn't the immersion part that had been strange. That wasn't it at all! That had felt amazing, liberating, and right. The weird part was that Chip *hadn't* actually been immersed. He had chosen not to go under the water completely because of his cast. Most of him had gone underwater; however, that awkward white plaster stuck right out of the pool like a sore thumb. Ettie knew that Chip's baptism was still valid; it was his heart surrendering to God that was important. His arm sticking out of the water seemed to be symbolic of something that wasn't quite right, and Ettie still couldn't wrap her mind around what it could be. Was it more than his anger? She didn't know.

Of course, to explain the cast and the baptism to Evelyn, Ettie had to backtrack and tell her mother about the argument from the night before. Evelyn listened politely and gave the right responses. As soon as manners allowed, she steered the conversation to a topic dear to her heart.

"It sure sounds as though you had a busy week. Did you and Chip have a chance to decide about Lydia coming here for the summer?" she asked.

"We did; and thankfully, he agreed. I'm glad that it is you who will be teaching Lydia chemistry and not me. You're an amazing teacher, Mom."

Evelyn was overjoyed to hear that Chip had acquiesced to the eight-week visit. She was also slightly surprised since he was often overprotective of her. This wasn't the time to dwell on that, Evelyn reasoned. The opportunity to teach Lydia the entire Honors Chemistry course over the summer was as exciting as a trip to Oahu! Evelyn adored being with her granddaughter, and she was inspired by teaching chemistry. There were many things that she wanted Lydia to learn, demonstrations that she wanted her to see, and labs she wanted her to experience. Evelyn would open Lydia's mind to the wonders of matter, subatomic particles, and energy. It would be a lovely summer. Evelyn was sure that there could not be a happier grandmother on the face of the earth, not even in Hawaii.

Although Evelyn hadn't intended to be a working mom, the role of a teacher fit perfectly with her role as a mother. Over the years she had taught in the same school as all four of her children. First, she had been a science teacher at Molly and Ettie's middle school. Currently, she was teaching Honors Chemistry at the Anglican College Preparatory School of San Diego; and Brittany and Ashton attended both middle school and high school there. Those days were some of the best moments of her life. From Molly's first step into kindergarten in 1974 until the moment that Ashton graduated in 2003, one of her life's main goals had been to be a part of her children's education. She had imagined that those golden days were over.

Now, thanks to God's goodness, Evelyn was getting another chance. She would be her granddaughter's teacher. Evelyn could hardly wait until the end of May when Lydia and Chip would fly cross-country together to attend Helen's graduation in Moreno Valley. Sam and Evelyn would attend too, and then drive with Lydia back to San Diego. Evelyn began telling anyone interested that she was going to have an incredible summer teaching chemistry to Lydia.

A week before their travels, Ettie and Evelyn talked on the phone about the location of the high school graduation and other details.

"Do you know if the family is having a get-together after the ceremony?" Evelyn asked.

"Yes, they sure are. Helen's grandparents are hosting the party at their house. There won't be too many people. They are planning a barbeque for dinner and swimming for the kids.

"That sounds nice," Evelyn said. "Of course, Dad and I won't want to stay too late, since we will still have the drive back to San Diego. Lydia can bring her pillow in case she wants to fall asleep in the car."

Ettie paused. "I'm sorry, Mom; Lydia won't be driving back to San Diego with you. Chip wants to be with her as much as possible before she is gone for the summer. He has already made reservations at La Quinta in Moreno Valley for graduation night. He'll bring her to your house the following morning."

The rest of the phone call was a blur for Evelyn. Her heart was the Arizona sinking in Pearl Harbor; her mind began to race. How peculiar that Chip wanted to arrange to be alone with Lydia in a hotel room. It didn't seem to matter that Chip's mother would be there too. It reminded Evelyn of the time that she had found him under the covers of his bed with Lydia. Thinking back, Evelyn could picture herself in the kitchen during the spring when Ettie was expecting David. Everyone had gone to visit Chip, Ettie, and Lydia after they had settled into their new home in Oak Harbor.

The house had been filled with the aroma of pancakes and sausage. Juice was being poured into glasses when Evelyn realized that Chip and Lydia were missing.

"Has anyone seen Chip and Lydia?" she had queried. Sam and Ettie hadn't seen them. Ashton, Brittany, and Molly shook their heads. Molly's daughter, Charlotte, had been enjoying an appetizer of Cheerios in her highchair. Evelyn had walked down the hall to the master bedroom. She had walked in, unannounced, and had found Chip under the quilt with his head resting on the pillow.

"Chip, have you seen Lydia? Breakfast is ready."

"She's in here with me," he admitted as Lydia poked out from under the covers.

"What are you two doing?" Evelyn demanded in confusion.

"Just cuddling; that's what we do," Chip stated calmly. Lydia happily jumped up and skipped to the kitchen.

Evelyn hadn't been calm; she had been outraged. If Chip wanted to be close to Lydia, couldn't he sit by her on the couch in plain sight? Evelyn wanted to bring up that incident with Ettie as they planned the cross-country trip. Instead, she kept her criticism and worry to herself, *Chip was a scoundrel before, and he is still a scoundrel now. Why does he need to be with Lydia in a private room? Is he hoping to cuddle with her? Is that* all *he hopes to do?*

When the day of Helen's graduation ceremony came, a monsoon pattern developed, and Moreno Valley was drenched in a rare torrential rainstorm. Everyone huddled together under the covered grandstand. The wet and windy weather could not dampen Evelyn's excitement about beginning a special summer with her lovely granddaughter. Lydia was sharing about her friend's birthday party and the movie they had seen. Evelyn loved hearing the details. She glanced over at Chip standing stiffly in his starched white uniform. For a while, he was engrossed in his discussion with his father, Henry, and he didn't seem to be eavesdropping on Lydia's bubbling descriptions.

However, after the pledge of allegiance, Chip leaned forward and glared at Lydia. "You need to quiet down. Stop talking so loudly and so fast." He nearly growled. "And sit properly."

Evelyn couldn't believe her ears. *How dare he reprimand Lydia in the middle of their conversation?* Evelyn fumed indignantly. *I am enjoying every moment of this time. If I think that there is a problem, I can address it.*

At the graduation and the barbeque, Evelyn completely enjoyed Lydia's company despite Chip's presence. Unfortunately, as Sam and Evelyn began the drive home along dark roads that night, her thoughts were overrun by nightmarish images of Lydia and Chip at La Quinta. Evelyn clenched her fists as she pictured Chip kissing Lydia and putting his creepy hands on her. It took every bit of her willpower to stop imagining that and worse.

Still, she wondered, *what is going on? Why is he harsh with her one minute and other times he acts as if Lydia is his wife? A husband and wife would want one more night together before a summer apart, but why a father and daughter? What evil is lurking behind the mask of that officer's costume?*

The farther they drove from Moreno Valley, the more Evelyn wanted to grab the wheel from Sam and turn the car around. She would march into that hotel room and whisk her granddaughter away from Chip's fawning paws.

Evelyn had spoken with Sam many times before about how she suspected that Chip was acting inappropriately with Lydia, and now she brought it up again. Sam agreed that there were instances when the snuggling seemed out of line. Nonetheless, Sam had never seen anything distinctly sexual; he wanted to believe that Chip was a good man with strong Christian principles.

"Remember that time I saw him touch her on her behind when she was getting into our van?" Evelyn asked in a voice near panic. "He was nearly caressing her right in public!" She took a deep breath and sighed as Sam took her hand. "My dear Lydia. I wish I knew what I could do to help her."

"You do, Evelyn. You've been praying for her faithfully over the years, and that is the best thing you can do. Keep lifting her up to our Heavenly Father; He is watching over her even as we speak." Sam replied encouragingly.

His heartening words soothed her for the rest of the ride. Yet when they reached home that night, Evelyn became overwhelmed with fear for Lydia. She replayed the innumerable times she had lain awake worrying about Lydia's safety. Twice she had gotten out of bed in her determination to call Child Protective Services and report her suspicions. She would stop short when she remembered that she had no proof. What would happen? The result might be that she would estrange herself from their family, and that would be unthinkable! Sam was right: the best thing she could do was to keep praying. Evelyn closed her eyes and spoke to God in her heart, "Dear God, please protect Lydia from harm. Take away any sexual desire that Chip has for her. Lord, I know that You can stop any sinful actions in that hotel room tonight." Evelyn took comfort in knowing that God was in control, and she finally fell asleep.

The following morning dawned bright and clear. Evelyn awoke with only a hint of the worry that had plagued her the night before. When Lydia and Chip arrived after lunchtime, Evelyn hugged her granddaughter with love and thankfulness. Chip stayed briefly, as he needed to catch a flight that afternoon.

Making sure that Lydia was comfortable in their home before their rigorous chemistry schedule began was important to Evelyn. First, they went shopping for groceries; she wanted to be sure that they had plenty of Lydia's favorite foods. As Evelyn put the groceries away, Lydia began to unpack her suitcase. "Lydia, when you finish emptying your suitcase, you can bring it out to the garage," Evelyn explained. "Since you won't need it for the rest of the summer, Grandpa will put it up in the attic."

By dinner time, Lydia had settled into Ashton's old room, putting some clothes in the drawers and others in the closet. She arranged her pictures on the dresser. A group shot of Lydia with several of her friends at the beach had a prominent spot in the middle. It was fun for Evelyn to watch Lydia settle in. She loved everything about her oldest granddaughter: her beauty, her smile, her chatty disposition, and her honesty.

"Tell me about your friends," Evelyn encouraged interestedly as she looked at the group photo on the dresser. "Who is this?" she asked as she pointed to a tall, graceful girl with long red hair and a sprinkling of freckles across her nose.

"Oh, Grandma, that's Marcella! She is the sweetest friend ever. You would absolutely love her. I hope you can meet her next time you come to Jacksonville. We have a lot of sleepovers together, and we share music too. This week, she gave me the best album for my iPod. I listened to it on the way here in the car this morning."

"Doesn't she dance with you at your ballet studio?"

Lydia responded, "Yes! We have classes together three or four days a week. And she is homeschooled like me. Her brothers are friends with David and Jonathan. We have a blast when we swim at their pool and when our families go to the beach together."

Evelyn listened as Lydia raved about her friend and remarked, "Yes, I remember meeting Marcella when we came to see you in the Nutcracker. I'm glad to hear you two are still close. And who's this?" Now Evelyn gestured to a brunette with a gentle smile.

"That's Laura; Laura DeBarry. I wish I could have brought her here with me this summer! She is the nicest person you'll ever meet! She was the one who was thinking about coming to take chemistry with me, but her ballet schedule got in the way. She dances at a different studio than me and Marcella, and she also teaches classes there to the younger girls. We took biology together this year from Mom; and Laura's mom, Ms. May, taught us Literature. Laura's dad is the worship pastor at our church: Pastor Don. He is such an amazing musician. Did you know he is giving guitar lessons to my dad? Mom gave him the gift of lessons for his birthday this year. I love the whole DeBarry family."

As Evelyn smiled and nodded, Lydia pointed out Camille, a bright-eyed Hispanic girl who had her arm around Lydia in the photograph. She told Evelyn about how they attended youth groups together and had sleepovers at one another's homes.

"Camille and I are in the same 'life group.' Ms. Brooke is our leader. She is a great listener, you know? She gave us these pretty journals to write down our ideas and prayers. Yesterday, I started writing about..." With these words, Lydia paused mid-sentence and concern clouded her eyes. "Oh, I miss them all already! How am I going to make it through these two months without them?"

"You're going to be fine, Lydia," Evelyn reassured her. "I'll keep you very busy working on chemistry during the day, and we can make sure that you have time in the evenings to stay connected to your friends on Facebook."

"Oh, can I?" Lydia looked so relieved her face shone like an apple on the first day of school. "Are you sure you won't mind me using your computer at night? You know, at home I have strict time limits for the computer and phone."

"Hmm, I have heard a little about that, Lydia. Let's go into the kitchen and start making dinner, and you can tell me more about it while we are cooking." As Evelyn spoke these words, a sense of foreboding gripped her heart. What else was Lydia going to share with her about her home life? Evelyn's fears from the night before began to surface again; then she remembered that she needed to address Lydia's question. "No, I don't mind you using my computer. I know it's important to you to stay in touch with your friends," she added.

As Evelyn and Lydia prepared a savory dinner of angel hair pasta with shrimp, broccoli, and Alfredo sauce, Lydia told story after story about Chip's house rules. She wasn't complaining; she stated the facts and affirmed that she loved her dad. This went on throughout the dinner hour. After everyone cleared the table, Sam washed the dishes while Lydia and Evelyn went back to the table to continue talking.

They pushed back their chairs and sat together for another hour. Lydia explained to her grandparents how she wasn't allowed to completely close her bedroom door; it always needed to remain open at least a crack. And she wasn't permitted to lock her bathroom door ever. An unspoken rule was that she could only invite friends over for a sleepover or go to their homes for sleepovers when Chip was out of town. Chip let her be on email and Facebook as long as she disclosed her passwords to him so that he could monitor her online activity.

With every detail that Lydia shared, Evelyn saw another red flag pop up in her mind: the bedroom door, the bathroom door, the sleepover restrictions, the online eavesdropping. Another flag arose as Lydia described how she was required to give Chip all the cash she earned from her many hours of babysitting for the families in their neighborhood. He told her that it was going into a "virtual" account that would be given to her when she entered college. Five thousand dollars of babysitting money sitting in an account that didn't even have Lydia's name on it? Evelyn found it completely suspicious.

When Lydia began to describe how she and her mother were required to turn in their receipts after shopping trips, even if it was a trip to the exchange to buy milk, Evelyn was shocked. She tried not to show the dismay she was feeling as Lydia poured out her heart. Lydia obviously did not find these facets of her life to be unusual since she spoke matter-of-factly. Evelyn, on the other hand, found it seriously disconcerting. She had known that Chip was overprotective and somewhat controlling; she just hadn't known to what extent. Weren't these attempts to control Lydia and Ettie a glaring sign of something amiss in their family life? It seemed to confirm her horrible conjecture of sexual abuse.

Once again, Evelyn wondered what she could do to help Lydia. There must be something she could do! As she spoke to God, her prayers became more urgent. *You have brought Lydia here for the whole summer, God. Please don't let me miss this opportunity. If there is a direction I need to guide her in, please show me.*

Evelyn kept her prayers in mind even when chemistry class took the front seat starting Monday morning. Math was not Lydia's favorite subject; however, she didn't complain when the first few days of work were primarily math based: scientific notation, metric conversions, dimensional analysis, and significant figures. Together, they moved through this section quickly and then began to explore the concepts through experimentation in the lab. One of the most remarkable reactions was one in which a penny disappears in nitric acid. First, a cloud of red gas is released, and afterward, the solution inside the container turns from clear to brilliant blue.

After a full afternoon of working in Evelyn's classroom at her school and using a Bunsen burner and a crucible to determine the empirical formula for magnesium oxide, Lydia sat down on the reddish-brown leather sofa next to Evelyn. "Can I use the computer when you're finished, Grandma? I can't wait to see the pictures that

Laura and Camille posted from the youth group picnic at the beach last night."

"Sure, you can. It'll be about another half an hour or so."

"Okay; that's totally fine. What are you working on?"

"I'm working on counselor training plans for the Ninth Grade Wilderness Adventure."

"Oh, you mean the trip to Yosemite?" Lydia replied enthusiastically. "That's the school trip I went on when I was three, right? I remember: Mom was the photographer and I wanted to be the 'cotagrapher' too. I walked all over with my pink camera." The two laughed together about the happy memory.

"Yes, your mom has helped twice in the eighteen years that I've been doing this trip. You went again when you were seven. With your mom and dad."

As she said the words, an idea flashed in her mind. It was as if her thoughts had remarkably turned from clear to blue as in the chemical reaction with the penny. Where there had been nothing before, suddenly a lucid strategy appeared. The plan was this: Evelyn could use the counselor training as a springboard for discussions with Lydia regarding sexual misconduct. This was her chance to educate Lydia about the insidious nature of sexual abuse and the innocence of young victims.

"Oh yeah, that's right, Grandma," Lydia answered, completely unaware of the ideas careening through Evelyn's mind. "I remember the picture that Mom took of me where I am holding white flowers and sitting by a stone bridge. I guess you guys thought I looked pretty cute with both of my front teeth missing. What part of the trip is that?" she wondered aloud as she pointed to the paused video on the screen of Evelyn's laptop.

"It's the video we show at the counselor training, Lydia. It's called 'Into the Light.' The idea is that anything inappropriate will not stay in the dark; instead, it will be exposed to the light. We use this video, and discussions too, to train the students to look for anything that could be inappropriate during the camping trip.

Our school requires that everyone in a leadership position must go through the training to be educated about the prevention of sexual misconduct."

She explained that in the film, actors and actresses describe how pedophiles develop close relationships with children with the intent of sexually assaulting them once a higher level of trust is developed. In one vignette, a teenage girl describes how a male friend of her mom's would invite her into his classroom after school. When the girl was seven, the visits were chats about the school day and included innocent goodbye hugs. As the months and years went by, those embraces escalated into sexual encounters.

"That man had tricked that sweet girl into thinking that their relationship was normal for two friends. It was disgusting to hear him recount the way he purposely planned their encounters," Evelyn described in dismay. "Children inherently trust the adults in their lives, especially when those adults are close family members. Unfortunately, sometimes grownups will wear a mask of kindness to cover up their horrible behavior. The video portrays lots of different scenarios; each one is designed to help the camping trip counselors understand what sexual abuse is and how to avoid situations that could be perceived as inappropriate."

The following morning as Evelyn prepared breakfast, she wondered if any part of the discussion about sexual misconduct had struck a chord with Lydia. If her granddaughter was living through a nightmare like the ones in the "Into the Light" video, Evelyn wanted her to be able to recognize the signs.

She had appeared young and naïve the night before sitting there on the couch with her hair pulled back in a ponytail. In her gym shorts and her church t-shirt, no one would guess that she was four months away from sixteen; she could still pass for fourteen. Maybe the conversations about the counselor training wouldn't be enough. What if her youth and innocence blocked her from seeing any correlation between her own life and the training video?

As Evelyn reached across the kitchen counter for the eggs,

a headline on the front page of the newspaper caught her eye: "Elizabeth Smart Testifies About Kidnapping." Elizabeth's account of abduction, rape, and brainwashing was heartbreaking. Still, Evelyn realized it would be a natural way to continue their talk from the night before. The tragic stories of Jaycee Lee Dugard and HaLeigh Cummings were also bound to be in the news more during the summer. She and Lydia could discuss the tragedies that these young women lived through as well. Maybe that would be enough to help Lydia open her eyes to anything amiss in her life. People often stood silent in the face of sexual abuse, but Evelyn would not. They would discuss these things even if it was uncomfortable to do so. She did not want anyone, and least of all her beloved granddaughter, to live through the wickedness and deceit of child sexual abuse.

God had answered her urgent prayer, the one she had prayed asking him to show her the way to guide Lydia. Evelyn felt that Lydia was almost certainly facing abuse at the hands of her stepfather. Now Evelyn had one more desperate prayer: *Please, God, help Lydia get out of danger. If she is surrounded by evil, help her to get out of the grip of the man in the mask.*

"He lies in wait like a lion in cover."

Chapter 10

LYDIA'S SWEET SIXTEEN

Taking the steps two at a time, Lydia leaped downstairs from her bedroom and rounded the corner into the kitchen to barely miss a head-on collision with Chip.

"How many times do I have to tell you to stop running in this house?" Chip roared. His dark eyes narrowed like a wild cat on the hunt as he spied his prey.

Lydia stopped short. She hadn't realized she had been running. It felt more like a happy kind of skipping. Not wanting to upset her dad any further, she ducked her head and trained her eyes to focus on his polished brown uniform shoes and the cuffs of his khaki pants. She stated the expected "Yes, sir" in her most apologetic voice.

Chip didn't give her another glance. He turned and huffed up the stairs. Nothing had gone right in his day at work, and now that he was home, he knew that things were going to get even worse. The fact that he was winded when he reached the top of the stairs did not improve his mood either. Sitting down in the wooden chair in the corner of his bedroom, he unlaced his shoes and pulled them off.

He stood and looked reproachfully in the mirror above his dresser. *What a loser,* he groused. *When are you ever going to get in shape? When are you finally going to get a promotion to commander?* Chip's anger didn't stay directed at his failings for long. Turning away from his reflection in disgust, he reached in his closet for

Levi's and a hunter-green polo and began to focus instead on this ridiculous evening his wife had planned for them. The whole night was going to be a huge fiasco. Thinking about making it through the next couple of hours made him want to throw something heavy and break it. That might give him some satisfaction. *Maybe I should throw this wooden chair through the upstairs window?* he plotted. *Ettie would have to cancel this awful dinner party.* The exhilaration of hearing the crashing glass and the thud on the front lawn was tempting as well.

Before he had a chance to reflect on that possibility any further, the bedroom door opened, and Ettie came in smiling. She was dressed for company in the red flowered kimono top Chip had brought home from his last trip to Misawa, Japan. If she saw the sour look on Chip's face, she didn't mention it. Instead, she reached her arms out in a welcoming embrace. "Hi, sweetie. I didn't hear you come in. I must have been outside getting the table set on the back porch. How was your day?"

"I'm not going to lie; work was rough."

"Oh, sorry to hear that. Do you want to talk about it?"

"No, I honestly don't."

"Maybe later?" Pausing, yet receiving no reply, she went on, "Well, I'm glad you're home. The salmon has been marinated and is ready for you to put on the grill. Drew's family should be here in fifteen minutes."

"Humph." Brushing past his wife, Chip walked toward the bathroom.

"Wait; is something else wrong?" she asked in concern.

He gave her a wilting look over his shoulder. "I feel like a fraud. I don't want to meet Drew. Or his parents. That's what." He started to shut the door behind him brusquely.

Ettie moved to intercept him and put her arms around him once again. "Don't worry; it's going to be fine. You'll be a fabulous dad as always." When she turned her face up to kiss him, the scent of her Cherry Blossom body spray reached his nose.

He knew she wanted to encourage him; however, he wasn't ready to receive it. Neither her soothing words nor her delicate smell could penetrate the aura of anger that surrounded him. He spoke quietly. His voice was more of a snarl than a whisper, "I don't feel like a fabulous dad. Lydia and I don't have anything in common anymore."

"Yes, you do, babe. This past month, you have been playing your guitar and singing worship songs together in the evenings. It's been completely wonderful to hear the two of you. You have music and Jesus in common. Oh, and kickball too. That family kickball game we had last weekend was the best. You and Lydia were a great team."

"*She* was a great team; she didn't even need me. I stink at kickball. Why is she better than me at sports?" Chip glowered at Ettie as he spoke. "Everything has gone wrong with her since she got back from San Diego. I can't believe she came home from her grandparents' house thinking about boys. It's absurd."

The bathroom door closed loudly.

Speaking through the door, Ettie continued to attempt to buoy his spirits. He covered his ears with his hands until her voice trailed off, and he assumed that she had headed back downstairs to finish preparing for their guests. His thoughts began to spin in circles, spiraling in a groove that had been etched deep into his mind. Now that Ettie had invited the Masters family to dinner, the circle had widened to include new and disturbing possibilities. *What if Drew finds out what I've done? What will I say? It isn't anyone's business anyway. I simply hugged and kissed and touched my daughter. Still, I wish I could go back and change it all. Ettie deserves better than this, David and Jonathan too. I can't lose them. No one can* ever *know. But what if they do? What if Drew and his parents see right through me? Lydia better not start talking.*

The spinning stopped abruptly. Lydia was always talking, he remembered with chagrin. He'd better hurry up and get downstairs to intercept her in case she started to divulge any information regarding his relationship with her. As he approached the landing to head down to the kitchen, Lydia's voice did indeed drift up to where he stood. He froze, wanting to hear what she said and dreading it at the same time. She wasn't speaking about him; she was talking about Drew.

He inhaled deeply and quietly then held his breath. Lydia's voice rose with emotion as she expressed to her mother how excited she was that Drew was coming over for dinner. He was bringing his guitar, she explained; he had written a song about the characters he was studying in his Shakespeare class. Lydia had read several Shakespearean plays the previous year and couldn't wait to hear his rendition.

Chip couldn't believe that anyone could talk constantly and say absolutely nothing of value. At least she hadn't mentioned the unmentionable. Lydia wasn't thinking at all about *him* that night. Only that Boy Scout coming over with his guitar. Chip wasn't convinced he could make it through the evening without hurting someone. Yet the dinner party wasn't going to disappear because he was angry and scared. As he did every day, he glued on his mask and made his way downstairs.

At first, the evening wasn't as awful as he had imagined because of all the delicious food involved. His wife had prepared a meal of his favorites: teriyaki salmon, consommé rice, sauteed zucchini and mushrooms, and fresh berry salad. How could he worry while he was eating a dinner fit for a king? Plus, Drew's dad was easier to talk to after Chip had finished his first glass of Pinot Noir. Chip appreciated that after his heart attack in 2004, his cardiologist had prescribed a daily glass of red wine. That advice was a cinch to follow except that it often led to a second or third serving. The second glass that evening improved his mood enough that he was cracking jokes as they sat on the porch watching the setting sun paint the sky pink and gold.

With the third glass, Chip's anger returned, because it was at that point that Drew took his guitar out of its case and began to strum and sing. Drew's family also attended Ocean View Christian

Fellowship, so he played a couple of familiar songs. Chip could not bring himself to sing along. It was obvious after the first verse that Drew was a superior guitarist to Chip. Jealousy flared up in the pit of his stomach. The second helpings he had wolfed down earlier turned into a fiery ball of indigestion and heartburn.

Drew introduced the third song by describing how he and his friend Kevin had written the parody as part of a project in their literature class. His wide smile was for everyone in the group. However, Chip couldn't help but detect that Drew's sparkling brown eyes focused primarily on Lydia. It made him want to punch Drew in the gut, especially once he started singing:

"Romeo and Juliet commit suicide, Tybalt and Paris get Romeofied;

Hamlet and Laertes are poisoned one day; so was everyone else in that play.

Macbeth kills everyone, but with Macduff, his reign is done.

Othello and Iago both die too, Julius Caesar is stabbed through and through.

Antony is smitten, Cleopatra by an asp is bitten.

Lear and Cordelia are given amnesty, they die anyway.

Coriolanus is killed for betrayal, Hector and Achilles die in their tale.

They did their best, and then there's the Titus Andronicus blood fest.

Everyone dies in Shakespeare, each and every day:

Everyone dies in Shakespeare, no matter what you say.

If you were in Shakespeare, you would die too.

Everyone dies in Shakespeare, so tell me why don't you?"

Chip wasn't blind. Even he had to admit that the tongue-in-cheek words and the teasing melody were amusing, and he could see that his family found Drew charming and witty. Nonetheless, Chip longed to be the one making the group laugh with delight. *Never mind the characters in that ludicrous song,* he seethed, *the young guitarist with eyes for my daughter is going to be the one facing death.*

What right does he have to look at Lydia with those winsome eyes? Chip couldn't even hear the fourth song begin over the anger drumming in his ears. Before he exploded, he excused himself, went into his study, and banged the door shut.

After the Masters family left and Ettie had headed upstairs for the night, Chip went into the dark kitchen and helped himself to an atypical fourth glass of wine. This last drink mellowed his disposition; thus, he was feeling contrite when he went up to bed. He showered, slid into bed, and snuggled up with Ettie. She was already breathing deeply, but he knew how to wake her. As he caressed her hair and kissed her neck, he wondered if he should make a clean breast of everything. He could go ahead and untie the weight of the millstone hanging around his neck. Ettie would be understanding. They could move forward with life as usual—minus the fear of discovery that had lately been crouching on his heart.

When Ettie stirred and responded to his touch, he whispered her name in a loving undertone. "Ettie, my beautiful bride. Something got into me tonight. Quite honestly, it was because parenting is difficult. Yesterday Lydia was learning to ride her bike, and suddenly she wants to have a boyfriend. It was better when she was my little girl. I'm losing her, and I'm afraid I'm going to lose you too."

"My dear, you'll never lose me," Ettie replied sleepily. "I'll always be right here. You've got me completely."

"Mmm, and repeatedly." Chip agreed, referring to the passion in their marriage. The wine had loosened his tongue, and he kept talking when he should have stopped. "I know you say that you love me unconditionally. I'm worried about making a big mistake though. I mean, what if I make a majorly wrong decision? You're going to leave me."

"What kind of big mistake, Chip?"

Chip paused. Here was his chance. He could make his behavior with Lydia sound completely innocent like he had with the good touch versus bad touch mishap in Oak Harbor. How could he make it work this time? What could he say to make his wife believe that his advances had been a sweet, fatherly gesture? His head was fuzzy with the wine, and he hadn't had an opportunity to plan out any explanations for his behavior. It was destined to come out sounding wrong. He'd better not say anything. Of course, he couldn't. *No one can ever find out. What am I thinking?! Am I going soft in the head?* Chip silently cursed his foolishness.

"Honey?" Ettie coaxed.

Chip blinked as if waking from a nightmare.

"Uh, with our finances or something. That's all. What if I invest in the wrong stocks and lose all our savings?"

"I would never leave you, Chip. There's nothing you could do to lose me. I do love you unconditionally."

"I love you too, babe."

Chip kissed Ettie fervently to show the truth of his love then rolled over onto his back and sighed. Filled with the reassurance of her promises and lulled by the food and wine in his stomach, he was snoring within minutes.

Ettie lay awake listening to the sounds of his repose. She was confused by Chip's erratic behavior that evening and by their conversation regarding mistakes. Thankfully, she and Joy had plans to meet the following morning for a prayer walk. For the past month, they had been exercising together before breakfast. Both friends were benefiting from the time set aside to share concerns, give one another counsel, and lift their voices together to Jesus. They had been praying often for their husbands; tomorrow would be no exception.

The sun was rising over the Brightons' house, and Ettie was sitting on the front porch buckling up her purple Chacos when Joy greeted her and her dog the following day.

"Good morning, beautiful. Hey there, Stella. How are you?"

"Hi, sweetie. I'm seriously ready for this walk. How 'bout you?"

"Ugh. It was tough to get out of bed this morning. Walker here kept me honest." Joy gestured to her coonhound pulling on the other end of the leash. "I was going to call you and tell you I was too tired to get up. This wild dog barked at me to tell me that I had better start moving."

"Aww, thanks, Walker." Ettie joked as they started walking along the sidewalk at a brisk pace. She added, "He must have guessed that I needed to talk to you today."

"What's going on?" Joy queried, looking at her friend with concern.

"There are so many things I need to be praying about with you. I'm not sure where to start."

"Ettie, that's me on most days. And that's what best friends are for. All right, it will be my turn to listen today. What's up?"

"Well, first, we need to be praying for my sister Brittany and her family. Her husband, Paul, lost his job. He's in construction management and has been building water treatment plants. The company that he works for in Imperial Beach went out of business a couple of months ago. Unfortunately, he hasn't been able to find any more work. They are renting out their house, and yesterday they moved in with my parents."

"Wow, your parents are the coolest," Joy interjected. "Do they have enough room for everyone? Your sister has two kids, right?"

"Yes, Madison and Micah. Madison is 3, and Micah is six months old. There is enough room; still, it will definitely be a full house. Especially since Paul doesn't always see eye to eye with my parents. We can be praying for him to find a job, and that there will be peace in the house while they are staying there." Ettie paused, and Joy asked her friend what else was heavy on her heart that day.

"The hardest thing is that I can't comprehend what's happening with Chip," Ettie began. She stopped in her tracks and focused on the empty school playground they were passing. After she collected her thoughts, she spoke sadly as they resumed their walk. "Could it be that I'm living with Jekyll and Hyde? One minute he's breaking a wine glass at the dinner table because Lydia rolled her eyes at him; the next minute, he's offering to buy her a sterling silver flute to play in the youth symphony. In the past three weeks, three items in our home have fallen prey to his temper: the wine glass, his favorite bonsai plant, and one of the back porch chairs which he heaved over the back fence onto the basketball court!"

"Oh no!"

"Right? What in the world is going on, Joy?" Ettie shook her head in disbelief. "And here's another strange thing—Chip has been leading our Bible study group in our home for our whole marriage. Yet two days ago, he told me that he can't lead anymore. He confided that it's too hard on him."

"Too hard? Why? He's a natural leader. Even Don has mentioned that he has noticed how real Chip is when he's facilitating, and how he's transparent with his faults and hang-ups. It's the first time Don has been semi-consistent about coming to Bible study with me. I'm sorry to hear that he won't be leading anymore."

"Me too." Ettie agreed. "When I asked him why it was hard, he said that on the days we are planning to meet, he is in a heated spiritual battle right up until the group starts. His words were, 'Ettie, it's like a fierce animal is attacking me. I can't fight it because I've got this huge weight pressing down on me, holding me back.' He says he needs to work through whatever is going on spiritually before he can lead our group again. He's asked Rhonda and Silas Mulligan to be our group leaders from now on, and they have graciously agreed."

Joy lit up, "The Mulligans are great! And they'll start this Monday night? Are you and Chip still going to host?" When Ettie answered in the affirmative to both questions, Joy continued, "All right, friend, let's do some serious praying for Chip in a few minutes. You said you had a lot of things on your mind though. What else?"

"Well, Lydia's birthday is in a month, and she is in the process of planning her party. She's a true organizer! I love all her ideas: she wants it to start at the beach for soccer, pizza, and a bonfire, and then back at home for cake and presents. Chip is saying that's too elaborate. Can we pray that they can agree on something that will be special for Lydia's birthday?"

"Of course, sweetie."

"And here's one of the biggest things: she's asked permission to start dating once she turns sixteen. She has a nice young man friend at youth group who is asking." Ettie announced enthusiastically.

"You mean Drew? The guy who came over for dinner last night?" Joy gushed. "How exciting for Lydia! He runs the sound board for the youth worship band, doesn't he? I met him a couple of times when I was volunteering with the youth. He's handsome and funny too. Oh my, Lydia must be thrilled. I can't believe she's turning 16. I can still picture her and Lindsey out on the basketball court playing their imaginary game, 'Journey to Atlantis.' I can see it like it was yesterday afternoon, can't you?"

Ettie nodded quietly as the two friends passed through a shady tree-lined section of the neighborhood. They strolled along pensively for a moment as they mused on the blessings and woes of their children maturing.

"Time has wings of a dove," Joy reflected philosophically.

"Yes, it certainly does. How amazing that you said dove!" Ettie assented. "The dove reminds me of God's promises; I've recently been thinking that the dove is a perfect symbol of how He has hope and a future for Lydia. This birthday is a unique milestone, and it's helping me to envision all the wonderful things God has in store for her."

Joy agreed with a smile, "Yes, she has amazing potential. I can't wait to see what she will do with her life. What did you and Chip decide about her request to start dating?"

"We're discussing it. He tends to agree with Pastor Don and his wife, May, who want their three kids to wait till college to begin exploring boy/girl relationships. I'm okay with her spending some time with Drew and calling it having a "boyfriend," as long as they are supervised and if Chip and I can stay in close contact with his parents. All right, sweetheart, thank you so much for listening to all these prayer requests today. You're the best. Now your turn; what's up with you and your family?"

Since the rising Florida sun was warming the morning air, Joy readjusted her thick, black hair into a ponytail. "My pleasure, Ettie. You remember that was me with all the prayer needs last week, right? Thanks for praying. I'm starting to feel closer to forgiving Don, yet I still cannot believe that he went out and bought himself a brand-new 300z without telling me first. He seems to be purposefully trying to make it impossible for me to forgive him because all he does is stand out there in the driveway gloating over that shiny car. Have you ever seen anyone wash and wax their car six times in six days?" Joy shook her head in disbelief. "I've been trying to do what you have suggested in the past: rest my head on God's shoulders. It's helping a lot. God has been faithful before, and He will be faithful again."

Joy continued to tell her family's news. She was extremely thankful that her mother was out of the hospital after a bout with pneumonia, and her nephew with autism had been introduced to a new food therapy that was proving to be beneficial. She asked for prayers for Justin who was struggling in middle school. She was trying to decide if she should bring him back home to homeschool as they had been doing while he was in elementary school.

When all their praises and concerns had been shared, Ettie and Joy took turns praying aloud as they walked. They included adoration, confession, thanksgiving, and supplication. Spending this time with one another and with God gave both women a fresh measure of God's peace and joy as they began another day. The homeschooling day at the Crews' home on Sea Robin Street flew by productively. It wasn't until the day was ending that the peacefulness gained by the morning prayer time was snatched away abruptly from Ettie's heart.

After a hearty dinner of homemade turkey chili, the three children traipsed out the back door to play in the yard with the Brighton kids. Ettie and Chip stayed behind to clean the kitchen. Clearing the dishes first, and next grabbing the sponge to wipe down the table and the counters, Ettie then moved to the sink to begin washing. Chip started in with his usual playful after-dinner banter.

"What are you doing, little miss?" he teased as he gently tugged on her braid. "You worked hard all day teaching our children. Why don't you sit back and relax tonight while I clean up this mess?"

"You're sweet to offer; you were working hard all day too. You're the one who needs to put his feet up." She flicked him playfully with a splash of water from the faucet.

"Okay, okay; my white flag is up," he relented in mock seriousness as he waved the blue and white striped dish towel. "You wash, and I'll dry. That way I can stand behind you and kiss your neck while we work," he smiled triumphantly.

Ettie loved that she and Chip argued backward, as they called it. Taking care of the chores was much more pleasant when they worked as a team. She was feeling blessed and thankful until Chip uttered something so outrageous that she suddenly felt sick to her stomach.

"I was talking to some of the guys at work today about Lydia's upcoming sixteenth birthday party. I had an idea why the birthday is called "Sweet Sixteen." It's got to be because oral sex is legal at that age." He chuckled.

Ettie dropped the sponge into the sink and turned to look at Chip. Her face was a mixture of disgust and confusion. He realized his words had been a mistake the moment they left his mouth. He attempted to backpedal but crashed into the wall of his wife's wordless disapproval.

"Well, you know what I mean. I just thought...One of the guys at work told that joke today." His explanation was met with a silent stare. "You're right, Ettie; it wasn't very funny."

Not even taking the time to wipe her wet hands off on the dishcloth, Ettie excused herself and went upstairs. Chip had told her a few crude jokes before, however, nothing that tactless. Her instinctive response was to run to Jesus for comfort. She shut the door to her bedroom and knelt by the side of the bed. Her eyes welled with unshed tears as she swallowed back the rising emotion. The unexpectedness of Chip's crass words was a slap in the face, especially since she and Joy had been focusing on Lydia's birthday from such a different perspective earlier that morning.

Ettie's prayers were fraught with questions: *Jesus, how is it that Chip could conceive of such an inappropriate idea? What is causing this change in him? What should I do?* She half expected Chip to come in and give another excuse for his behavior. She was both disappointed and relieved that he didn't. God's words were certain to be more helpful than any lines Chip could try to finagle into sounding reasonable. Her bible lay open to Psalm 62. "Find rest, O my soul, in God alone; my hope comes from Him. He alone is my rock and my salvation; He is my fortress, I will not be shaken." Meditating on these strong promises, Ettie was able to regain her composure.

By the time she headed back down to the kitchen, Chip had finished the dishes and closed himself into his study. His comment was left undiscussed that evening, and neither he nor Ettie brought it up again. However, Chip's sheepishness at speaking crudely about his daughter's upcoming birthday cleared the way for Lydia to be able to plan her sixteenth birthday party the way she had hoped. After his faux pas with Ettie, Chip simply agreed to every request that Lydia made regarding her beach celebration.

Thus, Lydia's party ended up being everything she had imagined. She and her twenty friends enjoyed a rousing soccer match on the shores of Mickler's Beach. After the game, pizza was delivered to the pavilion by the dunes. As the sun set, everyone worked together to build a bonfire. Gathering chairs around the blaze, the youth sang to the acoustic melodies of Drew and two other friends who had brought their guitars to the beach.

For Lydia, the highlight of her sixteenth birthday was that her parents had agreed that she and Drew could start dating. They acquiesced nearly a full month before the date of her actual birthday. Lydia had been in disbelief when they had told her. Now that she and Drew had been boyfriend and girlfriend for several weeks, she felt that the timing had been preordained. On October 23rd, when the day of her sweet sixteen dawned, she and Drew had spent enough time together that they felt quite comfortable in each other's company. It was as though they had been friends forever.

Lydia's stomach fluttered with excitement when the beach portion of the party began to wrap up. Drew had been hinting that he had a special present for her that would be quintessential for her sixteenth birthday, and she had a guess what it might be. She smiled in anticipation as everyone made the short drive back to the Crew house for cake and presents.

When the partygoers had settled into the living room, Laura started to hand the gifts to Lydia one by one. She opened—among other things—silver earrings and a journal from Camille, two music CDs from Marcella, and footie pajamas decorated with panda bears from Laura. After opening each gift, Lydia gushed over how thankful she was to receive the present and how it was a blessing to have such thoughtful friends.

"Oh, Camille, this journal is fabulous! I love the details of the dainty birds etched into the leather on the front! How did you know that I had just finished writing on the last page of the journal Ms. Brook gave us? You're the sweetest, Camille! Thank you so much!"

"Laura! You knew that I needed some footie pajamas to match you and Megan at our next sleepover! We're going to be super cozy! These pandas are the cutest I've ever seen!" Lydia held up the pajamas in front of her to check the size. "Oh good, they look like they are going to fit! Thank you, Laura, I love them! You're the best friend ever!"

Lydia's appreciation overflowed, and she received each present as though it were the best and only one at the party. Drew's gift was in the final festive bag that Laura passed to Lydia. She unwrapped the layers of tissue paper to find a teddy bear costumed as a pirate and holding a mug of chocolate kisses. Drew had told her privately beforehand that there would be two gifts: one that she could open at the party which would symbolize the second gift that he would share with her later.

Holding the mug of kisses in her lap, Lydia perceived that her intuition had been correct. Blushing to the roots of her auburn hair, Lydia thanked Drew. They laughed together over the inside joke that had led him to find a bear dressed as a pirate: their ongoing debate over who was supreme—pirates or ninjas. When the last guest departed, Drew took Lydia by the hand and led her to a romantic spot under the large Live Oak tree in the front yard.

Unbeknownst to the two young sweethearts, they were being watched. Chip had subtly stalked their every move that evening. As they headed outside, he crept into his study where he lifted one slat of the window's blinds to have a clear view of the moonlit tryst. Jealousy and anger roared deafeningly in Chip's mind as he peered out at Drew kissing his daughter; nevertheless, he forced himself to remain hidden. He would bide his time until the time was right to pounce. He let the slat fall and sat in the dark room brooding over his glass of wine.

Lydia came back inside, and after helping her mother clean up the remains of the party, she went upstairs to write in the journal Camille had given her. She described her sixteenth birthday party in vivid detail. Her writing flowed smoothly until she reached the part about the end of the evening. Drew's kiss had unexpectedly surprised her, and she wasn't sure how to put her feelings into words. *His kiss was tender and affectionate,* she mused, *but it lacked the passion and expertise of my dad's kisses. Hmm, maybe I won't include the reference to kissing my dad; it's probably a weird comparison,* she concluded.

Continuing to journal until bedtime, Lydia filled the first five pages of the notebook. Just as she was closing the leather-bound book, her mom knocked on her partially opened door.

"Come in."

"Hi, birthday girl. What a wonderful evening! Your friends are all lovely. Did you have a good time?"

"Yes, Mama. It was exactly what I had been envisioning. Thank you so much for helping me plan and organize, and for making my birthday special. It's super cool that Camille gave me this journal tonight," Lydia shared enthusiastically as she waved the book in the air. "The timing is perfect! I finished writing in the other one from

Miss Brooke yesterday! So tonight, I wrote down all the details of the party; I hope I didn't leave anything out."

"My pleasure, Lydia," Ettie replied to her daughter's words of gratitude. "You know, you are truly a gift from God, and I'm grateful to be able to celebrate this beautiful milestone with you. Speaking of your journaling, I've noticed that your writing is improving in your schoolwork. Maybe you should consider writing a book someday. You could use your journals to help you compose the story of your life; you have so many interesting things going on."

"Ha-ha, that's funny, because didn't Grandma always tell you while you were growing up that you should make a book about your life too?" When Ettie agreed, Lydia added, "Writing a book would be a lot of work. I'd rather be a missionary in Africa or a dance teacher. I think you should write the book, Mama, just like Grandma suggested. What if I tell you all about my life, and you can include it in your book?"

Mother and daughter chuckled together because neither of them imagined that this would ever be a possibility. They hugged and said good night, never suspecting that Lydia's words had been spoken as a prophecy of what was soon to come.

"If God has shown us bad times ahead, it's enough for me that He knows about them. That's why He sometimes shows us things, you know–to tell us that this too is in His hands."

Corrie ten Boom

Chapter 11
THE DREAM

November 2, 2009, Ettie awoke after a terrible nightmare. As she mixed the pancake batter at breakfast, she started to tell Chip that she had dreamt of being tied with ropes and put into a box. The person who was tying her was telling her that she was going to the zoo to be sniffed by a lion. As she was speaking, Ettie suddenly realized that Chip was the lion in the dream.

She stopped right there and didn't tell him anymore; she felt that the vision had been sent by the Lord to warn her of something. For as she had started telling Chip, she recalled that Lydia was in the dream too. They were being tied together, hand and foot, and put into a very small box. The person who was tying the ropes was answering Ettie's questions. "If the lion attacks us, will you save us?" "No." "If the lion starts to eat us, will you shoot it?" "No." Then the box started to move. Yet rather than heading to the lion's den, the box kept going and went far, far to another distant part of the zoo. The box stopped; after a while, small things started to crawl around on it.

Ettie had experienced weird dreams before. Although that one was stranger than most, she tried not to worry about it. Besides that nightmare, the week her world fell apart started the same as any other week.

After their whole wheat pancakes, all three children worked on finishing up an art project modeled after Piet Mondrian's

Neo-Plasticism. Ettie had cut out strips of black paper; Lydia, David, and Jonathan had each designed his or her grid of vertical and horizontal lines. They cut out colorful squares and rectangles to fill the spaces that they thought needed color. It was different from Mondrian's work since his artwork was painted, and theirs were paper. The results were certainly still eye-catching, and the process was fun.

They had lunch on the basketball court with Joy and Benjamin. They brought out their trays of pasta, fruit, and cold water from the water cooler. As they ate, Joy regaled everyone with the antics of her children from the night before. Benjamin ate slowly, and when he finished, he and the Crew boys rode their scooters around in circles on the court while Lydia and her mother studied Early American History. The Jacksonville sun was delightful even in November.

Normally, they would bring out some tasty chocolates too. However, about two months before, Ettie had begun fasting from sweets to focus on praying for their daughter. At the beginning of the fast, Ettie had also heard God direct her to resign from her work at the church nursery so that she would be prepared in heart and mind for their adoption. She knew that when they brought Eva home, it would be a blessing to have the extra time to bond with her.

Many prayers had been lifted up for Eva during the four years they had waited to be matched with her. For most of that time, Ettie and Chip had her name chosen and prayed very specifically for her by name. During those last two months of fasting, Ettie was not led by the Spirit to pray for Eva by name. Instead, she was seeking God's plan for "their daughter" and for the changes that were approaching for their family. How could she know that the upcoming changes were to be the antithesis of the family growth and togetherness that she was anticipating? How could she know that it was actually her older daughter that God was calling her to lift up in prayer? She couldn't know—because from Ettie's perspective, their life seemed almost perfect. She never suspected that a volcanic eruption was roiling under the surface.

Tuesday afternoon everything began to shift. The world began to tilt just slightly so that at first it seemed like another minor upset. That afternoon when Chip came home from work, Ettie took David and Jonathan for a walk to the Navy Exchange on the corner. David had received birthday money from Chip's father back in September that he was planning to spend that day. While the three of them were at the store, Drew had invited Lydia to the youth group at Ocean View's second campus on the other side of town. Since her parents were not allowing Lydia to ride alone with Drew, she was trying to make arrangements to ride with another friend or with a youth leader.

David and Jonathan walked home from the exchange with Ettie, bouncing the new birthday basketball between them along the sidewalk. As they neared home, Lydia came skipping out of the front door at her "something exciting is happening" speed and started to tell her mom about the plans she was trying to make.

Chip was close behind her, scowling and correcting, "I am already helping you with your plans for the evening; you don't need to involve your mother."

In thinking about this moment afterward, Ettie couldn't remember what they said or did in response. Ettie didn't yet know about the plans—perhaps she had asked for clarification. Maybe Lydia had acted frustrated that her excitement was being doused by her father's desire to keep her mom uninvolved. Something caused Chip to snap into a fit of anger. He snatched David's new basketball, charged into the open garage, and flung the birthday gift against the wall. He yelled incoherently as the ball crashed and clanged into the lawnmower.

Moving quickly from speechless and surprised to seeking safety and peace, Ettie told the children that she was leaving the house to go early to church. Over the years, they witnessed many similar outbursts. At the moment, Ettie couldn't begin to deal with the questions of why this was happening again. David and Jonathan got into the Honda Pilot with their mom, but Lydia stayed put.

She very much wanted to go to youth group and hoped it was still a possibility. Her desire to be with Drew and her friends overrode any concerns she had about upsetting her dad further. The class Ettie was teaching was at Ocean View's main campus not at the Riverside campus where Lydia's youth group was meeting.

As they pulled out of the driveway, Chip was at the basketball court shooting the new basketball into the hoop farthest from the house. He didn't turn around to look as they left.

Taco Bell was their first stop since it was still an hour before they needed to be at church, and they hadn't had dinner yet. Ettie made sure that David and Jonathan had enough to eat, yet she couldn't eat more than a couple of bites. Fear gripped her heart, and she felt cold in the core of her chest. It made her feel shaky down to her fingers and toes. She was terrified for her family when these fits of anger occurred. Could she convince Chip that he needed to get help? During dinner, she tried to smile at the boys and act calm so that they wouldn't be worried. It wasn't a burden that her children needed to carry.

When they arrived at church, Ettie's friend, Sandy, came into the four-year-old classroom where Ettie was setting up her lesson for the evening. Ettie tried to answer Sandy's friendly greeting with honesty. She told her that their family was having trouble at home because Chip and Lydia weren't seeing eye to eye. Ettie had no idea that the cause of Chip's outbursts was much deeper than that. Sandy held hands with Ettie, and together they prayed for the Crew family.

That night, Lydia told her mother that her youth leader had given her a ride to youth group and that Chip had picked her up when it was over. No one even mentioned Chip's tantrum.

By Thursday, their family life seemed normal again—back to the "almost-perfect" feeling. However, the mirage soon shimmered into nothingness. In a few days, Ettie would live through the most horrendous day of her life, but Thursday night had the distinction of being the worst of the nights.

Ironically, it started with a lovely dinner date with Chip at the quaint Mexican joint next to their church. Dinner was followed by an inspiring church meeting to announce the opening of a third church campus and a brand-new name that would fit all three of the campuses: "Redemption Church."

Afterward, Chip and Ettie chatted with friends as they stood under a night sky twinkling with the eyes of heaven. The grassy square in front of the church was as familiar as a second home to Ettie. They joked with Pastor Isabella about Ettie coming back on staff since the new campus nursery would need a director. Then they spent some time talking to their friends, Pastor Don and his wife, May, who described their opinions on teenage girls and dating. When Chip squeezed Ettie's hand to signal "Let's go," they offered their good nights, walked to the truck, and drove the mile and a half home.

Back at Sea Robin Street, Chip got onto the computer, and Ettie went upstairs to tell Lydia about the excitement of the meeting. They got cozy in Lydia's room on the edge of her sleigh bed: talking, sharing, and laughing. Their church was growing; the youth group's name was changing too. After a half hour, the conversation turned to Lydia's blossoming relationship with Drew. Lydia mentioned something that she remembered telling the leader of her small group at church.

She had told Ms. Brooke, "Daddy wants me to stay his little girl. He doesn't seem to want to face the fact that I am growing up."

Immediately after she shared this with her mother, Chip's desperate and furious voice cried out, "I think I'm doing fine with that! Thank you!" Ettie and Lydia looked at each other in dismay as they heard his feet clomping down the stairs like hammers. They realized in confusion that Chip must have been eavesdropping from the top of the stairs next to Lydia's room. In the next moment, crashing noises echoed from the living room as something was thrown against the wall. The front door slammed. From outside, they were shocked to hear a terrifying primal yell.

Ettie and Lydia continued to search each other's fear-filled eyes, each wondering what could have possibly caused such an explosion of emotion. Ettie's stomach began churning. She was cold, scared, and shaking all over again. The perfect world was tilting too far to ever be considered nearly perfect again. What had just happened?

Ettie's wobbling legs carried her downstairs. She quietly perched on the blue velour loveseat. Chip had come back inside and was in the study facing away from the door. He turned intuitively and looked at her with disdain. For the first time in their nine years of marriage, he declared that he was leaving her. He seethed, his voice barely controlled with deep emotion, "I'm leaving you, and I'll pay you whatever you want."

Ettie could not reply. Sitting on the edge of the loveseat, she was frozen like a deer in the headlights. She could not form a coherent thought; there were no words to say in response to this betrayal of all their promises. She sat mutely in her terror. Ettie did not even recognize his face, contorted and red with rage, as he spoke those words. Silently, she questioned who that man was. Could it be her husband? She had certainly seen him angry many times, but never to the point where his face was distorted and unrecognizable. He charged out of the room and up the stairs. Ettie heard dresser drawers banging. She didn't move, almost didn't even think—cold and petrified.

Only five minutes later, he was back in the living room apologizing, "I don't know why I spoke those horrible words. That wasn't me. You know I could never leave you. I just can't live like this with you and Lydia trying to analyze me."

Ettie certainly didn't know at the time what he meant about "analyzing him." *What was he talking about?* she wondered in confusion. She reminded him that when Lydia said he wanted her to be his little girl she was simply repeating a phrase that he had told her sweetly on many occasions. *Why would that upset him? Why did he think they were trying "to figure him out"? What was there to figure out?* He was a dad; Ettie had heard that many of them struggle with the emotions that come with watching their daughters grow into the world of boyfriends. Even though he had been acting strange lately, prayer had been Ettie's ally, not psychiatry.

They met face to face across the coffee table, Ettie on the loveseat and Chip on the couch. The couch where they had—over the years—snuggled, loved, and read books to their children. And now the couch where they were sitting to discuss for the first time and only time in their marriage why Chip was threatening divorce. They started by talking about his anger. Ettie wondered aloud if he would consider getting help. Maybe another counselor?

Chip cried in reply, "You'll never know the things my mother did to me." This sounded as though he was about to expose a childhood trauma he had never mentioned before. At that moment, Lydia walked in; he left his disclosure unfinished. Lydia apologized contritely for upsetting him. The nightmare scene ended with a sigh of forgiveness.

Joy came over early the following morning. She shared that she had heard the door slamming and Chip yelling. It was loud enough even inside her house that she had been afraid that the exchange was being robbed next door. When she realized it might be Chip in a fit of rage, she prayed for Ettie and her children. Ettie felt a bit better after talking to Joy about her concerns; later, she called her sister, Brittany, in San Diego for more encouragement. Both Joy and Brittany were wonderful listeners. Still, she couldn't forget the dreadful look that she had seen on Chip's face. *What was happening to their beautiful family?* she fretted. *How was it that Chip could change from that ranting monster to an apologetic husband in only five minutes?* Was *there something she needed to figure out? What was Chip hiding? Perhaps an event from his past with his mother?*

Ettie was starting to worry. After that miserable Thursday evening, she was thankful that Friday and the rest of the weekend passed without any other disaster. Friday after work, Chip brought home a cheerful bouquet of orange tulips for Ettie. Her favorite. God provided a quiet moment before the storm. Even with this respite, no one was prepared for the tempest ahead.

"You say we could lose our lives for this child. I would consider that the greatest honor that could come to my family."

CASPER TEN BOOM

Chapter 12

PACK! NOW! RUN!

On Monday night, November ninth, Chip and Ettie were in bed, leaning back on their pile of pillows, reading the Bible together. Chip was reading aloud from the book of Isaiah. This was different as they didn't usually read together before tucking in for the night. Often Ettie would read by herself in bed while Chip was downstairs in his study on the computer. It was Ettie's habit to turn off the light between ten and eleven; Chip often stayed on the computer till twelve or one.

Since the computer was available that Monday, Lydia was having an unprecedented turn at night—rather than in the afternoon—to connect with her friends on Facebook. When her ten-thirty bedtime approached, she logged off and went upstairs to go to sleep. She found her parents reading together with the door open.

"May I come in?" she asked. She went over to the side of the bed near the window and stood next to her mother. "Good night, Mama."

Before Ettie had a chance to wish Lydia goodnight, Chip interrupted. "How long have you been on Facebook, Lydia?" he questioned with a scowl. Then he added, "An hour and a half? Don't you think that's ridiculous?"

Lydia's smile dissolved into a look of confusion. She looked frightened and unsure of how to respond. Ettie wanted to help her;

what could she say? It didn't seem absurd to Ettie, especially in light of the way that Chip normally spent several hours on the computer every night. Surely it wasn't the time to make that comparison! He had already shown his rage twice that week! Was there anything they could do to turn away his wrath? She didn't know what to do that would avert his anger, so Ettie said nothing, and bewildered Lydia shrugged her shoulders.

Without warning, Chip flew into his third tirade of the week, demanding that Lydia leave his presence, "Get out! Get out! Get out of our room!"

He picked up his pillow from the bed and threw it around the room yelling incoherently. He smashed the pillow onto the bed, the dresser, and the floor.

For the first time in her life, Lydia felt that her father might hurt her physically; his body language and his voice were menacing. Lydia sobbed that she did not have a chance to wish her mother goodnight, then she ducked out and went to her room. Chip thundered down the stairs. Ettie yearned to go to Lydia and comfort her, but the icy hand of fear had gripped her. Instead, she curled up in bed and let the hot tears roll down her cheeks because the rest of her was frozen with terror. It took her almost an hour to muster the courage to cross the hallway.

When she did, all she could do was sit on the edge of her daughter's bed and whisper, "Something has to change, Lydia. Please pray with me that we will know what to do."

For the first and only time in their marriage, Chip spent the entire night on the couch. Early the next morning, Ettie heard him come upstairs. He opened his closet and his drawers and got out his uniform, socks, and shoes. He shaved, dressed, and stood silently next to Ettie's side of the bed.

Ettie looked questioningly at him. She wasn't sure what she expected him to say—maybe not his usual sweet words of endearment—but his abrupt "See you later" was another hurtful blow. He always told her that he loved her as he left for work. She wondered: *why is he sleeping on the couch all night and why is he forgetting to kiss me goodbye?* It was so unlike her husband; Ettie knew that he was in trouble.

She was so afraid for him, for their family, and for their safety. Therefore, she asked, "What are you going to do to get help?"

A sarcastic "Wow," was his only retort; he turned and walked out of their bedroom—not looking back. These were to be their last words to each other face-to-face. Ettie didn't know yet, but the force of the storm that was approaching was growing stronger, and their lives were about to be irrevocably changed. Even though the current moment seemed awful, its bitterness paled in comparison with the impending revelation.

After he left, Ettie's fear for the security of her family escalated. He was targeting Lydia with his outbursts, thus Ettie decided that the safest course of action was to quickly get Lydia out of harm's way. Ettie went downstairs in her pajamas to check the prices of airfare to San Diego. Chip had never physically injured their daughter in the past. Now—after three fits of rage directed at Lydia—Ettie worried that he might easily lose his cool enough to hurt her. That was unthinkable! She knew she must get her daughter to safety immediately before a tragedy occurred. Lydia could stay with her grandparents until the danger passed.

Next, Ettie picked up the kitchen phone and called Rhonda and Silas Mulligan, their small group leaders. She knew she could count on them to help her make a wise decision for the well-being of her family. They were both available to come over within the next hour. "Please come and pray with me," Ettie requested in desperation. "I don't know who I am living with anymore."

Crawling back into bed, Ettie soaked her pillow with a flood of tears. Her heart was breaking. How could they possibly find a way for Chip and Lydia to get along? Ettie felt that she was at an impasse because she didn't know what was causing his deep anger to surface. Ettie cried out to God for wisdom and help. Thinking of the psalm on the lovely black and white photograph in the kitchen, she knew that God would prove Himself faithful again: "I lift up my eyes to the hills. Where does my help come from? My help comes from the Lord, the Maker of heaven and earth."

As she lay in her bed that fateful morning, Ettie was thankful for the promise of that verse, for she knew that only with God's help would she make it through the remainder of the day. She rested in His strength and allowed herself to feel the peace of His presence.

Lydia came into her mother's room at eight-thirty; she didn't seem surprised to find her mother crying. Together they sat on the queen-sized bed and began to discuss the possibility of Lydia traveling to Grandma and Grandpa's in San Diego. Lydia did not want to go. She had already been away for the whole summer, she argued. Her tears began to fall as Ettie's tears continued. Always the social butterfly, Lydia listed many reasons why she couldn't leave: her friends, her brothers, her dance classes, her youth group, and the symphony. Ettie felt her daughter's love when Lydia declared, "I can't leave you either, Mama."

Ettie did not want her to leave at all! Yet, she was extremely scared for her daughter's safety. Maybe there was another way; Ettie hoped that perhaps she could help Lydia and Chip reconcile if she understood the root of the problem. She asked Lydia if she knew what might be causing her father to be infuriated with her. That is when their world exploded forever.

Lydia began hesitantly, "Well, nothing has ever been the same since that stuff happened."

"What stuff?"

"You know—the things that happened in Oak Harbor."

Ettie had no idea what "stuff" Lydia was referring to. At her mother's request, Lydia started to explain what had happened to her as a young child. Of course, Ettie did not know! Her face registered her utter shock. How confusing the next few minutes were as Lydia tried to remind her mom of something she never knew about. Lydia thought her mother knew about the horrible series of three incidents in which Chip had touched her private area when she was seven years old.

Lydia tried to jog her mother's memory saying, "Remember, we sat down in my room and all three of us talked about how it would never happen again because that is not what dads and daughters do?"

Oh, yes, Ettie did recall that conversation; however, the reason for that serious talk must have been completely different than what she had been told. Ettie scrambled through her mind: what had Chip explained to her all those years ago? In 2007, Lydia had been attending Oak Harbor Day School. Her school had started to teach about good touch versus bad touch. Chip had come to Ettie one day to tell her that in an effort to clarify Lydia's questions about good touch versus bad touch, he had mistakenly tapped her on the outside of her clothes in her private area. That was all Ettie knew! She had imagined *that* was what they had discussed with sweet seven-year-old Lydia in her room.

That wasn't what they had talked about at all! Ettie's husband had touched her daughter in a very inappropriate way. The waves of shock that came with this horrific news caused Ettie to suddenly feel nauseous and lightheaded. She tried to remain calm for Lydia's sake as she asked, "Was there ever anything else that happened?"

Her next response was as unwelcome and unexpected as her first disclosure, "Well, there are the birthday suit hugs."

"WHAT is a birthday suit hug?"

Lydia's explanation was brief but sickening. What had Chip done to her child? He had hugged her while she had no clothes on?! All Ettie could utter in reply was, "Pack." That was all that made sense to her at that moment. She knew they had to leave; she had to get her family to safety. It was the only possible choice. Something big and persistent was suddenly behind her, compelling her to get out NOW as if a semi-truck were pushing her to gather up her children and RUN!

But Lydia didn't feel that insistent push. In fact, she didn't even grasp why her mother was upset. "Pack? Why?"

"I think I am going to throw up. Lydia, you are a victim of abuse. We have to leave now!"

"I am?"

Her sweet, innocent girl didn't understand that the things that had been done to her were grossly wrong. Ettie explained briefly; however, a more serious talk would have to wait. "Hurry and get out" was thrumming so loudly in Ettie's pounding heart that she began to tremble. What if Chip came home and found out that she knew what he had done to Lydia? What would he do in his anger? She was terrified to find out. She no longer knew what to expect from Chip: the man she had known him to be had vanished like smoke into the air. What monster was rising out of the smoke? She did not want to know. They could not stay at home a moment longer than necessary.

The next three hours were a blur of tears and suitcases. Ettie was trying to make major decisions when all she wanted to do was scream and cry out. The feelings of unfairness and betrayal were trying to gain a strangling hold of fear in her mind. Why did he do that to her daughter?!

Where should they go? Ideas swirled like dissonant chords through her mind. First, Ettie thought about going to the Browns for help and tried to reach Deb, but she only got her voicemail. At that point, Ettie knew they would all have to get on an airplane because Joy's house wasn't far enough away to be safe. If Ettie purchased their plane tickets with a credit card…. This idea collided with the frightening reality that Chip often checked the credit card activity from his work computer during the day. What if he saw the charge for the tickets? What if he tried to stop them at the airport? Would he attack them in anger? Since the option of using her own card was out, Ettie tried to call her dad, and next, her brother, Ashton, to see if either of them could buy the tickets. Unfortunately, they didn't pick up either. Her mother would fall apart in the middle of her school day if Ettie told her why she needed the tickets, so contacting her was out. She knew that her sisters would help if they could, but the tickets were going to be too expensive.

She would have to call her mother-in-law. Not her first choice; nevertheless, if she was home, she would help. Before she called Meg, she made a second call to Rhonda and Silas to tell them there was a change of plans. Yes, she needed them to pray with her; she also needed them to come over and help with the packing. How could Ettie function with this panic suffocating her? She knew she couldn't do it alone.

In the bathroom, staring blankly into her jewelry box, Ettie dialed her mother-in-law, and she answered. Even as they began to have the most awful conversation imaginable, Ettie sorted through the few necklaces and earrings she owned. They were making plans to leave for who-knew-how-long and she needed to start packing. Her brain was having trouble functioning: the jewelry all reminded her of Chip. She had worn that sparkly blue necklace on their last date; those lovely silver earrings had been a Christmas gift from him. How could she bring any of it with her? Maybe she would never be able to wear any of that jewelry again—too many associations with a love lost, a heart betrayed, and her child losing her innocence. She turned away from the jewelry and didn't pack any of it.

Instead, she spoke in a voice that sounded eerily like it was coming through a dark tunnel, "Mom, I am leaving and taking the kids away from here; and I need you to buy the plane tickets for us."

"Oh, Ettie. Is it that bad? Surely you can stay and work things out." Meg suggested in her quiet southern drawl. Ettie knew she was supposing that perhaps Chip had simply lost his temper again.

"No, I can NOT. Listen, please; I need you to be brave now. We will cry later." Her voice was shaking. She felt anything but brave. "Chip sexually abused my daughter, and we will NOT stay here."

Because of the desperation she heard in her daughter-in-law's voice, Meg agreed to help. They discussed options several times over the next hour because Meg's computer was slow pulling up the one-way flights that Ettie had found. Eventually, the tickets were purchased. They were to leave at two in the afternoon—that gave them about three hours till they needed to get to the airport.

Somehow, they had to be ready. They had to get away before Chip knew that they were leaving. Ettie became terrified that he was going to come home from work early and find them in the midst of packing. What would he do in his anger at finding them? Would he hurt Lydia when he realized that she had told Ettie what he had done to her? Ettie became even more nauseous and afraid.

Thankfully, Rhonda and Silas arrived to begin helping. Joy came over about the same time; Ettie was immensely grateful for her best friend at that moment. Joy looked at her friend's tear-stained cheeks and reached out to give her a reassuring embrace. Rhonda and Silas also hugged Ettie. Lydia, David, and Jonathan came downstairs and there were more hugs all around. They stood in the foyer, held hands, and prayed together: for strength, for protection, for guidance. Ettie knew God heard because He always does; and because at the end of the day, as she looked back, she saw that He had blessed them with all three. Strength to make the difficult decisions, protection on the journey, and guidance from friends and family. He gave them just what their hearts needed to rest in Him.

Joy offered to buy a dog carrier for Stella. She went to Petco and picked one out so that they could bring their sweet dog on the plane. When she came back with the carrier, she and Rhonda went upstairs to help Ettie decide what to pack. Picking out the clothes to put into the suitcase proved to be almost as difficult as sorting through the jewelry: all the clothing items had a memory attached. Ettie started to put things into the suitcase only to discard them onto the bed a moment later, thinking "I can never wear *that* again." Her room became uncharacteristically a mess; the bed was unmade and clothes were scattered around. Whose room was this? Who was this horrible thing happening to? Ettie's morning felt like a living nightmare.

After nine and a half years of marriage, only a few items were simply clothes and not memories. These were the only ones that made it into the suitcase. Unfortunately, it was the navy-blue suitcase that had been Chip's since he had graduated from college. Ettie certainly did not want to take it, yet she had no choice. The children were using the other two suitcases they owned. Ettie didn't want to take the cell phone either; Chip and Ettie shared a phone. It would break her heart every time she saw it. Joy and Rhonda were more practical, and very resolute, and convinced her that she would most definitely need the phone on their trip west.

Packing for David and Jonathan was easy for Ettie since Lydia took over that job. Chip was so frugal that the boys didn't have many clothes, and Ettie told Lydia to pack it all. Their entire two wardrobes fit into one carry-on suitcase. They each had only one pair of shoes: Floridian flip-flops. Ettie forgot to ask Lydia to pack any toys. The idea of playing didn't enter her terrified mind. They were fleeing; she was utterly in shock and merely trying to do one thing—get away.

Was it in any way a normal morning for David and Jonathan? When they first awoke and played Legos together in their room, did it feel like the start of a regular day? When Benjamin came over and joined them, the three musketeers ran up and down the stairs with their wooden swords. It couldn't have felt like an ordinary day for long, because suddenly Ettie was telling them that they were going on a trip to visit Grandma and Grandpa in San Diego. They were full of questions and persistently wanted answers. "Why are we going? Why are you crying? Are you okay, Mama? When are we coming back?" Dare she try to explain?

Even at their young ages, David and Jonathan were sensitive and in tune with the emotions of their family members. They saw the fear in their mother's eyes. When Ettie gave them only a vague response to all their questions, they asked again; and their eyes began to mirror her distress. Ettie felt she had to give them an explanation: the truth, but only the uncomplicated and necessary truth. The truth is a strong rock to stand on in a storm. Stronger than a story anyone might make up and have to change later when it didn't fit the circumstances anymore. She wanted her boys to have the truth to hold onto, and she needed them to trust her. Everything was falling apart around them. They needed each other. They could help each other if they were all facing the gale standing together on the rock of truth.

She told them simply, "We have to leave. Your father has hurt your sister, and it is my job to keep her safe and to keep you safe. We are going to Grandma and Grandpa's house, and they will help protect us."

"Mama," Jonathan argued, "You can't leave Daddy. God doesn't like divorce."

Ettie was blessed that Jonathan remembered what God's Word teaches about the sanctity of marriage. She reassured him, "I am not divorcing Daddy. We are leaving so that we will not be hurt. Daddy is not safe right now. As your mother, God has also given me the very important job of keeping you away from danger. That is what I am going to do."

Even in her shock, and although she didn't remember any toys, the strong sense of responsibility to be a dedicated home-schooling teacher compelled Ettie to pack a fourth bag full of schoolbooks: Jonathan's first-grade readers and workbooks, David's second-grade books, and Lydia's sophomore textbooks. Had she known the emotional state she would be in over the next few months, she may not have packed any books. Ettie thought they would be able to continue their schooling at home—certainly slowly at first, but eventually with the same focus and enjoyment. She had no idea how wrong she was.

One of the last things Ettie noticed when she took her final look around their beautiful two-story home was that she had left the breakfast dishes unwashed. Ettie had poured herself her customary bowl of Honey Bunches of Oats, then had been too nauseous to eat more than one bite. She had atypically left the full bowl sitting in the sink. They always did the dishes before they left the house; this day was different in every way. Even the dishes reflected the horrible mess they were in.

Ettie's fear that Chip was going to come home and find them at any minute inspired Rhonda and Silas to suggest that they spend an hour at their home. As they were getting ready to leave, Ettie began to worry about another possibility. What if, in his rage, Chip did something rash when he arrived home? Like hurt himself? Or destroy their home? Or even come after them with a gun? It seemed like anything was possible. To minimize the harm he could do to himself or anyone else, the Mulligans took Chip's gun from the shelf in the garage where he stored it and put it in Silas' trunk. They would bring it to their home for the time being.

Together with their friends, the Crew family took one last look around their home. Seeing the children's art projects and the family photo albums on the bookshelf made Ettie yearn to gather those priceless belongings and somehow squeeze them all into her suitcase. As she shut the door, Ettie considered all she was leaving behind, emotionally and physically. Yet, the goal of getting her children to safety was so encompassing that it was as if the rest were a single drop of water in the seven oceans. If God's only Son could give up his glorious home in heaven to save her, surely she could give up her own earthly home for the security of her children. God's greater love was her guide and her inspiration; his greater love was her strength. She remembered Jesus' words, "Greater love has no one than this, that he lay down his life for his friends." Could she have that kind of love for her children? Yes, with God's help, she knew that she could. She locked the door and walked with them out to the sidewalk.

How do you tell your best friend goodbye when you don't know when you will see her again? Joy hugged Ettie tightly, and their fresh tears were a reminder of the closeness of their hearts. Joy asked Ettie to call as soon as she could when they landed in San Diego. They lamented about how sad Joy's two older children would be when they came home from school and heard that the Crews had gone.

With heavy hearts, the Crews piled into the Mulligans' cars. Lydia rode with Rhonda. Ettie, the boys, Stella, and Silas followed in his Suburban since it had room for Stella's new dog carrier.

Red flags kept signaling in Ettie's mind to hurry and get her family to safety. She had a terrible sense of foreboding that Chip was going to intercept them: on the highway, at their friends' home, or more certainly at the airport. Her nervous stomach clenched. She hoped desperately that her bad feeling was wrong; but what if she was right?

"*How many times have you heard me cry out,
'God, please take this'? How many times have
you given me strength to just keep breathing?
Oh, I need you, God, I need you now.*"

PLUMB

Chapter 13

TAKING THE TEMPEST

On the drive, Silas counseled Ettie to take out a large portion of the money from her savings in case Chip decided to close her accounts. They stopped at the nearest branch of her bank, and Silas thoughtfully walked up to the teller with her. Ettie hardly knew what to ask the lady behind the counter in her nervousness. Were they actually running away from home? She couldn't say that! How much should she ask for? She didn't even know how much was in her account. Because she rarely went to the bank, she didn't know what information the teller would need; Chip had total control over their finances.

Silas' company gave Ettie the confidence she needed, and she left the bank with several hundred dollars—enough funds to make the journey to her parents' home. And perhaps to sustain her family for a couple of weeks. Until what? Until the money ran out? Until Chip found them? Ettie closed her mind to images of what the future held. The present trial was enough weight on her heart and mind. Instead, she considered the fact that even if there had been no cash, they would be leaving anyway. Money or no money, she had to get the children to safety. Nothing could stand in the way.

Once at the Mulligans' home, David and Jonathan relaxed in front of cartoons on TV, and Stella went into every corner sniffing around curiously. Rhonda started cooking macaroni and cheese for lunch with Lydia helping, but Ettie could only sit at the kitchen table in complete shock. Now that the panicked rush of packing and leaving their home had passed, she felt incapable of doing anything. She was merely waiting to get her family on the airplane. And she wanted to go soon because the waiting was terrifying.

Ettie looked around at her three children—thankful that they were safe for the moment. Unfortunately, that brought her back to how Lydia had not been safe before; and she hadn't known. That was the hardest thing, suddenly learning that her dear child had been abused all those years. Had she failed in protecting her daughter? She felt as though she had! She wouldn't fail anymore! She *would* get her to safety. In the strength of her resolve, a prayer of longing rose in her heart, *Jesus, please help us.*

God blessed her prayer; immediately, she was clear-headed enough to try calling her brother, Ashton. As Silas was busy choosing their seat assignments at the computer in his home office, he noticed that their layover in Atlanta was very short, and their flight out of Jacksonville had been delayed briefly. They might miss their connecting flight. Ettie knew that Ashton, who was living in Atlanta, would meet them at the airport in case they needed a place to stay for the night.

Ettie dialed his number, and Ashton answered.

At first, Ettie couldn't speak when she heard Ashton's voice. She attempted to say "hello," but it came out sounding more like a muffled cry.

"Ettie, is that you? Is everything okay?"

"Hey, brother," she paused, trying to collect her thoughts. What exactly should she tell him? "No, no, definitely not okay. We are in a serious crisis, so I am taking the kids to Mom and Dad's. Chip was inappropriate with Lydia, and we can't stay here." She had tears streaming down her face as she struggled to speak. "If we get delayed in Atlanta, could you possibly meet us at the airport?"

"Oh no! I'm so sorry, Ettie. Of course, I can meet you. When will you be arriving?"

"About 3:30."

"Alright, I'll plan to be there either way. Is there anything else you need?"

Ettie realized that her parents still didn't know she was coming. That was going to be a difficult conversation. If she asked Ashton to let them know what was happening, it would be one less emotionally demanding thing she had to do. She felt she needed to conserve her strength for her kids because she needed to be brave for their sake. "Yes, would you please call Mom and Dad for me? I haven't told them that we are coming yet."

The conversation with Ashton was short and Ettie was thankful for her brother's quiet, unruffled demeanor. However, she continued to feel anxious about needing to leave the Mulligans' house; the hour of waiting at their home stretched on endlessly. After Ettie got off the phone with her brother, Rhonda served lunch. Lydia and her brothers appreciatively ate the mac and cheese; Ettie could only sip a glass of water. Urged by Rhonda and Silas to eat a bit, she nibbled a Saltine. Her stomach was too busy turning somersaults to want any food, and she could barely finish one cracker.

Driving away from the house after lunch, Ettie felt a moment of relief that Chip hadn't discovered them there. As they rode the familiar highway, her eyes scanned the lanes for his white Ford F-150. What an unfamiliar task! Hoping NOT to see her husband. It completed the nightmarish quality of the day. In bad dreams, things always went wrong. In a nightmare, Meg would have called Chip to tell him that his family was fleeing. Did that mean he was speeding toward the airport at that very moment to obstruct them from getting onto the plane? Again, Ettie hoped that her premonition was mistaken; nevertheless, her hopes couldn't prevent the deep fear that had taken root in her heart.

They made it uneventfully to the airport, and with trepidation, Ettie searched the nearby rows of parked cars for Chip's truck. Not there as far as she could see. She breathed another short-lived sigh of relief. She got out of the SUV on shaky legs; could they possibly make it onto the airplane without Chip intercepting them?

Unloading the Suburban, Silas offered to carry Stella's new crate. It was a bit tricky to get her in since she had never been in a carrier before. Once inside, she peered out pitifully from behind the bars. She looked almost as miserable as Ettie felt. Rhonda, Lydia, David, and Jonathan each offered to pull a wheeled suitcase. All Ettie needed to carry was her shiny black backpack. Picking it up and moving it to her shoulders, Ettie remembered that this was the backpack that Deb had given her to bring to China when their adoption of Eva was final. How disheartening that now Ettie would never use the backpack for its intended purpose. How heartbreaking that she would never get to shower little Eva with love.

Ettie had been planning for the last few months that the next time she flew would be to travel overseas *with* Chip to meet Eva for the first time. Instead, here she was escaping to the airport with her children to flee *from* Chip; the weight of her emotional burden suddenly overwhelmed her. No wonder she was in shock. Could she find the strength to keep taking one step after another toward the airport doors? Could she find the strength to keep breathing? Every heartbeat was painful.

What if you find something to be thankful for? the Holy Spirit whispered to Ettie's heart. At the same moment, a gentle wind blew across the sidewalk like a breath from heaven. Ettie slowed her steps a bit to lag behind the group. Ah, there, right in front of her was a blessing: her healthy, young sons willing to help with the challenge of the heavy suitcases. Just as God was equipped to help her with her weighty burden. He was always there with her, in the lovely days and the miserable ones; and she would try to learn to trust Him and praise Him even through this tragedy. Job had understood this lesson; could she? "The Lord gives, and the Lord takes away; blessed be the name of the Lord."

However, this crisis crushed her more profoundly than anything else she had lived through by far. So much was being taken away.

Her daughter's innocence. Her marriage. Her children's father. Her home. All those years, and she hadn't known. *God, please help us.*

Lydia turned and saw that her mother had fallen behind, and she stepped to the side to wait for her to catch up. Concerned, she asked, "Are you okay, Mama?"

"Yes. Well, yes and no. I'm pretty scared, but I am trying to find something to be grateful for. Are you doing okay?"

"I think so. This feels unreal though. It's hard to believe we are leaving; I was supposed to be meeting Laura for dinner tonight. And this afternoon, I am going to be missing ballet class. You already called Ms. Daphne and told her I won't be there, right?"

"Yes, and you can use my phone to call Laura."

"Thank you, Mama. Well, speaking of being grateful, I'm really thankful for the Mulligans, aren't you? I mean, they are helping us so much today. It was amazing that they helped us pack and made us lunch and brought us to the airport and everything. And I don't think they are judging me either. When we were riding to their house, Ms. Rhonda was telling me that she volunteers at a women's crisis center. Did you know that? She said that you are doing the right thing to get us out of this situation." Here Lydia lowered her voice, "I told her that last night, I was terrified that Chip was going to hurt me when he was screaming at me to get out of your room."

"Me too, Lydia. We are going to be okay now." She repeated this phrase hoping that she could begin to believe it. "We're going to be okay. Have you talked to Drew yet? Do you think you…"

Ettie's question was left unfinished as mother and daughter were caught up in the mass of people and suitcases entering through the airport's automatic doors. She knew that they would have another chance to talk, and her question could wait. With the Mulligans, the Crew family turned left and ascended the escalator to the second floor. Heading to the Delta counter, Ettie pulled her ID out of her purse and got ready to hand it to the flight agent. The first minutes of the exchange went smoothly, but Ettie wasn't prepared for the agent's next query, "Can I see the vet papers for your dog?"

"Pardon me?"

"For your dog to travel, I need the health certificate from your veterinarian, not more than 10 days old, and your pet's shot record and proof of current rabies vaccination. Do you have those with you?"

Looking down at her faithful friend in her carrier, Ettie shook her head regretfully. She hadn't known that she needed these papers; Stella had never flown before. In their rush to pack that morning, no one had considered looking into airline rules about dogs traveling. Until four and a half hours before, they hadn't even had an inkling they would be traveling that day. What would happen to Stella now? Ettie looked back up at the flight agent with tears welling in her eyes. Crushing emotion made her voice stick in her throat. She could only shake her head again.

Mentioning their one-way tickets, the agent suggested that they reschedule their flight for the following day so that they would have the opportunity to bring Stella to the vet before their departure. Waiting till tomorrow was impossible. Chip would certainly find them by then. A vision of his volatile anger flashed through her mind. No, they couldn't wait. Still mute, Ettie glanced at Rhonda and Silas for help. Silas stepped up to the counter and explained, "Please go ahead and process their tickets. They will be traveling today because of an emergency. We thank you for your consideration." He turned and spoke quietly to his wife about keeping Stella for a while, and Rhonda nodded in agreement.

Ten minutes later near the entrance to airport security, Ettie and Lydia expressed their heartfelt thanks to their dear friends for all their invaluable help. They knew that God had sent the Mulligans, and Joy, to be like their guardian angels that day. It was with tearful goodbyes that they parted: the Crew family headed toward the metal detectors and the Mulligans down the escalator with Stella's carrier in tow.

Walking down the hallway toward gate 21C, Ettie resisted the urge to grab her children's hands and bolt for the gate. She didn't want to draw attention, and they weren't late, but safety beckoned frantically. Now they were so close. The possibility of boarding the airplane without Chip stopping them felt real for the first time that day. Her pace quickened as she was carried along by her near panic. *"Hurry! Hurry!"* the mad pounding of her heart counseled her. Fortunately, Lydia, David, and Jonathan were oblivious to the force that felt like a semi-truck pushing Ettie from behind. To remain near her children, she slowed her steps. She didn't want to rush them. David and Jonathan paused to point to the 757 parked on the tarmac outside the large airport window. Ettie closed her eyes and took a deep breath as she prayed, *Spirit of God, please help me walk in your peace.*

When she opened her eyes, David was asking, "Mama, is that our airplane? Is that the one we are going to take to San Diego to see Grandma and Grandpa?"

"No, sweetheart; ours is at the end of the terminal. We still need to walk a bit. Ready?"

Ettie took David's hand, and Lydia took Jonathan's. They walked four abreast on the right side of the hallway. Ettie felt surrounded by love, and suddenly she knew without a doubt that they were going to make it. These were her precious children; they trusted her completely. She would bring them to a haven because their God was leading the way. There was David on her left: sensitive, helpful, and earnest, walking straight and tall, in many ways already like a young man. And there was Jonathan: enthusiastic, philosophical, and imaginative with the childlike faith they all needed. And Lydia: graceful, exuberant, and hard-working, braving it through the beginning of this storm with courage. A family. Their family. And they were about to board the plane! Ettie's newfound confidence surprised her. *Thank you, God!* Aloud she added, "Hey guys, let's pray that we can board our plane soon after we get to our gate. I'm ready to go see the rest of our family; aren't you?"

She made her voice sound light, but she was praying for the possibility of immediate boarding with all her strength. One step in front of the other, past the magazines and paperbacks, past Starbucks coffee and muffins, past the souvenir shops with Florida t-shirts for sale. Past women and children with their strollers and overflowing diaper bags. Past teenagers lolled back in their chairs with their earbuds dangling from their ears. Past men with mustaches or plaid shirts or briefcases. And with… what? From a distance, that man looked like… Could it be? When they had made it all this way? The same broad shoulders and black hair, the same confident stride. The man approached closer and closer till Ettie could see the shape of his face. No! It wasn't! It wasn't him, and they were still safe and on their way to their gate.

One minute more and they were standing together by the circular water fountain sculpture at the entrance to gate 21C. Lydia used this moment to call her friend, Laura, to apologize that she would not be meeting her for dinner. She had only gotten the first words out when she got choked up with tears. Handing the phone to her mother, Lydia sat down on the edge of the fountain and covered her face with her hands.

"Hi, Laura; it's Ms. Ettie. Is your mom there, please?" She waited while Laura went to get May. "Hi, May; I'm sorry, but Lydia won't be able to come over for dinner with Laura tonight. Thank you for inviting her. We have had a family crisis, and we're unexpectedly leaving town." She paused again while May offered any assistance that the Crew family might need. As her friend spoke, Ettie's eyes began to well with tears.

"Now boarding flight 563 to Atlanta at gate 21C. We will begin by boarding families with young children and those needing special assistance. Again, flight 563 to Atlanta with continuing service to San Diego now boarding at gate 21C." The interruption of the gate attendant's voice was at this moment one of the most welcome sounds Ettie had ever heard. She wiped her eyes and explained to May that they would call again soon, and meanwhile what they needed most was prayer.

As she hung up the phone and slipped it back into her black backpack, Jonathan stood close and looked up into her tear-shining eyes. "Mama, we're boarding the plane already. It's a prayer come true!" He was right, of course; and although Ettie didn't normally take advantage of the pre-boarding for families, that day she did. It was such a huge relief to get on board! The whole morning had been leading up to this moment. They took their seats near the back of the plane. Ettie sat with Jonathan on the left side of the aisle while Lydia and David found their seats on the right. Both rows had a third seat by the window that was thus far unoccupied.

Passing time as their fellow passengers embarked, Ettie replayed Jonathan's comment in her mind. He had said that their prayer had come true. Not that their prayer had been answered, or that their dream had come true. Because of Jonathan's adorable rewording, the phrase took on a whole new meaning for Ettie. God already had a plan in mind for Ettie and her children, and He was going to make that true too. If only she could hold onto that hope right now. She wavered between holding on to hope and being scared to death. "A prayer come true" reminded her of Jeremiah 29:11, "'For I know the plans I have for you,' declares the Lord, 'plans to prosper you and not to harm you, plans to give you hope and a future.'" What would they do without the word of God to stand on? Ettie knew that in this fierce gale, she would have already been swept away if she didn't have God's word to cling to. Yet how could they believe that their Father had good plans for them after what they had just learned about the secret behavior of Chip? God's good plans seemed to have been snatched out from under their feet. How could they reconcile their understanding of God with the affliction that had overtaken their lives?

The slamming carry-on compartments jarred Ettie out of her contemplation. Passengers jostled in the aisle. The flight attendant walked by with fleece blankets; Lydia got an extra one for her mother and passed it across the aisle. Ettie immediately wrapped the navy-blue fleece around her shoulders. Her jeans and hoodie weren't warming her up nearly enough. The cold, nervous sensation that she had since first hearing the shocking news hadn't subsided a bit even though she was trying to rest in God's strength. Feeling normal again was going to take time. For her and her children. How much time? She didn't know; they couldn't know the road that lay ahead for them. God was only revealing one step at a time on this difficult road, and thus far all she knew to do was get her family to safety. That was the first step, and they were almost there.

A smiling, curly-haired woman in her forties made her way to their row and eased into the window seat next to Ettie. Jonathan was busy talking across the aisle to his sister; Ettie closed her eyes. She didn't want to invite any conversation at present, not even with her friendly-looking seatmate.

She sat waiting and waiting—another wait that should have felt short but was interminably long. Finally, the jet lurched forward and began to roll. Ettie opened her eyes. The mixed-up gust of emotions that filled her heart and mind swirled faster than the trees and houses rushing past the window. Anger, hopelessness, sadness, anxiety, and fear all welled up inside needing an escape. Faster and faster the wheels sped forward; faster the emotions whirled. As the wheels lifted off the ground, Ettie knew for certain that *now* they were safe. She looked at her three beautiful children buckled into their seats, happily pointing out the window to the ground shrinking below them, and she leaned her head forward onto her knees and burst into tears. Not quiet, subtle tears but the mournful wailing of a woman who has lost a loved one. Her sobs came pouring out of a heart nearly broken. A heart broken by the man she had been married to and had trusted completely for nine and a half years.

A small hand tenderly touched her right arm; that was Jonathan comforting her, she knew without glancing up. A larger hand rubbed the center of her back in slow, reassuring circles. That must be the window seat passenger. How considerate that this woman she hadn't even met was attempting to calm her. Ettie purposefully slowed her breathing, and her weeping began to subside. She searched her heart and felt relieved that with her tears some of the vortex of feelings had been released; at least enough so that she could compose herself and give Jonathan a thankful hug. Across the aisle, Lydia and David were looking at her with concern. She exchanged a slight wave with them to let them know she was going to be okay.

Turning her head to the left, Ettie met the gentle blue eyes of her new acquaintance. The kindness Ettie had felt in her touch was mirrored in her voice as she asked, "Hi there; I'm Flora. This must be a difficult time for you; is there anything I can do to help?"

"Oh, thank you." Ettie pulled out tissues from her backpack and wiped her eyes and nose. "You're right; this day has been a nightmare." She focused out at the rectangle of blue sky now drifting past. "Well, do you pray?"

"Yes, I surely do. I have already been praying for you and your son."

Ettie gestured toward Lydia and David. "Those two are my children too. We are on a hard journey because we have had to leave their father. He wasn't a safe person for us to be with anymore. We are heading west to stay with my parents." She sighed heavily. "Thank you for praying for us; that makes all the difference in the world."

The warm-hearted woman promised to be praying for them throughout their journey: both the literal one and also the figurative one that was merely beginning. She and Ettie discussed a few of the many painful steps they would need to take along the road toward healing. As Flora shared her knowledge about the healing process, Ettie welcomed these companions of compassion and wisdom.

If she could take only *the compassion and wisdom on their trip,* she thought. However, there was no getting around it: the trauma, the nightmare, the tempest of what had happened to her daughter, and to all of them, was coming on the journey too. Ettie did not get to choose, David and Jonathan did not get to choose, and Lydia certainly did not get to choose. Like it or not, they were taking the tempest.

"All this pain, I wonder if I'll ever find my way;
I wonder if my life could really change at all."

Michael Gungor

Chapter 14

Broken

Upon landing in San Diego, Ettie checked her phone and found the voicemail full of urgent messages from Chip. In the first two, he sounded confused: why was the house a wreck when he arrived home from work? Where were his wife and his children? His voice became more agitated and aggravated in the next couple of messages as he began to discern that they had left for good. He had noticed that they had taken their clothes and demanded to know where they had gone. Finally, in the last voicemail, he spoke regretfully, asking "Won't you come home again?"

She had closed the phone knowing that she wasn't at all prepared to face a conversation with him. That had been several hours ago. They had made their connection in Atlanta after all and had arrived in San Diego shortly after dinner time. Meg, Sam, Evelyn, Brittany, Madison, and baby Micah had all met Ettie and her children at the airport. Their reunion had been tearful on the part of Lydia and all the adults. After crying, Lydia buoyed her spirits up. She had even pointed out the one positive on her heart: they were all together again. She had never been as thankful as she was at that moment to have a family that loved her unconditionally.

For the Crew family, it was still east coast time, so David and Jonathan had been ready to get to sleep after the half-hour ride to the Zellers' home. Sam and Evelyn had set up a cozy futon bed for

David and Jonathan at the foot of their own waterbed. After getting the boys washed up, Ettie picked a book out of the wicker basket in the corner of the bedroom. It had been Madison's library book, *The Lion and the Mouse*. She had read the classic tale to the two drowsy boys and had tucked them in with a reassuring hug.

Now it was past midnight, and Ettie sat cross-legged on the kitchen floor with Lydia and Brittany. The house was quiet except for their soft voices, the whirr of the refrigerator, and the ticking of the round kitchen clock.

In the stillness of the night, Ettie noticed that the weight that had been like a semi-truck pushing her from behind was finally gone. She didn't feel a need to hurry anymore; however, she was still frightened of what the future held for her and her children. She wondered how anyone could possibly begin to deal with this kind of betrayal and loss. Along with the fear of the unknown, the excruciating pain of her broken heart was pressing down on her like the gravity of Jupiter. It could only help to talk things over; once everyone else was asleep, the three women gathered in the kitchen where their voices wouldn't wake anyone.

Thankfully, Brittany was one of the best listeners God had ever created, and she patiently sympathized with Ettie and Lydia as they divulged the dramatic crises of the past week. Talking through the tumultuous events was draining and tearful. After a few minutes, Brittany got up to fetch a box of tissues from the bathroom counter for all of their tears and running noses. It took over two hours to share the details that were spinning wildly through their minds.

As their impromptu therapy session wound down, Lydia leaned back against the kitchen counter and sighed deeply. "You know, Mama," she began, "as awful as this whole mess is, I am so relieved that now you know. You were in the dark about what was happening for so long; and even though I didn't know you were in the dark about it, it's reassuring that you're not anymore. Does that make sense? I mean, I keep going over in my mind how this is such a shock for you. I think this must be harder for you than it is for me because

I've known all along what was happening to me. Seriously, I'm just surprised that you didn't know for all those years."

"Well, in a way you didn't know either, Lydia," Brittany interjected wisely. "Although you knew literally what was happening, you didn't understand the implications. And how could you? You were simply following the lead of Chip. You didn't know it was wrong or that it was abuse."

Lydia and Ettie both agreed with Brittany, nodding their heads and murmuring their assent. Brittany continued, "And remember, you're not alone. Many, many girls go through this kind of deception and are taken advantage of by men in their lives that they trust. Often, since it starts when the girls are young, they don't even know that it's inappropriate. I guess that's why you had no idea why your mom was telling you to pack." Here Brittany turned to Ettie and asked, "Do you mind if I share with Lydia what happened to me at a party when I was in college?"

"No, of course, I don't mind."

"I had gone to a house party with some girls from my dorm, and a guy who was a friend of my friends put a drug into my drink. Then he brought me out to my car and raped me. It was especially awful because I was not completely incoherent; I could see and feel what was happening to me, yet I had no power to make it stop. Afterward, I fell asleep; when I woke up, I felt sick and dirty. It was one of the hardest things I've ever gone through. After a while, I learned I wasn't the only one to have such a horrid experience, and neither are you: one in three girls are sexually abused before they turn 18."

"Oh, are the statistics that awful now? Last I heard, it was one in four." Ettie spoke sadly. She, too, had been a victim of rape—when she was only thirteen years old. As Lydia was growing up, Ettie had always hoped that she would never need to share that dreadful story from her past with her daughter. Now she knew that it was time because she wanted to be sure that Lydia would not feel all alone in the pain of being molested. It seemed that God had created the fellowship of suffering especially for moments like this.

Ettie looked upward to the ceiling to gather her thoughts and her strength. She began to recount her memory of the hot, sunny day she had ridden her bike to visit a friend. The seventeen-year-old young man, Grady, was the son of Ettie's youth group leader. He had been a trusted family friend; however, when Ettie had arrived at his house that July afternoon, he had been home alone, and he had raped her.

Lydia listened to the stories with tears glistening in her eyes, and she replied sympathetically, "How terrible for both of you. I am so sorry; I didn't know that you had both lived through those awful things."

"Yes, sweetheart, and we feel the same way about you. I am so very sorry that no one knew what you were living through either." Ettie's voice caught in her throat as she began crying again. Hadn't they all shed enough tears that day? With all her heart, Ettie wished she could go back through the years and keep her daughter safe and sound through all of them.

Brittany's Akita, Sky, padded onto the linoleum of the kitchen floor and settled right between Lydia and her mother. When Lydia began to stroke the velvet fur of Sky's ears, the grateful canine looked up at Lydia with complete adoration. Sky's whole body relaxed as she closed her eyes and began to breathe heavily. Her presence and her peaceful repose brought Lydia and Ettie both comfort.

Ettie grabbed a Kleenex and blew her nose. "Hey, Sky," greeted Ettie as she joined Lydia in petting her, "Hey, girl; what a good girl. Did you come in to help us feel better? What a sweet puppy." Then she turned her attention back to her daughter, "Oh, Lydia, I remembered something I wanted to ask you about when we were at the airport this morning."

"What?"

"Do you think you are going to keep your relationship with Drew as it is, at least for now?"

"Hmm, we did talk about that tonight. I called him when you were reading a bedtime story to David and Jonathan, and we discussed that for quite a while. We pretty much decided that we are going to keep dating for now. I hope that in the long run, we have made the right decision. At the same time, it's not going to be at all like dating because we won't be together, you know. He doesn't want to rush into any big change in the middle of this mess. It was a relief to hear him say that. I can't imagine breaking up with him right now: he's been my best friend for a while. It's all so confusing because now we're on completely different sides of the country. He really is a good friend, Mama, and he encouraged me a lot tonight."

"That sounds like a smart decision, honey. I'm glad that he was an encouragement to you too. What did he say?"

"You know, I told him what happened to me; I hope you don't mind. It seemed like the right thing to do since he was wondering why we had suddenly left Jacksonville. I didn't give him details. I told him more in a general way. And so, he wanted me to know I can still have a full life. Even though Chip did those awful things to me, Drew says I can still go on to live as a completely whole and happy person. You know, that's what he thinks. And I am pretty sure that advice is going to stick with me for a long time."

"Absolutely I don't mind that you told him. I'm glad that you felt comfortable talking to him about it, especially since he gave you such inspiring counsel. You can tell whoever you feel safe telling, Lydia, because you don't have to be ashamed: the crime was done to you. You did not do anything wrong. Okay?"

Lydia nodded her head and was thankful that her mother had this perspective. Her discussion with Drew had been a beacon of hope to her on this dark day, and she believed him when he had encouraged her to live fully. But the part that her mom had mentioned about it not being her fault, could she accept that as true? Probably not. Because it sure felt as though she had done something horribly wrong, a lot like her Aunt Brittany had shared about waking up feeling sick and dirty. Now that she had become aware of the abusive aspect of her physical relationship with Chip, she could not consider herself clean and innocent anymore. She was ashamed, and surely it was at least partly her fault? Would she carry the baggage of that shame forever?

Lydia glanced at the clock; it was almost three in the morning. It probably wasn't the right time to bring all of that up since her mother and her aunt seemed to be getting sleepy now, Lydia reasoned as she watched them both yawning. As Lydia began thinking about heading to bed, Sky snorted loudly and twitched in her sleep as if she were chasing a renegade squirrel. It lightened the heaviness of the mood when they giggled together about her dream time antics. They decided they needed to get to sleep too, and Brittany and Lydia headed to their rooms. Ettie walked wearily to the leather couch in the living room. She lay down and covered herself with the warm quilt she had found in the linen closet.

As tired as Ettie was, sleep would not come. Lying there in the dark, she realized that she hadn't yet returned Chip's calls. She fluctuated between the dread of hearing his voice, and the desire to get the phone call over with. Getting it over with won out. She didn't want to bother anyone, so she wrapped the quilt around her shoulders and walked through the kitchen to the garage. The two-car garage had no vehicles in it. Rather, it was filled with boxes and bikes, beach chairs and rakes, and Brittany and Paul's currently unused furniture. The bare cement floor was cold. It wasn't a particularly inviting spot; nevertheless, it seemed to suit the moment. Ettie plopped down on the garage's single step and stared at her phone. *This will not be pleasant,* she reflected. As if in a trance, she dialed.

"Hello," she grimaced as she envisioned who was on the other end of the line.

"Oh my! Ettie! Where are you? Where are the kids? I don't know why I got angry and exploded again. My mom said that you got on an airplane; please, come home."

"Chip, I didn't leave because you were angry."

"You didn't?" He asked in confusion.

"I left because you sexually abused my daughter, and that is NOT okay," Ettie countered emphatically. She couldn't believe the strength of the emotion rising inside her—she was a mother bear keeping danger away from her beloved cubs.

"What are you talking about?"

"Those three events that happened in Oak Harbor when Lydia was seven years old, and you touched her private area."

"I don't know what you mean."

"And what in the world is a birthday suit hug? I don't know what that is, but it is not okay either. Oh, what have you done?"

"The birthday suit hugs were just a little joke between us. I didn't mean any harm; they were like an inside joke."

"A little joke?" Ettie choked on the offensive choice of words. To her, it was utterly and completely the opposite. "Do you think if I had ever seen that, I would have thought it was funny?"

"No." Chip's voice sounded defeated as he admitted this.

Ettie was shocked and horrified. Had Chip really given his opinion that it was funny to hug a young child while she was naked? He had, and she was repulsed. She couldn't bear to continue talking to him for another instant. "Then I have nothing else to say," she ended their conversation abruptly and snapped her phone closed.

Dear God, how are we going to make it through this? She stumbled back through the kitchen and collapsed onto the couch. That had not gone at all as she had expected. She had been convinced that he would deny everything; instead, he had actually admitted that he had hugged Lydia when she was naked. The insanity of his admission was that he had said it was acceptable. How could a sane person utter those words? Sane people hug their children with clothes on and give them the courtesy of a private moment when they are undressed.

The fear, shock, and sadness that had pursued Ettie all day were suddenly joined by another unwelcome emotion: anger. How dare he do that to her daughter and call it a joke? He had stolen her innocence and had blown it off carelessly. What callousness! For all those years, he had masqueraded as a caring and devoted father and husband; now it seemed to her that his heart had been a giant void.

She had not known. She had imagined him to be prince charming. The dark anger rising in her from this next betrayal matched the gloom of the pitch-black living room. Although the house was dark and quiet, they weren't shadows that she could rest in. She couldn't even begin to fall asleep with this resentment churning in her breast.

Another hour passed as Ettie tossed and turned on the couch and wrestled with her anger. The bitterness taking root in her heart seemed to be trying to push away all the love that had been there before. The demons of fury, spite, and hatred haunted her. Being by nature a forgiving person, Ettie wasn't familiar with the emotions of this deep anger. Never had she felt so alone. Never had she felt so far from God's goodness. She felt that her heart was completely broken. She stared into the darkness feeling the bony hand of hatred gripping her heart.

In her anguish, she suddenly remembered to whisper God's name. The power of His name was a healing balm. The bitter root lost its grip, and Ettie asked her heavenly Father to take it away. Anger was not a part of the path to healing for her or for her family. She had to forgive Chip, or she knew that the anger would return more fiercely than before. Could she honestly forgive her husband for what he had done to Lydia? To their whole family? *Yes, Lord,* she prayed, *I forgive him just as you have forgiven me for my many sins. Your grace is greater than any sin.* Hatred would put them in bondage; forgiveness would set them free. As she lay there on the couch, Ettie made a firm decision not to let the foulness of those dark passions into her mind or soul again.

Instead, she began to fill her heart with the truthfulness of God's word. Ever since David and Jonathan had been infants, she had followed the bedtime routine of silently reciting Bible verses in alphabetical order. Most of the verses were put to a tune; thus, in a way, Ettie was singing herself to sleep. Sometimes she fell asleep quickly after the first two or three verses, and other times she had prayed through thirteen or fourteen before she drifted off. Either way, the devotional time kept her mind from turning circles around the worries that faced her. And she needed that new focus desperately on this night, November 10th, so she began.

"And we know that in all things, God works for the good of those who love Him, who have been called according to His purpose." Romans 8:28—beginning the routine already felt a bit calming. At least something was normal on this miserable night. But did the verse apply even to child abuse? Could God bring good even out of that? Could He give Lydia back her innocence? Since Ettie didn't have the strength to wrestle with that question at the moment, she moved on to 1 John 3:1 for the letter "B."

"Behold, what manner of love the Father has given unto us, that we should be called the children of God." The truth of this verse spread warmth through Ettie's heart as it began to soothe her fears for Lydia, David, and Jonathan. They had lost the faithfulness of their earthly father; however, God was an upright and holy Father who loved them completely and for eternity.

"Come to me, all you who are weary and burdened, and I will give you rest. Take my yoke upon you and learn from me, for I am gentle and humble in heart, and you will find rest for your souls. For my yoke is easy and my burden is light." *Oh, thank you, Jesus, for giving rest to the weary.* Ettie tried to lay the burden of her brokenness down at the feet of Jesus, only to take it right back up again. Leaving it there was going to take time.

"Do to others what you would have them do to you, for this sums up the Law and the Prophets." As she prayed through the golden rule, she realized that doing to Chip as she would have him do to her meant that she would need to learn to forgive him over and over again. She had forgiven him wholeheartedly moments before, and perhaps that had even been a miracle. In your own strength, how do you forgive the person who has wronged your beloved daughter so horrendously? Wouldn't she need to pardon his behavior again tomorrow when her resentment tried to resurface? The golden rule would give her a goal and a model to strive for each day.

"Every good and perfect gift is from above, coming down from the Father of the heavenly lights, who does not change like shifting shadows." Remembering the good gifts that God had given her came naturally, even on this bleak night. Her children, her parents, her family, her friends, salvation, God's Word. Yes, she could think of many gifts from God that would steer her through the shifting shadows all around her. In her meditation, she moved gratefully to two of her favorite verses for "F" and "G."

"For God so loved the world that He gave His one and only Son, that whoever believes in Him shall not perish but have eternal life." Singing through this pivotal verse several times began to assuage Ettie's wounded heart.

"Greater love has no one than this, that he lay down his life for his friends." Only that morning, she had discovered how God was calling her to lay down her life for her children; God's greater love would continue to be her guide and her strength.

"H;" When she reached the letter "H" she was stuck; she could not remember the verse. That never happened during her prayer time because the verses and their tunes were all very familiar. There was a block keeping her from that verse. What could it be?

Then the realization hit—the verse for "H" was "Husbands, love your wives;" and oh, how she started to weep. She hadn't been loved! Where had the love been for nine and a half years? Suddenly, the weight of the deception that had marked her marriage with Chip dragged her back into the darkness of the abyss she had been attempting to climb out of. Ettie's sobs echoed with despair.

As she wept, an amazing breakthrough occurred: God helped her to understand the nightmare she had experienced more than a week before. In the dream, she and Lydia had been in bondage; they were tied together and put into a box. They had been put in the box to be sent to a lion, and the lion had been Chip. What had happened next? They had been sent far away from the lion to the other side of the zoo and far away from danger! Now, Ettie understood! God had sent them all the way across the country to bring her and Lydia to safety!

The last part of the dream had been that something small was crawling on the box. Ettie could hardly believe that she now understood that the "somethings" were mice that were going to chew their ropes and set them free! It was parallel to Madison's library book, *The Lion and the Mouse*—the book that Ettie had read to her boys that night. God had even chosen the bedtime story to help Ettie interpret the dream: the mice had been chewing the ropes of bondage that had held Lydia and Ettie captive. How thankful Ettie felt; her spirit soared once again! *God, thank you for setting my little girl free!*

The night that had been dark and fearsome became a beautiful and glorious morning because, at that moment, Ettie saw a glowing vision of God's profile. She had never seen a vision before; its power overwhelmed her. The nearness of the Lord's presence flooded her with warmth and all-encompassing love more fulfilling than anything she had ever experienced. The vision lasted only a moment, yet in it, she lived the truth of Psalm 34 that "God is close to the brokenhearted and saves those who are crushed in spirit."

Because God had sent this dream ahead of time, Ettie knew that He had prepared her heart for the crisis. The Lord knew that she would not be able to fathom how the abuse could have happened and that she would be in total shock. When He sent the meaning of the dream on her darkest night and filled her with the warmth and love of the vision, the love that she *did* understand manifested itself as more powerful than the years of betrayal and secrets that she did not.

On that daybreak, God displayed His love for them in a glorious, healing way. Ettie began to see that nothing, not even the present darkness, could separate them from God's great love. His love was greater than anything she had ever known. Humbly, she prayed that the truth of this moment would continue to be present in their lives as they faced the uncertain future together. She knew that if they did not cling to God's love tightly, the unforgiveness and hatred that had haunted her that night would return to stake a claim in their hearts. Only the truth of God's great love could keep those bitter demons from crushing her family. God's love would be enough. Would they have the strength to hold onto it through the pain?

"When you smile and you laugh but you're fakin'
Cause you don't know how you're gonna make it
You feel so much pain
And you can't see your way."

JAMIE GRACE

Chapter 15

THE MASK

The love that enveloped Ettie in the vision she saw of Jesus gave her a spark of hope. That fiery spark helped her to be brave enough to move her feet one step at a time. It buoyed her spirits enough to make it through the daily tasks that needed to be done. Unfortunately, much of the time, Ettie was so sick to her stomach that she could barely walk. Taking even just a few steps jostled the empty, cramping feeling that had landed itself in her middle.

When she was a child, Ettie's family visited the east coast during hurricane season. A menacing storm bore down on the coastal states and the meteorologists cautioned everyone to board up their windows, buy supplies, and stay inside. Thankfully, the hurricane ended up passing them by. If her body was a home, this miserable feeling in her stomach felt like a hurricane had ripped through breaking all the windows and leaving shards of her life splayed in every direction. It was a storm she hadn't been prepared for, and its destruction was taking its toll.

The first week back in San Diego was a whirlwind of emotionally draining visits. The day after their arrival, Pastor Evan got Lydia and Ettie connected with Maria Windsor, a therapist who specialized in helping sexual abuse victims. This first therapist session was exhausting as Ettie and Lydia replayed the events of the past week that led to the abrupt flight from their home. Maria Windsor, in turn, referred the Crew family to the Navy's Fleet and Family Services where Lydia met with a counselor who asked Lydia to recount as many details as possible of the nine and a half years of hidden exploitation that she could remember. That visit lasted three and a half hours. A social worker from Child Protective Services came to visit the Zellers' home the following day. Once again, Ettie and Lydia retold the awful story of abuse and betrayal that had swept through their lives.

In addition to these appointments that nearly depleted Ettie of hope and energy, several burdensome phone conversations took place during that week. Calling Natasha, the coordinator at their adoption agency, to inform her that they would no longer be able to bring their daughter home from China, was heartbreaking. The situation and timing were extremely unfortunate, Natasha agreed. The Crew family was only three months from being matched with their child. Ettie spoke to Natasha through tears all the while whispering to her infant daughter in her heart, *Sweet baby Eva, wherever you are, I'm so sorry I will never meet you.*

Then there were the calls to Lydia's adult mentors: Mr. Tharpe, her flute instructor; Ms. Lu, the conductor of the Jacksonville Youth Symphony; Ms. Brooke, her small group leader; and Ms. Daphne, her ballet teacher. Ettie also spent time on the phone with her friends, Joy, Deb, Sandy, and May, and with Pastor Isabella and Pastor Greg from Redemption Church. Each call included an explanation of why Ettie and her family had left Jacksonville and how they would not be returning. Depending on the depth of the relationship, the explanation was sometimes brief; however, a few of the conversations were long and painful. Most people expressed their deep sympathy for their plight. Surprisingly, the most frustrating phone calls were with Deb and with Pastor Greg.

Ettie was shocked by Pastor Greg's response. His family had been dealing with the physical mistreatment of his teenage grandson, Gunner. They had been trying to get Gunner out of his father's home after Gunner had been punched in the face by his dad. When

Ettie called Pastor Greg, she had been expecting empathy of the most soothing kind: godly wisdom from a heart of understanding. Instead, his initial comment, "How do you know that she is telling the truth?" had left Ettie reeling to such an extent that she couldn't reply. She didn't even remember to say that Chip had admitted to an ongoing "inside joke" with Lydia. Of course, she knew that Lydia was telling the truth!

When Deb called to check on the Crew family after their arrival back on the west coast, Ettie was in the kitchen talking to her mother. Carrying the phone out the back door, Ettie settled onto a white patio chair by the pool. The water shimmered azure and inviting. Ettie dipped her foot into the fresh, cool water and swished her leg back and forth as she tried to keep her focus. Deb prattled on about her state of confusion during the last few days. The more Deb spoke, the more muddled her words became. Finally, Ettie interrupted to seek clarification.

"Wait, Deb; did you say that Chip called you on Tuesday afternoon to see if you knew where we had gone? What time was it?"

"Yes, I'm telling you, Ettie, you shouldn't have left him like that," Deb remonstrated. "It was around two o'clock. He said he got home early from work and saw that you were gone. He was worried about you and the kids. You should have stayed and worked it out with him. He sounded so distraught on the phone-it just broke my heart. I told him I didn't know a thing. When I called the house to see if everything was okay, he told me you had flown west to be with your family."

Ettie's foot froze in the water. "Did he tell you why we left?"

"He explained all about that. He said you accused him of touching Lydia in her private area. Ettie, don't you trust your husband more than that? Chip is a good, Christian man. He swore to me with his hand on the Bible that he fell asleep with Lydia when she was seven, and when he woke up, his hand was on her private area. One other time, he went into the bathroom and hugged her before she had her towel wrapped around her. But that was such a long time ago! Do you think it was necessary to leave him after that?"

Chip's deception reminded Ettie of the fetid waters of a drainage ditch. She pulled her foot out of the water abruptly as if the pool water were suddenly contaminated with his lies. His betrayal made her want to gag. Her husband had turned one of her closest friends against her.

Fortunately, unlike her talk with Pastor Greg, during this conversation, Ettie remembered that Chip had confessed his behavior to her with the perverted excuse that it had been a joke. After explaining that fact to Deb, Ettie hung up with her emotions churning. She remained sitting on the patio, yet she refrained from putting her foot back into the water.

Soon Brittany came outside holding little Micah. Even though Micah was crying hard, he was completely adorable with his rosy cherub cheeks.

"May I?" Ettie asked as she stood and held out her arms.

Brittany smiled and handed her infant son to her sister. Responding to Ettie's swaying and humming, and to the beauty of the bright, wide sky, Micah calmed down. Ettie pressed his chubby cheek against hers and thanked God for the gift of babies. Having Micah to care for and love was wonderful therapy.

"I'm grateful you and your family are here with us, Brit. What would we do without you? David and Jonathan needed to have Madison to pal around with. And although we have such a full house, it's been a lifesaver to have you and Mom and Dad to lean on." Ettie sat back down, joining Brittany on a white chaise lounge. She sighed as she bounced Micah up and down on her knee. "I just got off the phone with my friend, Deb. She was not as supportive as you have been."

"That's unfortunate, sweetie. Just keep remembering what you have brought Lydia out of. You're certainly doing the right thing. Did I hear you having a difficult conversation with another friend earlier too?" Brittany asked sympathetically. "I thought I heard you crying in your room."

"You did. Lydia and I called her small group leader from church, Ms. Brooke. They have gotten closer over the last year. We found out while talking to her this afternoon that Brooke had been molested by her stepdad when she was younger. Because of her experience, she started to suspect that something was amiss in Lydia's relationship with Chip. She was sorry that she hadn't been able to speak up soon enough to help Lydia."

Brittany's brown eyes filled with understanding as Ettie continued, "Brooke was able to be an encouragement to Lydia today. The more Lydia realizes that she is not alone, the better." Ettie placed Micah back into his mother's arms where he could reach the pool water and amuse himself with splashing. Putting her head into her hands, Ettie whispered solemnly, "I spoke to Brooke privately afterward. Her story is heartbreaking: her stepfather sexually assaulted her for many years—until she left for college. Her mother was aware of what was going on, yet she said she couldn't leave. She never got Brooke away from him."

Ettie's sobs suddenly overwhelmed her. It broke her heart to realize how many children must be trapped in abusive homes. When she could speak again, her voice trembled with sadness, "Brittany, what does 'couldn't' look like? If Brooke's mom couldn't get her to safety, what does that mean?" She began to answer her own questions with more questions. "Well, maybe she didn't have the financial resources to leave? Maybe she had no family to run to? Perhaps, she was afraid her husband would follow them and physically harm them?"

"Any of those could have been true, or all of them," Brittany confirmed.

"Brittany, I don't understand. *Nothing* could have stopped me from getting Lydia away from that man, absolutely nothing. I would have left even if we hadn't had a single dollar or a single friend to help us. We could have gone to a family crisis center; we could have gone anywhere. We just had to go. I forgive Chip, but I couldn't stay. I will never, ever trust him again."

"You're right, honey. It's going to help Lydia heal knowing that you believed her and that it was vital to you to protect her. How is your friend, Brooke, dealing with her past?"

"With God's help, she has forgiven both her mother and her stepfather. She and her husband had to go through a couple of years of intensive counseling early on in their marriage. She said they are doing well now. They have three healthy children, and she is pregnant with their fourth. At the end of our conversation, she spoke a truth that I hope will someday become a part of Lydia's self-image as well."

"That's fabulous! God is faithful," Brittany replied. "What did she say?"

"'It's part of my story; it's not who I am.'" As Ettie repeated Brooke's words, their significance shifted her burden of sadness and brokenness to the strong arms of Jesus. Her identity was in him, Lydia's identity too; they were both daughters of the one true king. Abuse may have been part of their story; nevertheless, who they were would not be defined as "abused." No; they were loved, cherished, and chosen as God's children.

Ettie turned sideways on the lounge chair so she could see Micah's laughing eyes. His toes were curled with delight as he pumped his plump legs and giggled at the splashes he was making. If she focused on her nephew's joy, the sparkling water no longer made her think of Chip's deception. The darkness of the past was going to fade as well. In time, with focused effort and therapy, she and her family were going to heal. It was just a matter of how they looked at their situation. God would help them shape the story of their future.

Brooke's perspective was empowering. Through it, Ettie was taking a step in her own journey of healing. Each day would have challenges; at least today she had taken one step forward. Realistically, she knew that tomorrow she would perhaps be journeying one step back. When would she be able to simply go forward? She hoped it would be soon. Their new therapist, Maria, had told Ettie and Lydia to consider themselves in a kind of "emotional ICU" for at least eight months to a year. That sounded rather pessimistic, but Maria had years of experience helping sexual abuse victims, and Ettie trusted her opinion.

The next morning, the sun peeked over the horizon with the promise of change. *Would the change be a step forward or backward?* Ettie wondered. Jonathan rolled out of bed hesitant about the plans for the day. Ettie attempted to cheer him up by cooking his favorite breakfast: egg and salami burritos. She let him pick out his favorite orange t-shirt with the surfboard on the front. David also donned his top wardrobe pick, a Sea World shirt sporting a menacing shark.

Both boys had gotten sneakers the day before since their Floridian flip-flops would not be acceptable footwear for their new school. The novelty of their light-up Spiderman shoes kept their attention for most of their half-mile walk to Antigua Elementary School. Then the inevitable questions began.

"Mama, are you sure we have to go to school?" This was David. Jonathan had already asked the same question twice that morning as they had gotten ready. Ettie resisted the urge to sigh because she wasn't convinced either. She loved homeschooling her children just as much as they enjoyed it. The flexibility and the family togetherness were a perfect match. Lydia coveted the opportunity to take the time to learn her lessons thoroughly. They could just continue homeschooling, couldn't they? She had been over the options a dozen times during the last couple of days. When she had prayed about it, the wisest solution seemed to be that all three of her children enroll in school. She did not have the emotional energy to teach them while they were all recovering from this crisis. It wouldn't be fair for the children to get behind in their education.

Stay positive, she coached herself. "Yes, David; I'm sure you *get* to go to school. It's going to be fun: a cool adventure. You must be missing Benjamin and your other friends from Jacksonville. At Antigua, you'll make lots of new friends."

Next, Jonathan tried his hand at persuasion. "Can't we stay home, pretty please? I want to go in the pool today. I promise I'll do my work after I swim!"

"Swim?" laughed Ettie. "It's the middle of November."

"It's not cold to me, Mama. It feels nice," Jonathan shared with a grin that showed the gap where his two front teeth should be.

"Ha, the water is sixty-eight degrees, buddy. You're a polar bear."

As they rounded the corner to the final stretch of their walk, they saw a white SUV backing out of a driveway. "Look guys," Ettie pointed. Instead of seeing a car, Ettie was inspired by the opportunity to give an object lesson. "Do you notice how that car is going backward and to the left? And then..." She paused as the driver shifted into drive and the SUV pulled forward. "Now, the car is headed in the other direction. That's kind of like us today. We may think that going to school is the wrong direction for you, but soon we'll see that it was just a few steps backward. We will be happily heading forward in the right direction—the one God has planned for us. Jesus is showing us the way because He is the way."

The rest of the morning went smoothly. A friend from the Zellers' old church was the administrative assistant at the elementary school. In an office full of filing cabinets, she quickly received the needed paperwork and told the boys about their prospective first and second-grade classes. Her kindness and efficiency were a blessing. Ettie and her sons left Antigua already feeling more positive. David and Jonathan would be ready to start school the next day.

The afternoon brought an unexpected detour. After lunch, Lydia and Ettie borrowed Brittany's Pontiac to enroll Lydia at the neighborhood high school. Ettie anticipated that everything would progress as it had at Antigua. Yet, instead of meeting an old family friend at the front desk, the receptionist at Clairemont Mesa High School seemed to have eaten nails for breakfast. She looked over the papers with an air of disdain and pronounced that it was not sufficient. Ettie's attempts to explain that the same paperwork had been acceptable at the elementary school were ignored. Ms. Nails sniffed. "Our school is full; we have twenty-five hundred students here. We cannot accept transfer students without proper documentation." She sent them on their way and shut the door soundly.

"What just happened, Mom?" Lydia asked in disbelief as they made their way down the stairs and back to the parking lot. "That lady was rude for no reason. I mean, I understand that she wanted us to have a notarized letter. Still—couldn't she have told us that kindly? I'm already nervous enough starting high school without being belittled on the first day too."

"Well, we won't let her ruin our day, Lydia. We'll get the letter and prove her wrong." Ettie glanced at her daughter. Lydia may have been feeling worried; however, it wasn't reflected in her confident stride. "I'm feeling sad too. What things are making you feel especially anxious?"

"Mama, I'm sad, because I am going to miss so many parts of homeschooling. For instance, getting to be relaxed while doing school—I mean, it's awesome doing my work anywhere. And hanging out with you and the boys. You guys are fun, you know? Going to school is what we have to do, so I'm not angry or anything, I'm just not thrilled about it. In terms of starting high school, I am pretty nervous because I don't really have any idea what it is going to be like! I haven't been to school since first grade!" Lydia broke off while they passed a gaggle of students headed in the other direction. She turned to study them after they walked by. "So, here's the funny thing; I have all these silly, horrible ideas in my mind about what high school could be like from movies."

Ettie chuckled inadvertently. "Movies aren't real life."

"Seriously, Mama, I know. But in the movies, there are always kids teasing you or people pretending to be your friend, then they actually have malicious intentions. Or you don't have friends to sit with at lunch, or someone comes along and pulls your pants down for a joke." Lydia joined her mom in laughing. "Well, maybe not that last one. I guess it can't be that bad. I do think it's going to be hard to be the new girl anyway."

"Yes, I understand, honey. I also know that you're going to make friends just as comfortably and easily as you normally do."

Ettie's phone rang when they reached Brittany's car. It was Evelyn, and she was bubbling with excitement. "I just left the office of our principal, Gail Jefferson; she says you are welcome to come work here as the laboratory technician in our science department after the winter break. And listen to this! She wants Lydia to come to our school as well!"

"Umm, I do too. There is no way we can afford the tuition at Anglican College Preparatory School though. We're currently in the middle of trying to get Lydia enrolled at Clairemont Mesa, remember?"

"Right, but Gail says she will do whatever she can to have Lydia here. She means that she will give her an extremely generous scholarship. She's thrilled to have Lydia join our dance and music programs. Lydia is so talented in the arts and also in academics; Gail sees that Lydia's gifts will be an asset to our school. It's a wonderful opportunity for Lydia too. ACPS has a lot to offer."

"This is an amazing opportunity, Mom. Let Lydia and I talk it over, and we'll call you back. Your timing is perfect. We kind of got kicked out of Clairemont Mesa a few minutes ago."

Evelyn gasped. "Kicked out?"

"Just figuratively, Mom."

Lydia's blue-green eyes were wide with questions. She had figured out why her grandmother was calling from hearing her mother's end of the conversation, and she wanted to get all the details. Ettie answered Lydia's queries and started the car. Crisp fall air blew through the open windows as Ettie and Lydia discussed the possibilities. Both mother and daughter agreed that God had effectively closed one door and opened another. In fact, he had flung the door to Anglican Prep wide open. They decided to take steps of faith and walk through it. Although the financial aspect was daunting, they knew from experience that God has unlimited resources. If he wanted Lydia at ACPS, he would provide the funds.

"It's going to be a fresh new start for you, Lydia. And it will be such a blessing to have Grandma at school if you need anything." As they merged onto the highway, Ettie smoothed back the tendrils of dark hair tossing around her face. She put up the driver's side window. "You know what? Speaking of a fresh start, I was thinking of getting a haircut. Do you mind if we stop by the hairdresser on the way home?"

"That's fine, Mama. I'll be happy to go with you."

At the salon, the stylist, Alma, ushered Ettie to her booth and fastened on a black drape. When Ettie requested that Alma clip her hair into a pixie cut, the middle-aged Bosnian woman was taken aback. She pulled out the ponytail holder at the end of Ettie's braid and ran her fingers through the loose hair. "What? No! You want me to chop off all this lovely hair?"

"I've got to leave the past behind me," Ettie explained as she regarded her reflection in the mirror. Her eyes still looked shell-shocked. Maria Windsor was right; it was going to take a long time to look and feel healthy again. "My family and I have walked through a nightmare. All the hair that will grow back will never have experienced that darkness."

Alma nodded in understanding. She offered no more resistance to cutting her customer's hair short. Hardship was something Alma was well acquainted with. As she worked, she described how the Bosnian War had displaced her family. Alma's life story was so engrossing that Ettie didn't notice how the haircut was progressing until Alma held up the silver hand mirror in front of her and asked, "How do you like it? You look nice; you have a pretty, delicate face."

Ettie didn't argue, although, in her opinion, she resembled a shorn sheep. She thanked Alma and was preparing to pay, when on a whim, Lydia decided to get her hair cut too. She chose a bob, and Alma went to work once again, this time trimming off seven inches of Lydia's auburn tresses. The hairstyle was becoming on Lydia; Ettie and Alma complimented her sincerely.

When the two returned home, Ettie called Evelyn and confirmed their decision for Lydia to attend Anglican Prep School. A few days later, Ettie met with the admissions director and the guidance counselor. Letting the counselor understand the story of Lydia's past and current situation was important to Ettie. If something triggered overwhelming emotions for Lydia, both Evelyn and the guidance counselor would be available to help her cope. Once the spring semester started, the lab tech job would begin for Ettie, and she would be at the school as well. It seemed to Ettie that all the details regarding school and work were fitting together as neatly as a puzzle.

Lydia thought so too until she walked into the lunchroom on December first—her first day at ACPS. The morning of classes had been fine. Lydia fit right into her Spanish class which had only twelve students. In Marine Biology, she sat with Teagan, a friend that she had met the previous summer when she had stayed in San Diego to take Chemistry from her grandmother. Lunch, however, was a different story. The O'Reilly Center, as the cafeteria/auditorium was called, was teaming with students who were busy eating, laughing, and chatting with their best friends. From where Lydia stood inside the glass doors, it appeared that all the tables were full. Plus, they were full of girls who all had long, flowing hair. Lydia suddenly felt ridiculous with her new bob hairstyle. She was an outsider. Motionless, she wondered where she should go to eat her lunch.

No one sees me here; no one knows I even exist at this school, she realized with a sigh. *Maybe I should just go eat alone in Grandma's office?* Suddenly, a flash of yellow caught her eye in the sea of gray and blue uniforms. It was the golden yellow scarf she had noticed a girl wearing in her biology class. The girl had been one of Lydia's friends many years before at San Diego Country Day. She had danced around the crepe myrtle tree with Lydia on the playground in kindergarten. Caitlin Kellogg was her name; she and Lydia had greeted each other briefly that morning as Biology was letting out.

Relieved to spot a familiar face, Lydia made her way hopefully across the lunchroom. "Hi, Caitlin. Can I sit here?"

Caitlin and her friends looked at Lydia in surprise. Caitlin glanced around the table with her eyebrows arched. No one responded for what felt to Lydia like a whole minute. She considered excusing herself and walking away.

"Oh, of course, you can," Caitlin finally replied with a catty grin. "We were just finishing. You'll have the table all to yourself."

Caitlin and her entourage gathered up their backpacks and their half-eaten food. Lydia was left standing alone-her face flaming with embarrassment. She certainly wasn't going to sit there by herself nor was she going to try to join another group! Oh, how she missed her dear friends at that moment! Laura, Lindsey, Marcella, Camille— she remembered each one with a lump in her throat. Her heart ached to be back in Jacksonville where she belonged. Making her way across the stone courtyard, Lydia realized that she and her friends would never have treated a newcomer so coldly.

When she arrived home that evening, Lydia was prepared to share the ups and downs of the day with her mother. Their recent crisis had brought them even closer than before, and Lydia was looking forward to her mother's wisdom and encouragement after her challenging school day. Unfortunately, when she walked in the door, she found her mother crying on the back porch. David and Jonathan were also wiping away tears. Something must have gone terribly wrong for her brothers to be crying!

"What's wrong, Mama?"

"Stella...A car..." Ettie struggled to speak. "I'm sorry, Lyddie. I'm so sorry."

Lydia looked at her brothers for an explanation. Jonathan blew his nose and announced soberly, "Our dog died. We won't see her again for a long time. Not till we get to heaven. I loved Stella very much, Lydia. I did. She was my best friend, and she loved peanut butter."

Jonathan's precious epitaph touched Lydia's breaking heart. She reached out to hug her family one by one and joined them in their tears. Once Ettie recovered, she recounted the story as she had heard it from Rhonda Mulligan. Rhonda and Silas had kept Stella for a week and then had arranged to bring her back to Chip. A tragic accident had occurred when they met him in the church parking lot after work that afternoon. Chip had put Stella into his Ford F-150, but she had jumped out and had run straight to the busy road where she had been struck and killed by a U-Haul truck.

Lydia's mom was distraught over the loss of their dog and was busy consoling the boys, so Lydia kept the troubles of the school day to herself. She balled them up into a tight fist of disappointment and fear that filled her chest. She kept asking herself *"Why?" Why did Stella have to die? Why did they have to move away from her friends? From her life? Why had she not known that she was being sexually mistreated? Why had she not told her mother what was happening to her? Why had the abuse happened in the first place?*

Her questions spiraled into the vortex of one horrible conclusion: *It's all my fault.* That night as everyone else in their full house slept, Lydia could no longer control the swirling cascade of emotions. The therapist had told Lydia that her insomnia was a symptom of the sexual abuse she had suffered for nine years. Finally, at sixteen years old, Lydia understood why she had always had difficulty sleeping. That night was exponentially worse. Awake for hours, she turned over all the scenarios in her mind. *My family has fallen apart. My best friends are across the country. My sweet dog is dead. I'm ostracized by the kids at school. And it is all my fault.* Tiptoeing out of bed, she found Sky nestled in the living room. Wrapping her arms around Sky's neck, Lydia hid her face in the ruff of white, fluffy fur and let the emotions pour out.

Exhausted, she finally climbed back into bed and closed her eyes. In what seemed to be a blink, Grandma was waking her for school. Groggily, she stood before the mirror and peered at the dark circles under her eyes. *No one can see the hurt inside,* she chided herself. *ACPS is a school where everyone has their lives together. Of course, everyone has their troubles. But those kids at least look good. I will too. I can cover up my brokenness with makeup and a smile. If I just hide all this pain inside me, no one will wonder what's wrong. Then they won't ask, and I won't have to talk about the hurt and confusion. If I don't talk about it, I will be okay.*

Lydia caked on a makeup mask, "her happy mask," to wear to school that day, and no one asked her if anything was wrong. Her broken heart was carefully and successfully hidden from sight. So, morning after morning, week after week, she penciled in a grin to wear for the day. She tried to train her smile to reach her eyes, but it would not; nor would it reach her aching heart. Nevertheless, things were not as they appeared. After a full day of pretending, the glow of the moon would reveal Lydia sobbing on the floor of her room—betrayed, hopeless, and confused.

"Where my heart becomes free
And my shame is undone."

FRANCESCA BATTISTELLI

Chapter 16

VICTORIOUS

"Grandma, can I borrow your blue duffel bag?"

"Of course, Lydia. It's on the left side of my closet." Evelyn glanced up from the papers she was grading to smile at her lovely granddaughter. "What time are you leaving?"

"We are heading out right after school gets out tomorrow. Hooray for spring break!" Lydia answered as she came out of the bedroom closet with the duffle slung over her shoulder.

"It was thoughtful of Sarah to invite you. She's been a good friend to you the last few months, hasn't she?"

"Right?! I'm not sure what I would have done if she and Teagan hadn't started to invite me to sit with them at lunch. It's super cool to reconnect with Sarah after all these years. Remember when she and I were in your Sunday school class together? That's the summer I did that still-life painting of fruit that's hanging up in your kitchen, isn't it?"

"Yes, it is; my favorite painting."

"Not mine so much. I *still* had a lot to learn. Oh no, Teagan's puns are rubbing off on me, ha-ha."

Evelyn chuckled; she was glad to see her granddaughter in high spirits. "Will you need a sleeping bag for this weekend too?"

"Oh my! You're right. I do! Thanks for thinking of that, Gram.

I totally forgot. It would have been a bummer to show up without one. Are they up in the attic?"

After Evelyn described where to find a sleeping bag, Lydia left to finish packing. Gazing out the window at the fading afternoon light, Evelyn gave thanks to God for this opportunity for Lydia. Moving back to San Diego had been difficult for her granddaughter in a plethora of ways. Evelyn had certainly noticed that Lydia had not been herself lately. Here was a chance for Lydia to revive during the heart-to-heart fellowship with her peers over spring break. The focused teaching and worship would certainly assuage her grieving heart. Pastor Juan from Christ the King would be leading the retreat called "The Journey." Many of the high school students from their church would be attending with other students from all around Southern California.

Maybe Lydia will have a breakthrough moment at the retreat similar to the one that I had at our chapel service on my sixtieth birthday last December, Evelyn reflected as she continued to look out the window. In her reminiscing, the orange tree and the date palm in the backyard morphed into the verdant view from her office at school. Her memories transported her back to Lydia's first week at Anglican Prep.

Lydia rushed into Evelyn's office moments after the third-period bell rang.

"I'm in a super big hurry, Grandma. I have to get all the way out past the O'Reilly Center for my theater class next period. And I don't want to be late. Do you have a three-hole punch I can borrow quickly? I need to put my homework into this binder."

Evelyn assisted Lydia with her papers and watched her dash out the door. Third period was free for Evelyn, so she spent the hour replying to emails and planning for a trip to Caltech with the juniors and seniors in her scientific research class. As she worked, thoughts flitted in and out of her consciousness like hummingbirds. The details of Evelyn's upcoming birthday party darted around in her mind although she couldn't focus on them completely at the moment.

The elaborate floral arrangement in the center of Evelyn's conference table was a reminder that this wasn't just any birthday—it was her sixtieth birthday. The flowers were more festive than any that Sam had sent before. He knew how significant this landmark was to her since she was leaving her youth and middle years behind. Together, they had planned a special dinner with friends and family that would take place over the weekend. Sam had also hinted that he had found the exact green and white hand-stitched quilt that she had been hoping for as a present.

As the next bell rang, Evelyn joined the flow of students and faculty heading to the O'Reilly Center for Wednesday chapel. The table on the stage was set for communion. Perfect for my birthday, Evelyn realized thankfully. Even though she had not told her colleagues or students that it was her birthday, there would be a celebration with God in the lead. She took her seat with her homeroom students and focused on the liturgy, the message, and the music. Knowing that God was present was relaxing and comforting to Evelyn. She had no inkling of the gift he had in store for her that day.

The message spoken by the chaplain highlighted the inspirational life of Nelson Mandela: "If a man tortured and imprisoned for nearly three decades could find in himself forgiveness, what lessons might we take from him on how to respond to acts of aggression and cruelty in our ordinary lives? Ought we forgive those who are not sorry for their cruelty and the pain and suffering it produced?" In his talk, the chaplain referenced a powerful quote from Mandela regarding forgiveness: "Resentment is like drinking poison and then hoping it will kill your enemies." Mandela had chosen to walk in forgiveness toward his oppressors even after years of unjust imprisonment.

Evelyn's conscience awoke at the references to forgiveness; however, she hadn't been able to let go of her searing anger toward Chip for his heinous behavior. This wasn't the time to dwell on the abuse. She simply wanted to focus on Jesus. At the end of the sermon, when the pastor mentioned Matthew 6:14 and 15, Evelyn realized that focusing on Jesus meant she would need to forgive Chip. Her Lord was quite clear in His teaching, "For if you forgive other people when they sin against you, your heavenly Father will also forgive you. But if you do not forgive others their sins, your Father will not forgive your sins." *Evelyn reflected on this truth and wondered if she would be able to follow Jesus' command; soon, it was time for communion.*

She knelt at the rail to receive the bread and the wine with the unwieldy weight of unforgiveness laying on her heart. Closing her eyes, she prayed, "Father, only you can help me let this go. Will you, please?" When she stood, Evelyn suddenly experienced a freedom she had not felt for months. The burden of hatred had been lifted away by the loving hand of God.

Returning to her seat with a new lightness in her step, Evelyn saw Lydia coming down the aisle towards the altar. Her granddaughter looked beautiful even though she appeared a bit nervous. Evelyn was overwhelmed with joy and gratitude. Lydia was a student at her school! She was safe! They were together. Evelyn gave thanks that she would be a part of Lydia's life in her high school years. She would be able to enjoy her granddaughter's achievements and talk to her about each day's activities. It was the best birthday present Evelyn had ever received.

God had orchestrated an incredible birthday blessing for Evelyn even amid the family's sadness. As she recalled the wonderful gift He had given, she pleaded with God once again. This time, she asked that Lydia would encounter His healing touch at the Journey retreat.

Midway through the spring retreat, Evelyn's prayer was answered. The students were enjoying some downtime between sessions. Lydia and Sarah relaxed together in their cabin. When their conversation turned to the abuse Lydia had suffered, they moved outside to a wooden bench in a quiet corner of the camp's garden. A carpet of pink and white pentas bloomed around the girls' feet. After listening compassionately to Lydia's story, Sarah looked at her companion and said, "Lydia, thank you for trusting me. You have been through a lot. What I don't understand is: why have you been hiding your pain from me? Why do I only see a super happy face all the time? I want to know the real you."

Lydia began crying in earnest. Her tears were rain on the hard seed of her heart. After six months of concealing her emotions from others, the shell around her heart finally cracked. Grace and hope sprouted inside her soul like the first tender shoots of the pentas flowers. Intuitively, she knew that this would be a moment that would forever positively impact her life. Her healing had begun. God had seen her confusion and brokenness; His hope had been available for her all along.

"You're right, Sarah. I've truly been a mess wearing this mask of fake happiness. I can't keep hiding. It's made me even more miserable. I'm ready to be honest with myself about how I'm doing. Life has been tremendously hard since we moved." Lydia choked back a sob. This wasn't going to be easy.

"Honesty with yourself is a great start. That is such an important first step. Do you suppose you could also be honest with everyone else?" Sarah pressed. "I'm not the only one who wants you to be yourself. Our whole youth group has been praying for you. We all care about you, Lydia."

"You think so?" When Sarah answered with a nod, Lydia hesitated only slightly before agreeing. "Yes, I'm ready for that too."

"I have a brainstorm. Since you are going to be the real you, you should stop wearing so much makeup to cover up your pain. It can be an outward sign of your inner change."

"You're right; I do want to stop wearing all this makeup. It's pretty uncomfortable." Lydia conceded while she gestured in a circular motion in front of her face. "What should I do then? I still want to be preventable." Sarah and Lydia burst out laughing. "What?! Preventable! I mean presentable." Lydia had been speaking so seriously that her slip-up sounded wonderfully comical. What a relief to giggle after all that crying.

"Girlfriend, you don't have to do anything. You are truly beautiful with a natural glow under that mask." She pointed to the pentas spread across the garden. "You are prettier than these sweet, dainty flowers," Sarah encouraged her friend. "Here, this is perfect timing. Since your makeup is already smeared from crying, let's go in and wash it off. It's time for a fresh start."

The Journey retreat had been aptly named. Lydia found herself on a pilgrimage back to being healthy and whole. On Sunday evening, Ettie arrived in a spring downpour to pick Lydia up from the camp and found her daughter with a real smile despite the pouring rain. Sarah had been telling the truth. The beauty and captivating radiance of the hope inside Lydia's heart shone through as she prepared to greet her problems head-on. It did take some time for her to get used to it. Lydia didn't see it at first. She felt exposed and ugly. She thought everyone would judge her for what she had been through. School was so hard for her because people wondered why she had changed. Lydia thought that to others it seemed like a change for the worse because she didn't seem to be as happy. Thankfully, her community of friends who were believers in Jesus loved her for who she was, not for how she looked. Their unconditional love and support buoyed Lydia. She felt as though she was walking on a cloud of prayers.

After two months of becoming more comfortable with her natural visage, Lydia pondered the steps of her odyssey in her journal. She sat on the couch late one quiet evening with her legs tucked under her. She wrote: *It feels good to wear no makeup and no happy mask. I see that those things were holding me back. Sarah helped me move forward when she called me out because that was the moment I stopped hiding and my healing began. It was in that instant that I found the grace to start over. I was finally able to be honest regarding how much I was hurting, and it was only then that people were able to start offering me help. I saw that it's okay to be me. I am finding true healing in Christ. God is faithful and He is holding our hands through all this mess. Each day, I am walking through those halls at Anglican Prep with Him right beside me. Every time I am with my youth group friends, I feel surrounded by family. Sarah, Zuri, Bradley, Emily, Carlos, Heather, Rebekah, Sonia, Danny—they all see me for who I am, and they still love me. God is giving me comfort and joy. I'm no longer scared. I feel God's strength with me.*

Lydia paused to pet Sky who had nuzzled up beside her on the leather couch. She looked out the back window without seeing anything except her thoughts trying to form like droplets in a cloud. Even though she had journeyed so far, something still didn't feel quite right. Something dark and heavy was still blocking her road to complete freedom. What was holding her back? As she stood and headed to bed, she hoped that she could gain some understanding about the roadblock soon. She felt ready to experience total healing.

The following afternoon, Ettie picked Lydia up from school for their weekly counseling appointment. Lydia did not particularly look forward to these appointments and always offered for her mother to go into Ms. Windsor's office first. This day was no different.

"You go ahead, Mama," Lydia coaxed as she settled into the waiting room and pulled her biology book out of her backpack. "I'll get a start on my homework. This is my last Biology assignment for the year," she added. "I'm super glad that summer is almost here."

Sinking into the big pillows in the therapist's office, Ettie sighed. These visits were helpful for her. She often cried through almost the entire session; nevertheless, she valued having time set aside each week to sort through the struggles she and her family were dealing with. Sometimes Maria said something insightful that caused Ettie to see things from a better perspective. The previous Monday, Maria had been a lifesaver. Ettie had been to visit Pastor Evan at two o'clock in the afternoon and had given him a brief explanation of what Chip had done to Lydia over the years. Shockingly, his response had been to counsel Ettie that she did not need to decide concerning her marriage to Chip during the current emotional trauma. "Take your time," he had suggested.

At four o'clock that same afternoon, Ettie had an additional appointment with Maria. Ettie had arrived shaken to the core. How could Pastor Evan expect her to remain in a covenant relationship with a man who had sexually abused her daughter? Was he right?

Could that ever be a possibility? What about Lydia's safety? They couldn't all safely live in the same house together.

"Pastor Evan meant to give helpful advice," Maria had explained wisely. "But he doesn't understand the extent of the abuse. Chip has given up his privilege of being a husband to you and his right to be a father to Lydia. You are doing a difficult thing to walk away from a marriage with him; despite that, it is the correct thing considering your daughter's safety. Choosing between your husband and your children is a choice you should not have to make; unfortunately, Chip has put you in that position. You have done well, Ettie."

Ettie had sobbed with relief. Keeping Lydia and her boys physically safe was a top priority for Ettie. Currently, Ettie needed to process her feelings of responsibility for Chip's well-being. She began the present counseling session by telling Maria some of the bizarre things he had said to her.

"I have spoken to Chip a couple of times recently," she began. "I appreciate that he had my car shipped out here, and I wanted to thank him. What a blessing it has been to not have to rely on everyone for transportation." Ettie sighed. "I'm thankful, but overwhelmingly confused as well. Why is he being nice to me in that regard and still lying to me about so many other things? I asked him about his conversation with my friend, Deb, the night we left Jacksonville. Deb had told me that Chip promised that he was telling the truth and that he had his hand on the Bible while he promised. How could he promise her one thing and tell me another? Because he certainly didn't tell me that he had fallen asleep with Lydia, only to wake to find his hand on her. He told me that touching Lydia was an inside joke." Ettie's voice rose in anguish as she described her confusion. Maria waited patiently while Ettie paused to gather her composure.

"Then yesterday, Chip says, 'I certainly wasn't holding a Bible when I called Deb that night. I had a bottle of whiskey in one hand and a pistol in the other.' How can his stories be that inconsistent, Maria? I tried to get him to tell me the truth; however, he changed the subject abruptly and started warning me not to let the Navy get involved with pressing charges against him." Ettie recounted Chip's outlandish caution word for word: "'I'm just waiting here at the house with my toothbrush in my pocket, Ettie, because the police are coming to take me to the brig. If they convict me of these felony charges, the penalty is death by lethal injection. Let that sink in!'"

Ettie knew that Chip's words were meant to snare her in uncertainty. As she spoke them aloud to Maria, they began to lose their grip on her mind. The absurdity of his claims made them impossible to take seriously; who had ever heard of the Navy killing someone for child abuse? Ettie had forgiven Chip the very first night they had arrived back in San Diego, and the forgiveness was real because the hatred and anger had been replaced by peace and hope. What a challenge it was to revisit the desert of anger over and over each time Chip told her another lie. She chose once again to walk deliberately back to the waterfall of forgiveness where she found Jesus' love waiting for her.

Maria had paused the writing she was doing in her notebook and was looking expectantly over the rim of her glasses. When she spoke, it seemed that she had been listening to Ettie's internal dialogue. "I know you have forgiven him, Ettie," she began, "And you will continue to forgive him since Jesus teaches us to forgive seventy times seven. Regardless, you do not need to feel responsible for changing him. Chip must find his own road to recovery and healing."

Ettie nodded. She believed Maria's wisdom to be true. "I can accept that," she acquiesced. "But what about David and Jonathan? Can they continue to be emotionally healthy without their father in their life? We've been back in San Diego for seven months, and he still hasn't even asked to speak to them on the phone."

"How do they seem to be adjusting?" Maria asked.

"Thank God—they are doing well. They have started counseling with a kind young woman from the Navy's Fleet and Family Services. She calls the visits "play therapy" and encourages the boys to use the puppets and toys in her office while she talks to them. They think it's a great time and can't wait to go. They are both excelling at their schoolwork too. One problem is that Jonathan has been expressing some unhealthy outbursts of anger when he is frustrated. We pray together after he has cooled down, and I am planning to talk to his counselor about it next week."

"That's good. And what is your opinion of how Lydia is recovering at this stage?"

"She is getting there. She is working hard to be herself and to allow God to heal her. She has an amazing amount of support from her friends—both here and in Jacksonville. She and her friend, Drew, are still in close correspondence. They had decided that they would not continue dating because of the distance, yet he still wanted to take her to his prom. She flew back last month to go with him, and they had a fabulous time. I'm thankful that she was able to connect with many of her friends while she was there." Ettie shook her head. "I know I'm not ready to go back to Jacksonville. She is a brave young woman. Something is still missing in her journey to healing though; I can tell because she does not want to get back into any of her dance classes, and that is very unusual. I do have faith that it will happen in God's timing, and I can't wait to see her transformation."

Lydia's mom came out of the therapy session looking refreshed and relieved. *It's my turn to go in,* Lydia reasoned as she stuffed her heavy textbook back into her bag. *I sure wish I didn't have to.* The therapy appointments simply weren't her cup of tea. She ended up describing things that made her feel deeply ashamed. Over the past months, as she had recalled details from her relationship with Chip, the counselor recognized more patterns of abuse that Lydia had not realized were molestation. For instance, all the times that Chip had kissed her on the mouth; the tick checks; the fondling he had pulled off in hot tubs and swimming pools; the caresses he had stolen while they were washing the car—those were memories she would rather not discuss. She left the counseling sessions feeling disgusted with herself for letting those things happen.

Sometimes the questions Ms. Windsor asked at counseling

allowed Lydia to focus on how her healing was progressing. Lydia did enjoy that part. It was amazing to reflect on how much support she and her family were getting. It was like God was choreographing all these people and events to help them heal. Sarah had invited her to the Journey retreat. Drew had brought her to his prom. Her youth group friends loved her unconditionally as she became honest with herself and with them. Lydia also knew that her mom and her brothers were experiencing exceptional support too. Pastor Juan and his wife had brought their children's extra Legos, scooters, matchbox cars, and magnets for David and Jonathan. Their longtime friends, Ms. Ruby and Lynn, had brought a thoughtful gift over for all the tears that were being shed: tissue boxes on which they had handwritten encouraging Bible verses. David and Jonathan had made two new best friends; one of them, Jason, was at their house so often that they had started calling him their "weekend brother." Most of all, her grandparents and her Aunt Brittany's family were there for them every day, at any hour. Lydia could go on and on recounting the blessings that were helping her and her family recover.

Even with that positive aspect, she still wouldn't name the therapy in a list of the top five most beneficial ways for her own heart, mind, and spirit to heal. Instead, the most effective solace for Lydia was found in the time she spent connecting with her friends and with God at Christ the King Church; and she couldn't wait for the worship service that weekend. Saturday would be the Fourth of July 2010, and the youth worship team was organizing a spectacular celebration of their country's independence and their spiritual freedom in Christ. The adults would be attending service in the main sanctuary, and then everyone would meet up to ride to La Jolla Shores for fireworks together.

Lydia climbed up into the risers with anticipation on the evening of the worship event. She greeted her friends and the youth leaders with a hug or a wave on her way up. Bradley and Zuri were already strumming their guitars; Danny was starting a gentle beat on the drums and Sarah was warming up at the keyboard. The lights were dimmed so the youth room felt especially cozy and inviting. Lydia was grateful that her youth group was small and that she was familiar with everyone there. They knew her story; they recognized that things had been hard for her. It had given her a consistent place to heal.

As Lydia settled into her seat, she bowed her head and quieted her heart to receive truth from God. When the band began their first song, God's presence surrounded her in a palpable way; He was the conductor of all the healing that had been orchestrated in her soul over the past months. The words she sang during the first three songs were fresh reminders of all that He had accomplished. Now, her heart was open to more because of the profound changes she had already experienced.

Worshiping with her eyes closed kept Lydia focused, but when the chords of the fourth song sounded, her eyes flew open. It was the anthem she had been humming for the past week as she had looked forward to this night of worship. The truthfulness of the words had brought her close to God all week and in her present moment, they washed over Lydia in a life-changing wave of hope: "God you give and take away; Oh, you give and take away; My heart will choose to say; Lord, blessed be Your name." Her heart soared in response, *Thank you, God! I will choose to still love you despite what has been taken away from me. I was violated, I was alone, I had to leave the life and the people I loved, but you have restored me. You have made me free! I will hold on to the truth that I am your daughter, healed and whole.*

After her fervent prayer, Lydia stood and raised her hands in thanksgiving. She would forever remember this moment. God's love was stronger than all her trials. Despite everything she had been through, she would choose to bless Him.

As the songs continued, Lydia felt that her expectations for the worship event had been surpassed. She had met with God in a deep and satisfying encounter. She never suspected that He had more in store for her.

"I'm trading my sorrows; I'm trading my shame. I'm laying them down for the joy of the Lord," Sarah's soprano and Bradley's alto rang out with triumph as they began the finale. Lydia's heart did a backflip at the word "shame." She had always loved this song, but suddenly the chorus had new meaning!

God had been preparing her for this next moment. Her spirit was finally whole enough to hear the gentle whisper of her Heavenly Father assuring her that the abuse was not her fault—none of it. Lydia received His word as bond. She searched her heart and saw no more questions about whether she was responsible for what had been done to her. She saw without a doubt that God had lifted that last burden. She was taking the culminating step in her journey to complete healing! The step that had been missing. God had been tuning her heart as you would tune a guitar: one string at a time. Her heart had been full of sharps and flats, and in His perfect timing, He had adjusted the final string. Now she could sing! Now she could dance again!

Her feet yearned to express her newfound freedom in grateful praise. However, the worship session had ended. The band was putting away their instruments and her friends were heading to their cars. This didn't seem to be the right time to start twirling around the youth room. Instead, Lydia started down the risers toward Sarah to share how the Lord had healed her completely.

Mid-stride she changed her mind. *I think my mom should be the first to hear that God spoke to my heart tonight,* she decided with a smile. Therefore, when she reached Sarah, she embraced her friend warmly and thanked her for the beautiful music. "I'll see you at the beach," she added.

Lydia rode to La Jolla Shores with two of her friends from the youth group. Her exciting news was nearly bursting out of her mouth. When the car parked, Lydia told her friends that she needed to find her mom and quickly skipped toward the boardwalk where she had arranged to meet her mother. "Mama! Mama! Guess what?" she called as soon as her mom was in view.

"What, sweetheart?"

"I had a remarkable time with God tonight! He told me the abuse was not my fault. I'm healed, Mama!" Now it was time to dance! Lydia kicked off her sky-blue Keds and pirouetted into the sand next to the boardwalk. After all her years of ballet instruction, the sauté arabesque, chassé, and tour jeté came so naturally it was as though she had never stopped dancing. Her spontaneous choreography was highlighted in the background by the first fireworks of the night exploding over the ocean.

"Oh, Lydia! I'm so happy for you!" Ettie exclaimed as she watched her daughter in delight. "You are shining with joy! What a wonderful gift from God! Yet, I'm a little confused; I've been telling you all along that the abuse was not your fault."

"You were telling me. Grandma was telling me. Maria Windsor was telling me too. But I didn't believe any of you. Then God told me, and I believe Him! There's a lot of power and weight in hearing it from God. His timing is perfect." Lydia extended her arms to the heavens and spun in a graceful circle. In the sparkling light of the holiday celebrations, Ettie could see that Lydia's radiant smile finally reached her blue-green eyes.

Ettie returned her daughter's smile. "Yes, it is. What do you think about writing that book of your life, Lydia? You have a special story to tell. You can be an inspiration to other young men and women who are healing from abuse."

"That abuse is only part of the story. It doesn't define me anymore. It's not who I am. I'm free now." Lydia laughed lightheartedly. "You've always been trying to get me to write a book—just like Grandma kept telling you to write one. I really do think you should be the author. If God has placed that on your heart, you should do it. Just be certain that you tell the rest of my story. Make sure you include the part where I am victorious so that other people can know they can be victorious too. With God, all things are possible."

Works Cited

"A Lesson from Nelson Mandela on Forgiveness." *Psychology Today*, Sussex Publishers, www.psychologytoday.com/us/blog/beyond-bullying/201306/lesson-nelson-mandela-forgiveness.

"A Quote by Nelson Mandela." *Goodreads*, Goodreads, www.goodreads.com/quotes/144557-resentment-is-like-drinking-poison-and-then-hoping-it-will.

Alexander, Lloyd. *The High King*. New York: Holt, Rinehart and Winston, 1968. Print.

"Beautiful Things Lyrics." *Gungor -*. Web. 5 Apr. 2014. <http://www.metrolyrics.com/beautiful-things-lyrics-gungor.html>

"Blessed Be Your Name." *We Are Worship*, www.weareworship.com/us/songs/song-library/showsong/779.

"Blessings." *Laura Story -*. Web. 5 Apr. 2014. <http://www.klove.com/music/artists/laura-story/songs/blessings-lyrics.aspx>

"Elizabeth Cotten Lyrics - Freight Train." *Elizabeth Cotten lyrics - Freight Train*. Web. 5 Apr. 2014. <http://www.geocities.co.jp/hollywood/1061/lyrics_freighttrain.html>

"Hide - Joy Williams." *SongLyrics.com*, www.songlyrics.com/joy-williams/hide-lyrics/.

The Holy Bible: New International Version. Grand Rapids, MI: Zondervan, 2005. Print.

"K-LOVE." *K-LOVE*. Web. 23 Aug. 2015. <http://www.klove.com/music/artists/francesca-battistelli/songs/holy-spirit-lyrics.aspx>

"Need You Now (How Many Times) Song Lyrics | Plumb Lyrics | Christian Music Song Lyrics, Christian Music | NewReleaseTuesday.Com."

NewReleaseTuesdaycom New Music. Web. 5 Apr. 2014. <http://www. newreleasetuesday.com/lyricsdetail.php?lyrics_id=76978>

"'Not Alone' Lyrics." *JAMIE GRACE LYRICS.* Web. 13 Apr. 2014. <http:// www.azlyrics.com/lyrics/jamiegrace/notalone.html>

"'Once Upon A Dream' Lyrics." *LANA DEL REY LYRICS.* Web. 5 Apr. 2014. <http://www.azlyrics.com/lyrics/lanadelrey/onceuponadream.html>

Sherrill, John, Elizabeth Sherrill, and Corrie Ten Boom. *Hiding Place, The.* Grand Rapids: Baker Pub. Group, 2006. Print.

Silverstein, Shel. *The Giving Tree.* New York: Harper & Row, 1964. Print.

"Tenth Avenue North - Healing Begins Lyrics." *SongLyrics.com.* Web. 13 Apr. 2014. <http://www.songlyrics.com/tenth-avenue-north/healing-begins-lyrics/>

"Trading My Sorrows by Hillsong United." *Lyrics by Hillsong United Song with Video and Bible Verses Notes,* sifalyrics.com/hillsong-united-trading-my-sorrow-lyrics.

Printed in the United States
by Baker & Taylor Publisher Services